Follow the heart through darkness . . .

As the Inquisition gains force, even the faintest rumor can brand one a heretic. In this world it is Sancha's gift—or curse—to be blessed with the gift of healing. But the villagers are in need of her arts more than ever, and she feels it is her duty to help them at the risk of losing her life. And at the sacrifice of her heart . . .

Enrique has never wanted a woman as he does Sancha. Determined to have her love, he woos her with exquisite passion, giving her refuge to pursue her healing in secret. But their very desire and escape from the ruthless forces of the world may be their undoing. And together, they must pit themselves against a jealous rival and archaic tradition to secure their place in a hopeful new dawn . . .

Visit us at www.kensingtonbooks.com

I0677322

Books by Tina Donahue

Dangerous Desires Series
Loving Lies
Wicked Whispers
Passionate Pursuit

Published by Kensington Publishing Corporation

Wicked Whispers

Dangerous Desires

Tina Donahue

LYRICAL PRESS
Kensington Publishing Corp.
www.kensingtonbooks.com

Lyrical Press books are published by
Kensington Publishing Corp. 119 West 40th Street New York, NY 10018

First Electronic Edition: February 2016
eISBN-13: 978-1-60183-587-1
eISBN-10: 1-60183-587-6

First Print Edition: February 2016
ISBN-13: 978-1-60183-588-8
ISBN-10: 1-60183-588-4

Printed in the United States of America

To the Book Escape Authors – you guys rock!

Author's Foreword

Ah, Spain. Warm, vibrant, enchanting. The first time I researched this wonderful country, I fell in love. The late fifteenth century was an especially volatile time for Spain with the battle against the Moors and the establishment of the Inquisition. A period that continues to fascinate me.

Acknowledgements

To Penny Barber for her wise and always accurate suggestions.

Chapter 1

Andalucía, Spain—1488
The castle of Don Fernando de Zayas

Of all the perils a man might face, Enrique de Zayas figured the worst was unending desire for a woman. Especially one whose heart he hadn't yet claimed, because the lady in question was being remarkably difficult. Heat had burned in Sancha's eyes the few times she'd deigned to meet his gaze. Of course, she had been busy tending to his brother Fernando's grave injuries, sparing him death and life as a cripple.

Isabella would never have forgiven her sister if Sancha had chopped off Fernando's arm and leg to save his life. He was a warrior knight and had proved his bravery by falling in love with and wedding Isabella, one of the Lopéz de Lara sisters, who appeared to be delicate Spanish flowers but were as hard as any man.

Steeling himself for whatever happened tonight, Enrique joined the other nobles in his brother's grand dining hall. Exotic spices, garlic, and onions scented the cavernous space. Rich tapestries depicting country life hung on the walls below ornate Moorish designs in gold and silver. The metal glinted from the flickering candlelight and oil lamps. A harpist, flutist, and a man playing a lute sat in the center area on red chairs. The musicians' vibrant Spanish melody was scarcely audible beneath too much converse and loud laughter from hundreds of guests, all dressed in their finest.

He spotted Isabella, regally attired in a gold silk gown that complemented her auburn hair and milky complexion. She saw him too and threaded through the crowd, heading his way. Numerous *señoritas* also edged close, eyeing him as the main fare for this evening's feast. Being a rich man in need of a wife was the second greatest peril a man could face. Isabella stood only as close as etiquette allowed to quell wagging tongues. Spaniards loved intrigue whether it involved the Crown or one of Spain's wealthy subjects. Her earlier abduction and near sale as a concubine for the Sultan's harem had certainly fueled enough gossip.

She turned into him, the top of her head reaching his shoulder. "Take heart. Sancha is here tonight."

His pulse pounded. Warmth rushed to his groin.

Isabella glanced around the opulent, red-walled room. "This time she promised not to take too long with the servant."

"Too long doing what?"

Isabella paled then shrugged. "Whatever one does with servants. Trust me, she will not keep you waiting."

She already had, repeatedly, in the few weeks since they'd met. To him the time seemed longer than most of his life. He wasn't a man who needed decades to determine his feelings for a woman. With Sancha, he'd fallen in an instant. Each day without her added to his torment.

He frowned.

"Oh no." Isabella regarded him closely. "Have you lost interest in her already?"

She'd made him sound like the worst sort of beast when he was the one in pain. "It would appear your sister has never shared my passion."

She flicked her hand dismissively. "You need to woo her as Fernando wooed me."

"When he believed you were Sancha, his betrothed, or after he learned your true identity?"

"Both." She grinned despite the hell she'd put him, Fernando, and two of their other brothers through. "Everything worked out as it should."

Indeed. Sancha had never wanted to wed Fernando. With Isabella taking her place, she remained blissfully unattached in order to torture Enrique with his endless yearning. "Where is my brother?"

"Resting before the meal. I insisted he do so until his strength returns."

"Fernando allows you to order him about?"

Her slender eyebrows lifted slightly. "You believe I or anyone could make demands of a warrior-knight? Never. I request and woo. Something for you to keep in mind with my sister." She searched the crowd and inclined her head. "There she is."

God help him, Enrique couldn't resist staring.

Bathed in the light of candles and oil lamps, she seemed unearthly, an angel sent to visit mere mortals, her complexion creamy and flawless, streaks of gold highlighting her auburn hair, a shimmering mass of temptation.

He locked his knees to steady himself, lost in her allure.

She stepped deeper into the room, emerald skirt swaying, her gown cut modestly, though still providing a hint of her ripe breasts and narrow waist. Unlike the other women here, she wore no jewels to prove her wealth, which was considerable. She was sole heir to her late parents' estate, her holdings as vast as his.

Caballeros watched as she passed.

She didn't glance at any of them.

Enrique wasn't about to suffer such treatment for himself any longer. Tonight he would change everything between them. First though, she had to look at him. To see him.

She stared into the distance, lost in her own world. A server passed too close and brushed her arm. Despite his heavy tray, he stopped and inclined his head in apology. She offered a gentle smile and stepped back to give him more room, her gaze touching Enrique.

He stilled, unable to draw a full breath. Pleasure registered on her lovely face, followed by the same longing he'd seen during their previous encounters, her dark eyes luminous with unmasked desire.

They wouldn't satisfy their craving for each other easily. She may have believed she was independent and even enjoyed playing a role more suited to a male. However, she still had a woman's need for a man to thrill and protect her within his strong embrace.

He fully intended to be that man. His inertia broke. He stepped toward her.

Her passion instantly turned to caution.

Fearing she might bolt, he prepared to give chase.

Isabella dug her fingers into his sleeve. "Give me a moment with her. My sister is shy."

Sancha's impassioned expression upon seeing him had said otherwise. Hunger had burned deep within her, simply waiting to be free.

"Stay here." Isabella patted his sleeve and brushed past the others.

Enrique waited a moment, lost patience, and followed. Another hand clamped on his arm. He gritted his teeth and turned.

Luscinda de Cortés held onto him, her strength surprising, her expression too eager. He would have expected such desperation from a homely woman, not her. She was remarkably beautiful, her snowy skin, long black hair, and dark eyes enhancing her sultry features. Her full lips had surely given many caballeros pleasant dreams. The scandalous cut of her red silk gown barely covered her ample breasts, quivering with each breath she took. Numerous pearl necklaces studded with diamonds graced her long throat.

From the rumors he'd heard, her clothing and gems represented the full sum of her family's wealth. A matter her *mamá*, Señora de Cortés, seemed determined to change, allowing her daughter to dress as she had tonight to catch a rich husband. The older woman stood to the side, watching closely.

He regarded Luscinda's hand on his arm.

A painfully long moment passed before she finally released him. "So good to see you here, Enrique."

Where else would he be with Fernando celebrating his and Isabella's union? Given how their wedding had come about, he'd suspected his brother might need help defending against any unkind comments or gossip.

He, on the other hand, needed to keep Luscinda and her grasping family away from himself. Rather than address him as Don Enrique, as good manners required, she'd addressed him as a betrothed or a man who was already her husband. He'd willingly face death before wedding her or anyone other than Sancha. Rather than explain the obvious, he bowed his head slightly. "Doña Luscinda."

Señora de Cortés snapped her fan and beat the air with the thing. He pretended not to notice the woman's outrage at his failure to add señorita to his greeting, affording her daughter even greater respect.

Luscinda's expression remained inviting and seductive. Color stained her cheeks, her pupils dilating unnaturally, possibly the result of using belladonna in her eyes and on her face. The poison was supposed to enhance a woman's beauty, if it didn't kill her first.

He hardly wished her harm, wanting only to have her bother someone else. Perhaps if he simply ignored her, she'd drift away. He glanced at Sancha. She neared one of the tables, speaking to Isabella as if no one else in the room existed, not even him.

He huffed.

"Poor Sancha." Luscinda looked to where he had and inched closer to him, her fragrance heavy and cloyingly sweet. "We must understand what she goes through and pity her."

His chest tightened with indignation, fury heating his face. "What did you say?"

She stepped back, her smile faltering. "I meant no harm. Everyone feels quite badly for her. Any woman would be shamed at having lost her betrothed to a younger sister, leaving her alone and unwanted at such an advanced age. Fernando surely had his reasons for spurning her and the great wealth she could have brought to their union. However, she has no recourse now except to enter the order and remain at the convent. As soon as she returns there, of course. Perhaps she prefers such a sad fate rather than fulfilling her duty as a wife and mother as the rest of us long for."

Señora de Cortés stopped working her fan despite perspiration dotting her fleshy cheeks and stout throat. "Our women have always carried out their duty in birthing the finest heirs. Nothing has stopped them."

Not even a man's disinterest. Poor Luscinda. She might have been a nice girl if not for her greedy mamá.

"Excuse me." He turned on his heel and left before her mother suggested he offer his future to Luscinda or threatened him if he refused to comply.

Sancha sat at a long table laden with tonight's feast. Isabella stood behind her sister, motioning frantically for him to fill the empty chair next to hers.

Was there any doubt?

He reached the spot. Another man put his hand on the back of the chair to make his claim. Isabella scowled, warning him away. Good thing. Enrique was ready to push the fool aside. He offered a slight bow to Isabella, acknowledging her assistance.

She grinned.

Once seated, he warned himself to give Sancha a chance to meet him halfway. He considered clearing his throat to capture her attention or asking her to pass the olives and boiled eggs, both slightly out of his reach. Of course, the servants who stood behind the chairs were well prepared to see to every need, except what he wanted most. Her in his arms.

She wore the same fragrance he'd come to identify with her. Her delicate rose scent brought to mind soft, heated breezes, a night sky in summer, threads of moonlight piercing the velvety dark, the silvery glow glittering off countless stars.

Perhaps a simple greeting would encourage her to look at him.

Before he could open his mouth, Luscinda took the seat to his other side with her mamá directly across from them. Both women regarded him intently. No different from beasts in the wild before those animals pounced on their prey.

He ignored them and filled himself with Sancha. No one else mattered. *"Buenas noches."*

She looked at him without pause, her expression guileless and wanting.

He smiled helplessly. Her eyes were more beautiful than he recalled, lushly lashed and expressive, the dark brown color unbearably warm. His brother had always boasted about Isabella's blue-green eyes as the most beautiful on earth.

Unique, yes, but more exquisite than Sancha's? Never.

Her cheeks grew rosy as they always did whenever he was near. If that wasn't proof of her attraction, what was?

He had much he wanted to teach her. The delights of their carnal play, the pleasure of wedding him, bearing their many children, their future filled with enough joy to last a lifetime. She only had to agree to his plan.

She inclined her head. "Buenas noches, Señor Don Enrique."

His stomach sank. Such formality when she'd already claimed his heart. She should take lessons from Luscinda, whose leg brushed his. He shifted in his seat to get away from her. She controlled herself for a moment, then slid her foot toward his. Their shoes touched.

Enough of this. He leaned toward Sancha to keep the others from hearing. "We must have a word after we eat. I insist."

Rather than acquiesce or demurely turn away, she studied him without reserve, her inner strength and resolve showing through. "Why must we?"

Expressing himself when they were alone would prove difficult enough. Doing so in front of this crowd would be impossible. He lifted one eyebrow. "The matter is not one I intend to speak of here."

Her cheeks darkened, but she didn't draw back, apologize, or try to change the subject as another woman might have. He liked her bravery in facing him even though her spirit rankled at times. Like now.

She straightened even more. "You know a chaperone has to accompany us if we speak alone."

If there were anyone else around, they would hardly be alone.

Isabella leaned down between them. "I will chaperone willingly."

Enrique had forgotten she was behind them. He gave her a hard stare, wanting her to go to her husband.

Fernando had arrived finally, thinner than he'd been before his brush with death, but his complexion matched Enrique's healthy bronze shade. They resembled each other closely, both tall with hazel eyes and dark brown hair. Only Enrique's white forelock set them apart.

Fernando waved away his guests' cheers and a servant's assistance, but he did take Isabella's arm. She led him to his chair at the head of the longest table. Rather than sitting at the other end, as custom dictated, she took the seat at his side, her full attention on her husband, father to the child she'd recently conceived.

Enrique wanted Sancha to treat him the same way and let him fill her with their babes.

After eating a bite of roasted pork, she peeked at him. A pearl of juice clung to the corner of her mouth. He longed to lick it away, then run his tongue over the seam of her lips, coaxing them to part.

"Dear Sancha." Luscinda leaned over. "How wonderful to see you out and about despite what occurred. Are you feeling all right?"

He turned to Luscinda and pulled back quickly at how close she was. "If you mean her health, as you must, she was never ill."

"Señor Don Enrique is correct." Sancha remained composed as always. "I am quite well."

Luscinda gave him a sweet smile, then looked around him and spoke to Sancha. "When do you return to the convent?"

"Tonight, surely." Señora de Cortés heaped more mutton on her plate and took the last of the white bread near them. "Prayers are important and should never be put off."

He drummed his fingers against the table. "Can she finish her meal first?"

"Of course." Luscinda grew as serious as he had. "We want her to be happy." She leaned past him again, her arm touching his, her breasts nearly falling out of her gown. "Eat, please. You have no reason to deny yourself now with your betrothal in the past. You can fatten up as widows do when they no longer have to worry about pleasing men."

Enrique shot Luscinda and her mother a warning look to say no more.

Both women kept their tongues. Once they'd stuffed their mouths with food, not words, he ate a small portion of bread and cheese, his hunger hardly for tonight's fare. He wanted what his brother had.

Fernando and Isabella held hands during their meal, sharing comments and quiet laughter, shutting out the rest of the world. Having witnessed what they'd gone through to come this far, including rogues intent on their destruction, Isabella's unfortunate deception, and a murderous uncle, Enrique was happy for them and sad for himself.

Sighing, he reached for an orange. So did Sancha. Their hands touched.

Bursts of heat raced up his arm, his skin tingling, throat constricting with desire. Before she could pull her hand from his, he folded his fingers around hers. Their softness and warmth stole his breath.

Others laughed boisterously, leaned back in their chairs, or indulged in the food and drink. She stroked his thumb.

His blood thickened with hard lust and aching tenderness. She wasn't like Luscinda and the other young women who flirted shamelessly, pursuing a man until they ran him down. A touch from her meant something.

He inclined closer to ensure no one heard them speak. "Will you join me after you sup? Please."

She stopped stroking his thumb.

Crushed, he prepared to make his case, even if hundreds watched and heard. Words swirled in his mind, none perfect or even adequate to begin his pretty speech.

She caressed his fingers again, much to his surprise. A faint sound poured from her.

"What?"

"*Sí.*"

"To what?"

"Meeting you."

The answer he'd waited a lifetime for. He had to keep himself from whooping in delight or hauling her onto his lap and kissing her senseless. Aware of how easily gossip could spread, he remained as close as protocol allowed to keep anyone from eavesdropping. "Are you familiar with the north balcony that faces the stand of olive trees?"

Sancha nodded.

"Meet me there as soon as you finish. But please, take the time you need for your meal." Even if the wait killed him, he'd endure anything to be alone with her.

He released her hand and ate faster than he ever had, far less too, neither tasting nor caring about his meal. The moment a bite of fig or beef stuck in his throat, he washed the offending morsel down with a gulp of wine.

Sancha picked at her bread and mutton.

"Can I get you anything?" He wanted to give her the world. "A slice of fowl or more honey?"

She folded her hands in her lap. "I want nothing more."

How wrong she was. They needed each other. "Leave this room when you feel you can. Then come to me."

He was ready to signal Isabella, reminding her to chaperone Sancha, at least until they arrived at the balcony.

Luscinda rested her hand on his arm. "You must try this." She offered an orange slice. "Its sweetness will stun you."

"Thank you, no. I need air, not food."

"Luscinda will accompany you." Señora de Cortés bit off another piece of cheese, her mouth crammed with it. "She could use some cooling air too."

The evening was as steamy as the room. "If she accompanies me, who will accompany her?"

Señora de Cortés smiled. "Her mamá, of course."

How clever of her. If they claimed anything untoward happened, like stolen kisses or more, the matter would rest on their word against his, followed by a wedding and a life of misery with a woman he would never want. "Remain here. I neither need nor want company this evening."

Both women glanced at Sancha.

Best he hide his interest in her. "I wish to remain alone unless my brother wants to visit with me. I should ask his lovely wife if she minds me stealing him away for a few minutes."

Señora de Cortés eyed him. "Indeed you should."

Ignoring her, he faced Sancha. "Excuse me." He left the table.

At his approach, Isabella smiled slyly.

Fernando rolled his eyes. "What are you two plotting?"

His and Sancha's future hopefully. "Nothing." He leaned down to Isabella and told her where he and Sancha would meet.

"Never fear, she will be with you shortly."

Fernando regarded them. "Bound and gagged if need be, no?"

Enrique clapped him on the shoulder. "She found you repulsive, dear brother, not me."

"We shall see."

Enrique turned to Isabella. "One last thing."

She held up her hand. "You have naught to worry about. She already knows how magnificent you are. Nearly as much as my dear Fernando."

Enrique smiled sweetly. "Keep an eye on Luscinda and her mother. If they make a move toward Sancha, fell them as you did the rogue who tried to take Fernando's life."

Isabella spoke through her teeth. "The dirty *puto*."

"Wife." Fernando pointed at her. "Must I keep warning you about your language?"

"Only this once."

"And until next time," Enrique said.

Fernando exchanged a glance with him, then bumped her arm with his. "He knows you too well."

"Go." She shooed Enrique away. "Sancha will come to no harm."

He left the dining hall, grateful for the cooler air and silence. Although Fernando's castle was half the size of Enrique's, the rooms were enormous, the halls long, candles and lamps everywhere, lighting his way. Soon, the only sounds were his shoes ringing against the stone floors. Colorful mosaics decorated many of the walls, the patterns breathtaking in their intricacy. Polished stone columns, as white as milk, flanked graceful archways.

Fernando had done well as a warrior. The Crown had granted him this castle and conquered land for his many battles against the Moors and spying for Spain in Granada.

As the firstborn son, Enrique never had to serve in battle, as he alone would inherit their *papá*'s great estate. In the past, he'd envied Fernando and their brothers for the adventures they'd known. Not any longer. Isabella's anguish had been hard to witness when Fernando had nearly died to protect her and Sancha from their murderous uncle. Enrique never wanted to bring Sancha such pain. He simply needed her love and would make his case tonight.

Upon reaching the balcony, he closed the doors and paced. A balmy breeze ruffled his hair, the scent of rich earth and vegetation surrounding him. An animal cried in the distance. The faint sound of horse hooves reached him, perhaps a late visitor arriving for the celebration.

He stopped pacing and listened for footfalls. None yet. Muttering an oath, he stalked from one end of the balcony to the other repeatedly. After an eternity of waiting, the handles rattled.

He strode forward, then stared, worried suddenly about Luscinda, her mamá, or both being here.

"Enrique," Isabella called. "The doors are stuck." She kicked the wood.

He pulled hard on the handles, opening them for her.

She stayed put. Although Sancha didn't race to his side, she did join him on the balcony.

"Fernando needs me." Isabella rocked on her heels. "When you two return, please do so at separate times so no one notices or discusses what might have gone on out here."

Sancha colored in the moonlight.

He spoke to Isabella. "Rest assured, I will protect her honor."

"You had better." Isabella winked. "Enjoy yourselves." She closed the doors and left.

Sancha turned to him, hands folded in front.

If he could have managed words, he would have told her how breathtaking she was, hair flaming in the gauzy light, skin looking softer than the finest velvet, her coloring as pale as a pearl. Her eyes filled with what he identified as wonder, the same as his.

Unable to help himself, he eased into her, cupping her face.

Her lips parted. She leaned into him rather than pull away.

Surprised and delighted, he brushed his lips over hers, astounded at their silky heat. Her breath smelled sweetly of orange, her usual rose fragrance mingling with a hint of musk. Her excitement as a woman.

He eased his tongue inside her mouth and waited for her response, praying she wouldn't move away at his bold move.

A soft, wanting sound poured from her. Sagged against him, she gripped his doublet and used his garment for support.

He wrapped his arm around her waist, holding her tightly to him, his thickened shaft snug against her mound. She stilled for a moment, then suckled his tongue, her need of him obvious.

This was heaven, the only reason to be alive. These moments would change everything between them. He'd claim her and she would be his for a lifetime.

Dizzy with joy, he deepened the kiss, working his fingers past her dark green caul and through her hair, caressing tresses softer than fur.

She clutched him more tightly, her mouth wanton and willing beneath his.

Exactly how he'd hoped their first moments alone would be, though still falling short of what he had to have. He cupped her breast, testing its weight and warmth, savoring her nipple pebbled against his palm.

She froze.

He tempered his passion and caressed her more gently.

She tore her mouth from his and pulled away.

He'd frightened her. Fool. He should have known better and did now. Despite his arousal, he remained where he was and dropped his hand to his side.

Sancha breathed as roughly as he did. She touched her mouth still damp from his lips on hers. He expected her to turn and run.

She cupped his face and claimed his mouth, driving her tongue inside.

He suckled her greedily. She returned his kiss, both of them pushing against each other to get closer. Unable to, Enrique wanted to howl in frustration. She moaned softly then pulled away again. This time she put out a shaky hand even though he hadn't moved.

He pulled in a deep breath. She stepped back again.

Before she could leave the balcony altogether, he stopped breathing. "Are you all right?"

"No. Enough of this."

Those weren't the words he wanted to hear, though he had expected something unpleasant. "Enough of what?"

She narrowed her eyes. "You kissing me."

He risked a smile. "When I stopped, you moved back into my arms and began again without me having to ask."

Her face went slack, gaze turned inward. "Is this what you wanted to speak to me about?"

"Our kissing and enjoying these moments? Not entirely."

"What then?" Fingers laced, she struck the same pose his mother had when he'd misbehaved as a child.

This wasn't how he'd envisioned the most important moments of his life. He'd imagined music playing, candles dancing in a gentle breeze, him holding her hands as she waited breathlessly for his words.

Sancha, like Isabella, needed to learn how women behaved around men, accepting that males ruled, females obeyed, and everything was as God, nature, and men had always demanded.

He lifted one eyebrow. "I would ask if you enjoyed our kiss, but I sense you did."

She opened her mouth then closed it.

Just as well. He wouldn't have accepted her denial. "Since you did enjoy our kiss and moved into me for another that I found even more delightful, I believe you and I were meant for each other. Much as Isabella and Fernando have found perfection in their union. Therefore, I want you to know I intend to woo, win, wed, and bed you."

Her face turned white.

He would have expected that reaction if he'd threatened her with death, not everlasting love or a blissfully happy marriage.

She stepped back. "No."

No? He crossed his arms. "Is it your habit to kiss men as though you have deep feelings for them, then say no to their offers of marriage?"

"Of course not. Only with you."

"What?"

She wrung her hands. "You, señor, are the first and the last man I ever intend to kiss."

How comforting, at least when it came to her not wanting to be with another man. "Then what part of my offer are you saying no to?"

"All of it."

He stiffened. "Why? I know you find Fernando repulsive. Are you saying I am too?"

"Never." Her gesture took in his entire length. "I have never seen a more glorious man."

He puffed up with pride and offered his sweetest smile. "You are unbelievably lovely."

She stepped back.

Unable to help himself, he approached.

She lifted her hand to stop him. "Señor Don Enrique—"

"Enough of such formality. We kissed. Call me by my Christian name or not at all."

She squared her shoulders. "Very well, Enrique. No matter what happened between us a few moments ago, I have no intention of wedding you or any man."

He didn't believe her for a minute. "Then why did you agree to come out here with me?"

"I suspected what you wanted to talk about and decided to tell you my feelings on the matter."

Not while they'd been kissing, she hadn't. "You intend to enter the order and stay at the convent forever? An odd choice for a woman who enjoys a man as you did me."

Her throat flushed, the rosy tint matching her cheeks. "I have no intention of joining the order."

"What then? You plan to remain independent?"

"Sí."

"Why?" A woman without a man to protect and guide her or the church to lead her through life was unnatural, unheard of.

She straightened even more than before. "For the same reasons you have yet to wed."

"Me? I was waiting to meet you. Now I have. Who are you waiting for?"

She pressed her fingers to her forehead. "No one." She dropped her hand. "Tell me, do you enjoy your days with no one telling you what to do or how to behave?"

"You make my life sound as though I have no duties whatsoever. I have countless obligations to the estate, my servants, the peasants, and more. I hardly spend my time doing precisely what I want."

"I never said you did. However, if you wished to study a subject, who would stop you? If you wanted to travel to a foreign land, would you need to take a chaperone? If you wished to run through the fields at night, would anyone dare tell you not to?"

"They might question my sanity for running through fields in the dark."

"You make light of this, but you know what I mean."

Enrique did. He held up his hands in surrender but did approach so they could speak softly, lest anyone was on the grounds below or inside the room with an ear to the door. "Does this concern your healing?"

She turned away.

"Sancha." He hesitated, his hands hovering before he risked resting them on her upper arms.

She tensed.

He stroked her gently until she relaxed. "If you want to heal, you can do so with me and our children, keeping us in good health."

She pulled away. "Only if you allow me to do so."

"Why would I stop you? You saved Fernando. You were magnificent."

"What if I wanted to save others?"

"My brothers, sister, and father? Your sisters?"

"Anyone who needed my—"

"No. Absolutely not. You know the Church targets women healers as witches. For you to expose yourself in such a way would put your freedom and life at risk."

"Both are mine to give, not yours. Unless you intend to tell the inquisitors what I do."

"You know I would never betray you. How dare you suggest otherwise."

Her frown hung on for a moment and then she slumped. "Forgive me. I never meant to wound you."

Of course, she hadn't. He'd never had any doubt yet had spoken so foolishly, railing at her when she needed comfort. He opened his arms. "Sancha."

She regarded him longingly, but finally backed away on a quiet sigh. "I need to do what I must. You need to find a woman who can give her all to you. *Adiós*, Enrique."

"Sancha!"

She flung open the doors, dashed through the room, and disappeared into the shadows.

Certain he'd catch up, he tore after her, but when he reached the hall, all six passages were inexplicably empty.

Chapter 2

Sancha climbed the steps in the secret passage she'd found out about earlier, thanks to her sister. Isabella said she and Fernando played games where she'd run and hide with him chasing and trying to find her. Once he had…Sancha had stopped listening at that point, trying not to groan or laugh at how silly her sister and Fernando behaved.

No different than her.

She'd been a fool to have met with Enrique. Running had been her only recourse, taking her here. Blindly, she negotiated each step in the dark, hoping he wouldn't hear her shoes tapping the stone, her rasping breaths.

She groped the wall on both sides to steady herself. Her hand slid into a depression on the left, fingers hitting nothing suddenly, that part of the wall gone. Shocked, she snatched back her hand, twisted, and nearly lost her footing. Clinging to the other side, she inched up the steps. Upon reaching the landing, she looked over into blackness. No one had opened the hidden door below, letting the light from a candle or lamp spill inside.

For the moment, she remained undetected and alone.

Always alone.

She slumped against the wall, its surface rough beneath her palms, the scent faintly stale.

Without wanting to, she recalled Enrique's clean fragrance. His freshly shaved cheeks had been smooth and hot beneath her fingers, breath sweet, mouth searching. His body hard and strong.

No. She shouldn't dwell on her memories of him and pushed them away.

The images returned, swift and sure, tempting her beyond reason. His broad shoulders beneath his dark blue robe and doublet, his sinewy thighs and calves clad in hose of a black-and-white striped design. He'd towered over her, his height imposing but never dangerous.

She'd been comfortable with him, wanting more of the man he was. Despite his obvious strength, he'd treated her with respect and gentleness, his male beauty impossible to resist. She'd longed to run her fingers through his thick, dark hair, the locks tumbling over his forehead and curling around his ears. His white forelock had mesmerized, begging for her touch, the same as his mouth.

While they'd been together, she'd kept thinking about stroking his bottom lip, damp from their kiss. In the moonlight, his eyes had seemed quite pale in contrast to his dark brows and tawny complexion. He was a magnificent man whose heat and strength had undone her too easily.

Even before agreeing to meet with him, she'd understood the folly of her actions, yet had persisted. Telling herself she would only speak with him, explain how his pursuit was hopeless and she'd never be his.

She'd forgotten her firm speech the moment she'd seen him on the balcony, his smile promising wanton delights and protection against the ills of the world.

She huddled closer to the wall, curling her fingers into fists, not caring how the gritty stone scraped her skin. The ache in her soul was far worse for desiring a man she would never have. Surrendering to Enrique would bring her carnal pleasure, an end to her terrible loneliness, and a lifetime of duty where she needed permission to indulge in whatever interested her. Tradition would reduce her to a childlike state again, where she'd have to wait for a man, a husband, Enrique, to make a decision on her life that met with his desires first, without considering her needs.

Never.

She beat her fists against the wall, frustration and sorrow battling within her. Resolve won. Refusing to weep, she brushed tears away and held her breath before she opened the door.

The hall was empty and shadowed, the candles in this part of the castle, where the servants resided, spaced far apart. Recalling the route back to her chamber, she hurried down the corridor and jerked to a stop before she ran into a maid.

The young girl jumped back, eyes rounded. "Forgive me for nearly harming you, Señorita Doña Lopéz de Lara." She took Sancha in and gasped. "Your fingers."

Blood ran down them from when she'd hit the passage wall.

The girl stepped closer. "Are you all right?"

"I am." She hurried past.

"Wait, please," the girl called. "I was coming for you. I just left the dining hall, thinking you were there."

Uneasy, Sancha turned, worried Enrique had asked the servant to search for her once he realized she hadn't returned to the celebration. "Who asked you to fetch me?"

"Juanita." She joined Sancha and scanned the hall in both directions. Although they were alone, the girl huddled close. "She has news of her niece. The child has taken a turn for the worse."

Sancha pressed her hand to her throat. She'd spoken to Juanita earlier on the matter. "Has she arranged for my travel to the village?"

"Sí. The child's uncles will accompany you. Forgive them for bringing a mule for you to ride. They lack the funds to own a horse."

"A mule is fine. Fetch me a male servant's clothing. Not what he wears during his duties here but his personal garments. Shirt, braies, hose, hat, and ankle boots. Clothing close to my size."

The girl's plain face slackened in apparent bewilderment.

"Go and do as I say." Sancha gestured to get her moving. "Return here."

She nodded and bolted down the hall.

Sancha paced as she waited. Every sound made her flinch. Repeatedly, she peered down the hall to see if Enrique approached.

He did not.

At last, the girl returned, arms wrapped around the garments.

Sancha took them. "Tell the men to wait for me in the olive grove."

The girl ran in one direction, Sancha the other, the journey to her chamber longer than she'd hoped. There were so many passages here, too many halls and rooms.

Once inside her own, she sagged against the door to catch her breath but didn't allow herself more than a moment. After dropping the clothing on the bed, she frowned at her silk gown. The garment had no end of buttons she might not be able to reach, the farthingale and kirtle each bore laces that were difficult to undo on her own.

She strained to reach the buttons on the back of her gown, her fingers falling short no matter how hard she tried. Growling, she grabbed both sides, prepared to rip the garment from her.

The door to her chamber flew open.

She froze. So did Isabella.

Sancha leaned over to see if Enrique had accompanied her sister.

Isabella was alone. She closed the door and frowned at the peasant wear on Sancha's bed. "What are you doing?"

"I need your help." After lifting her hair, Sancha turned her back to her sister. "Unbutton me."

"Why?"

"So I can remove my gown."

"Why?"

Sancha stormed away. "Never mind." She grabbed the back of her garment and tugged as hard as she could.

"Wait." Isabella grabbed her wrists. "What did you do to your fingers?"

"I scraped them on a wall in a secret passage."

"Why? What were you doing there?"

"Trying to find my way here." She shook off Isabella's hands and tugged on her gown once more.

Isabella clucked her tongue. "You ruin your hands and now you intend to rip your clothes to get them off?"

"I have no choice if you refuse to help me." She spoke quietly. "A child lies wounded, possibly dying, in the village."

"Wounded how?"

"Older children found a sword. While they were playing with the weapon, the little girl came too near and the tip slashed her leg. I need to go to her without delay."

"Of course you do." Isabella glanced at the other garments. "But dressed as a man?"

"I learned the trick from you. The deception served you well after your rescue when you traveled with Fernando."

"Exactly. I was with him, not alone."

"The girl's uncles will accompany me. I have no time to discuss this. I must hurry."

"Keep still so I can help." Isabella's fingers fairly flew over the buttons and laces.

With her sister's assistance, Sancha pushed the gown, farthingale, kirtle, and chemise off. Naked, she padded to the servant's clothing.

Isabella joined her. "Does Enrique know about this? Did you and he argue over your plans to help the little girl?"

"He knows nothing of her." She pulled on the braies. "I learned of her worsening condition after I left his side."

"Did you enjoy each other?"

Isabella's expression was so hopeful, Sancha warned herself not to encourage any romantic dreams. However, she couldn't be dishonest. "Far too much."

"Wonderful." She clapped her hands, stopping quickly. "Why did you two argue? I know you did. When Enrique came to me, he was quite concerned about you."

"Did he say what we discussed?"

"No. He left to find you."

Sancha stopped pulling up the hose. "Will he come here?"

"Not right away. He has no idea which room is yours. Tell me what happened."

Too much. Losing herself in Enrique's arms wasn't like her. All her life, Sancha had been the demure one, dismissing passion in favor of books and knowledge. Love was for other women who wanted nothing more than a man to rule their days. "I told him his hope for our union was impossible and to woo another woman."

"What? Since when do you find him as repulsive as you did Fernando? Is it because they resemble each other so closely?"

"No. I find Enrique too thrilling. We kissed and I wanted more."

Isabella laughed gaily, turning a fast circle only to stop. "You said you wanted more. Why then are you denying him and yourself?"

"To save others, as I did Fernando. If he had been anyone else's husband save yours, and I had wed a man who refused to allow my healing, Fernando would have died. How can I permit such a thing? How can anyone, and for no other reason than I happen to be a woman?"

"Sancha." Isabella embraced her. "I fear for your safety. The Inquisition has spies everywhere. Many of them are probably here tonight, eating my husband's food and enjoying his drink."

"Those spies have always been around, even when I tended Fernando."

"You had me to protect you."

Fighting a smile, she cradled Isabella's cheek. Her little sister was more warrior than she, both of them battling the constraints of their sex. "Protect me during my absence. Tell anyone who inquires that I felt ill and took to my bed. Surely, no one will come in here to see proof of my sickness."

"Enrique might."

Enrique would. He was not a man to let anyone deny him.

She should have been disturbed at the prospect of them in this room alone, both bared to each other's sight and touch, him wanting, seeking, demanding everything she could give.

Warmth coursed through her. She recalled their kiss, his thickened shaft pressing against her mound. A dull ache had filled her then, her channel growing increasingly congested, needy of a man to fill and possess that part of her. Even now, moisture lingered on the soft folds between her legs, proof of her desire for love and physical pleasure despite what good sense told her.

This had to stop. "If Enrique does come here, send him away." If he refused to be strong in this matter, she'd have to be for both of them.

Isabella sighed. "You have no hope of a future with him?"

Sadly, no. "I explained my position and he refused to see matters as I do. He would stand in the way of my healing anyone except him, our children, and the rest of the family."

"He wants to protect you. In time, you may change his mind on the matter."

"How many will die as I wait for his decision? No man, even a good one, has a right to ask such a thing of me." She pressed Isabella's hand to her cheek. "I trust you with my secret and life, little sister."

Isabella hugged her fiercely. "I will never fail you."

* * * *

Enrique checked dozens of bedchambers, each empty of guests though filled with their clothing and other personal articles. A quick search told him none of the items belonged to Sancha. The silks and gems were garish, nothing like her.

She had to be somewhere in the castle, no doubt with Isabella, who'd left the dining hall never to return. Hopefully, she was trying to change Sancha's mind about what she and Enrique had fought over.

He closed the last door, sensing even the most impassioned speech or his kisses and ardent lovemaking wouldn't change Sancha's mind on anything for long. She was as stubborn as Isabella, perhaps more so, her willfulness nearly as bad as his.

He'd never acquiesce to her plans to save the world. The danger she faced was incomprehensible, his determination as great. Whatever it took, he'd keep her from harm.

He bolted down the hall and checked balconies this time. He hadn't expected her to return to the one where they'd met, though there was always hope.

She wasn't there.

He slammed the doors and searched five more balconies, each seeming to be a league away from the others. On the last at this level, he leaned against the stone railing, gulping air. The hour was late. He was tired and wanted naught but comfort in her arms.

Ha. Her loving embrace wasn't likely to happen this evening.

He pushed away. A slapping noise sounded below. He scanned the grounds but found nothing amiss in the olive grove. Moonlight had turned the green leaves ashy. Twisted trunks left long shadows across the grass.

Something moved in the corner of his eye.

A peasant rode a mule on the grounds, his back to Enrique, hair hidden by an acorn hat. How curious that the guards had allowed the man this close to the castle.

Enrique leaned over the railing again for a closer look at the next peasant, also on a mule and departing this place. This individual was the size of a boy fourteen years old or so and wearing a sack hat. He carried something in a cloth bag tethered to his mule. From this distance, Enrique couldn't make out the contours of whatever was inside. Another peasant came into the scene, as large as the first fellow.

Enrique studied the bag, guessing that Fernando might have given food to those in need. If so, one of the men, not the boy, should have carried the items. Given their superior age, they'd be in charge, distributing any meal to others in the village. If that was their destination.

The first in line stopped, his hand lifted to signal the others. Their mules also came to a halt. The fellow in front turned to the boy and said something Enrique couldn't hear. The boy in turn twisted around to speak to the man behind him.

Enrique blinked then stared. Moonlight touched the boy's face, which was decidedly female and quite beautiful with dark eyes, delicate features, and a mouth he'd never forget.

Sancha.

Despite the odd scene that should have had him questioning his eyes, he recognized the way she gestured when speaking, how she glanced to the side while gathering her thoughts, then met the other person's gaze once she knew what to say.

Enrique opened his mouth to call out but didn't, sensing she and the others would flee. He raced from the balcony and down the great stairs to the castle entrance, intent on following her the moment he gained his horse.

Upon arriving here, the stable boy had taken the steed, presumably to the stables. Enrique had no idea where they might be. Isabella hadn't given him a tour of them.

He rushed to the dining hall and Isabella's side. At his fast approach, she and Fernando looked up. The others were busy getting happily drunk and fat to pay him any heed. Save for Luscinda and her mother. Both waved.

Enrique bent down to Isabella, so those surrounding them couldn't overhear. "Where is she going?"

Fernando frowned. "Where is who going?"

"Sancha." He spoke to Isabella. "Tell me. I saw her outside, dressed as a boy, leaving with two men."

She leaned away from him and Fernando, whose frown had deepened. He pressed closer. "What have you helped Sancha to do?"

"Nothing. If she dressed as a boy, she gained the clothing on her own."

"You know her destination and what she intends to do there." Enrique planted his hands on his hips. "Admit it."

"Why?" She lifted her chin. "Do you intend to stop her?"

"My goal is to protect her."

Fernando narrowed his eyes. "From what? Who?"

Enrique gestured helplessly to Isabella. "Tell me. Please. I promise no harm will come to her from me or anyone else."

"Do as he asks." Fernando rested his hand on Isabella's arm. "If you refuse and anything untoward happens to Sancha, will you be able to forgive yourself?"

"Nothing untoward will happen. It never does."

"Never?" Enrique's gut cramped. "How often does she do things like this?"

Isabella averted her gaze. "How would I know?"

He growled.

She sniffed. "Quit hounding me."

"Not until you tell me what Sancha is—"

"Tonight, she goes to the village at the edge of the estate to help the peasants." She grabbed Enrique's sleeve even though he hadn't budged. "Follow her if you must, but do nothing to stop her. She will fight you. If you win, Sancha will hate you for all time."

He wanted to bellow his frustration at her and Sancha but simply nodded. Any argument on his part would take time he didn't have. "Where are your stables? I need my horse."

Isabella called a servant over, instructing the young man to assist Enrique in gaining his steed and to give him directions to the village.

Fernando shook his head at Enrique. "Perhaps you should forget about Sancha."

He frowned at the notion, the same as Isabella had, and followed the servant.

The boy who tended the horses saddled the Arabian as quickly as he could. Even with Enrique's help, the task seemed to take them an interminable amount of time. Mounted, he wheeled his horse around and rode hard until the moon ducked behind a thick cloud cover.

He was some distance from the castle, unwilling to return for a torch, and cursed himself for not taking one. The same as Sancha and her companions had failed to secure any for themselves. If they hadn't arrived at the village yet, they were travelling as blindly as him. A dangerous venture. Something could alarm her mule and make the sorry creature throw her. Thieves could lie in wait. A snake might strike.

Swearing, he waited for the moonlight to return before prodding his horse to a faster pace. If he were to have an accident during his heated pursuit, his injuries would keep him from protecting her. As Isabella had warned, he couldn't stop Sancha, rail at her, or try to talk reason. If he dared do so, she'd hate him for eternity.

Clenching his jaw, he left the last fields and vineyards, entering an untended part of Fernando's property. Overgrown olive trees and orange groves flanked both sides of the dirt road. With one hand on the hilt of his sword, he scanned the surrounding areas and searched for anything untoward.

For the moment, he was alone.

Recalling the directions, the servant had given him, he turned to the left at a point where the road branched in several directions. Something moved ahead. He stopped and squinted at the individual, on foot and alone.

Couldn't be Sancha, unless something had happened to her mule and companions.

Sweat broke out on his face and neck. He rode as quickly as the road allowed and reined in his gelding at what he'd mistakenly believed was her. A cow ambled along the path, as if Enrique and his horse didn't exist. He passed the creature and growled at Sancha's foolishness.

How dare she put herself at risk, thinking of naught except helping the peasants. As though no one in the village was capable of doing anything for them save her.

He'd see about that, no matter Isabella's admonitions. The community lay ahead.

Crudely constructed mud huts mingled with simply designed wooden structures. Given the late hour, there wasn't much activity. Two men with uncombed hair and unshod feet stood at the village entrance, pitchforks in hand, keeping guard.

Enrique rode to them and identified himself. "Have two men and a boy arrived? The boy's mule carried a bag laden with goods."

The peasants exchanged a glance.

"I mean no one harm." Enrique pulled a *ducat* from his pouch and held the gold coin for both men to see. "The boy forgot something he needed. Whichever of you tells me where he is, so I might deliver it to him, receives the coin."

"What was forgotten?" the younger man asked.

Enrique warned himself not to frown or argue. He tried to recall what Sancha had used on Fernando when she'd treated him. The stench of illness had been horrific, though not as daunting as the scent of death.

"Wine." He remembered having seen a bottle in Fernando's room and something else. "Vinegar too." He patted the leather *alforjas* behind him, indicating where he had the items, hoping neither man would ask to see them or tell him the village was already in possession of the things.

The older man pointed. "The last hut to the right."

"*Gracias.*" After tossing the coin to the fellow, Enrique directed his horse through the village. Dust and mud seemed to cover everything, smoke permeating the air. No candles burned here. Light came from the moon and a few torches placed at such a distance from each other, he couldn't determine what they were meant to illuminate.

Although the village was grim in comparison to a castle, the people had tended the property well, keeping their chickens and pigs in pens. Tattered clothes hung on a limp rope strung between two sorry looking cork trees.

He stopped at the last hut, its windows shuttered. Faint light spilled through separations in the wood. The mules Sancha and the men rode were off to the side, tethered properly.

Before Enrique could dismount, a man left the hut, slammed the door behind him, and strode into the darkness.

After debating whether to knock first, Enrique slipped inside quietly, prepared to deal with an argument from Sancha or the men she'd travelled with.

Shadows darkened most of the room. Torches shone on a rough wood table with a little girl lying on top. Eyes closed, and moaning, she couldn't have been more than five or six years old. A rip in her homespun dress showed ribs as prominent as Fernando's had been during his recovery, the child's thin body nothing like those belonging to the nobility's sons and daughters. Their skin was olive or pink, not gray like this child's. Their arms and legs had never been as spindly as hers.

A pungent smoke smell was as strong in here as it had been outside, along with the odor of decay. Someone had hiked the child's garment above her right thigh to reveal a large wound, angry red around the edges, yellowish pus oozing from the center. Given how swollen the injury was, Enrique sensed there was far more pus inside. He'd heard Fernando and their other brothers speak of injuries like these when relating scenes from their battles.

Men had died from similar wounds, as Fernando would have, if not for Sancha's skilled help.

She, the two men who'd ridden with her, and a woman stood to the far left side of the table, their backs to Enrique. Several of Sancha's tresses dangled from her sack hat.

The woman wore a frayed kirtle and worn shoes, her hair uncombed, shoulders drooping.

The taller of the men asked, "Will you listen to him?"

"How can I?" The woman spoke to Sancha. "No matter what my husband said, you must save my daughter's life whether you can spare her leg or not. He worries if Maria loses a limb, no man would want her. I will. So will her uncles. We can see to her welfare."

The men promised they would.

Sancha nodded. "What did the woman who usually takes care of these things do for Maria?"

"She died recently." The mother pushed lank hair behind her ears. "Her daughter took her place. Under her care Maria has grown worse."

Sancha placed her bag on the table and emptied it.

Enrique frowned at her scraped fingers.

"I need several containers of water." She glanced at the pots hanging from hooks over the crude hearth. "Both the water and containers must be clean." She placed a stack of snowy linen napkins on the table, followed by a bottle of vinegar. "Two of you will need to hold Maria down when I cut into her wound to drain it."

"Cut? Drain?" The woman shook her head. "We were told never to do so. What flows from the wound would harm other parts of her body."

"Whoever told you so was misinformed." Sancha gestured to the wound. "See how red the skin is at the edges, how swollen the center of her injury is? The yellow matter inside causes both. Your daughter's body is trying to expel the vile liquid. Once removed, the wound will have a chance to heal."

The mother stroked her child's leg. "Will she live?"

"I will do everything in my power to help her. Please fetch the water."

The woman grabbed a battered pot and spotted Enrique in the darkness. She lifted her eyebrows. He put his finger to his lips, asking for silence. She gave it. So did the two men who followed her outside, pots in hand.

Hurriedly, Sancha pulled other items from her bag. There was a brass container, wine as she'd had when tending Fernando, a dagger, thread, and a needle.

Staring at the last items, Enrique stepped closer. His arm hit a broom. The smack of the handle against the packed earthen floor sounded louder than it should have.

She looked over and gaped at him.

"I mean no harm." He held his hands behind his back to prove his words.

The child squirmed and opened her eyes. "Mamá?"

Sancha stroked the little girl's cheek. "Your mamá is fetching water. She should return in a moment."

The child's face reddened with her strained breathing, fat tears sliding down her face. "My leg hurts."

"Of course it does." Sancha smoothed the girl's hair. "I promise to make it better."

No words would console Maria. She cried loudly without end. The moment her mother returned with the water, she put the pot on the table and held the girl to her breast, rocking her.

Sancha touched the woman's shoulder. "We need to begin now, before the infection grows worse."

"Should we give Maria some wine?" the smaller man asked. "The drink may quiet her some and make what you do less painful for her."

"No. Given how weak she is, the wine could do more harm than good."

"What did you give Fernando?" Enrique asked.

Everyone glanced at him.

Sancha looked away first. "Fernando had already swooned when I tended to his injuries. Nothing I did roused him in the least."

After rolling a napkin into a ropelike shape, she handed the item to the mother. "Have Maria bite down on this to help ease the pain."

Sancha pushed up her sleeves, washed her hands in the water, and dried them on yet another napkin. She uncorked the wine and vinegar, showing both to the mother. "This is to cleanse your daughter's wound."

The moment the liquids touched her, Maria screamed around the napkin. Immediately, the men held her down. Swiftly, Sancha washed her knife blade in another pot, then ran it through the torch flame. Upon her return, she spoke to the men. "Hold her firmly. She will fight the pain and me."

Maria spat the napkin from her mouth and wailed. Sancha hadn't even touched her as yet. Didn't matter. Screaming now, the child struggled against her uncles' hold. Footfalls and voices neared the hut. Enrique stuck his head outside. Women and men stepped back.

Not only was he a stranger but a noble. "All is well."

The child's ear-piercing shrieks turned to gasping sobs.

"Tell the same to anyone who asks," he said. "Especially Maria's papá."

Enrique closed the door. Sancha finally sliced into the child's wound. Blood and pus spurted out. The girl shrieked louder than before.

His stomach rolled.

Sancha mopped up the mess with the napkins. She used so many, the crumpled linens fell off the table. Despite the gore, she never flinched or became ill as he would have. At last, she'd exposed the raw core of the wound and poured vinegar over the dark red flesh.

The little girl stiffened and swooned.

"The worst is over." She looked at each family member in turn. "Do keep holding her should she awake without warning."

Weeping, the mother made the sign of the cross over herself.

Sancha opened the brass vial. The moment she brought the container to the wound, the mother put out her hand. "Wait. What is that?"

"A mixture of wine, garlic, onion, and cow bile to keep the injury from infecting again."

Enrique went to her. "Bile helps against an infection?"

"Physicians have used this for centuries as I did on Fernando." She poured the mixture on a fresh napkin and applied it to the wound.

Once the area was fully saturated, she ran the tip of the needle through the fire as she had the dagger and pulled thread through the eye. Then she held the edges of the wound together with one hand while stitching with the other. The same as she'd do when repairing a rip in fabric rather than a child's skin.

The mother covered her face.

Maria moaned several times but never awakened fully.

He'd never seen anything to match Sancha's actions and knowledge. She'd performed similar healing with Fernando but Enrique hadn't witnessed the actual methods. After snipping the thread with her scissors, Sancha washed the wound with more wine and vinegar, then wrapped several napkins around it. "You must keep the area clean." She gestured to the dressings. "In my experiments—"

"Your what?"

She ignored him. "During those times when I was faced with a similar problem as Maria's, if the wound became dirty, the infection returned." She handed the remainder of the napkins and the brass bottle to the woman. "You can care for her during the next days using these."

"What if she grows worse?"

"Send for me." Sancha pulled several loaves of bread, a wheel of cheese, and a container of roasted pork from her bag and put each on a shelf to the side. "Make certain your daughter eats as much as she can during the healing period and drinks plenty of water to prevent a fever."

She put out her hand to Enrique. "Give me any ducats or *reals* you have."

Sensing she wasn't in the mood for questions, he handed his money over.

She gave the coins to the mother, dug into her bag once more and produced even more gold and silver. "Use the coins to purchase whatever food you need for Maria and others in the village. If you eat well, you are less likely to fall ill."

"I could never accept so much."

"You can and you will. Señor Don Enrique insists." She glanced over. "Do you not?"

He lifted his hands. "Of course."

She fought a smile. The mother wept.

"Do you leave now?" Enrique asked Sancha.

She regarded Maria. "In time. I want to wait and watch. You may go, of course."

He would stay.

Chapter 3

Sancha tried to concentrate solely on Maria, as she should, but kept failing to do so. With the child quiet for the moment, Enrique's presence was too potent for her to deny. Each time she glanced over, he regarded her, his gaze thoughtful rather than possessive or filled with disdain.

She bathed Maria's face to keep her cool. He drew near, watching the child, then her. The moment Sancha sank to her knees and gathered the soiled napkins, Enrique joined her, seeing to the task.

Turned to Maria's mother, he lifted his hands filled with filthy linen most nobles would have been loath to touch. "Where should I put these?"

The woman was far too concerned about her daughter to answer him. Maria's uncles sat on the floor, backs against the walls. Their heads repeatedly fell forward. They flinched each time and tried to stay awake.

Seeing no receptacle for rubbish, Sancha held out the sack she'd brought. "Use this."

After dropping the napkins inside and washing his hands in the pot, he pulled a chair over and gestured to Maria's mother. "You should rest."

She regarded him gratefully, tears in her eyes.

Enrique placed his hand on the woman's arm, guiding her to sit. "Maria will be fine."

He brought the other chairs over and offered Sancha one. "You should also relax while you can. Maria may need you later."

Sancha didn't argue. Her shoulders and legs ached with tension even as weariness washed over her. After tending the ill, she always experienced crushing fatigue driven by her intense concentration over their maladies, coupled with worry that she wouldn't succeed in keeping her charges alive and whole.

The moment she sank to the chair, Enrique grabbed two clean napkins and dampened one with vinegar.

She couldn't imagine what he was doing and hoped he wasn't planning to treat Maria.

He dropped to one knee in front of Sancha. "Give me your hand. Either one, as I intend to see to both."

She buried her fingers in her homespun shirt. "My hands are fine."

"You hurt them. How?"

She wasn't about to say until he glanced at the table, its rough wood possibly the source of her injury. "Whilst I was at the castle collecting the items I needed for Maria, I moved too quickly and tripped. Not wanting to drop anything, I scraped my hands on the kitchen wall."

He accepted her lie without challenge, taking great care in cleansing her fingers with the vinegar. At the first sting, she winced. He blew on the hurt, easing her pain.

Moved by his tender care, she curled her fingers around his.

After giving her a fast smile, he used his dagger to cut the other napkin into strips and wrapped the linen around the scrapes to protect them from further damage.

"You should take more care with yourself." He knotted the last strip. "You know what an injury can do."

Her hands weren't her biggest concern. Her future was at stake, and yet she wanted him more with each passing minute. Already she'd allowed Enrique far too many liberties with their relationship. As she would a husband who had the right to follow her, remain here, and see to her physical comfort.

How pleasant she found his touch. He was a good man. Certainly chivalrous. But he wasn't her destiny. People like Maria and others in this village were. They needed her more than he ever would. There were countless women who'd want him, giving him heirs.

Too few saw to the needs of the ill and poor.

"Gracias." She eased her hands from him and gestured to his chair. "You should rest."

With a sigh, he sat. "This evening has been long."

She smiled. Given his stricken expression earlier, she was surprised he hadn't swooned as the child had. Although the scene had disturbed him, he'd kept his peace, affording Sancha the same right to do what she wanted as he would a man.

Because no vows bound her to him. He had no right to demand anything. Yet he had helped. Wanting to reward him for his kindness, she left her chair.

He stood. "Where are you going?"

She pointed at the table.

He sank back to his chair, let out what sounded like a relieved sigh, but remained alert.

Perhaps she was too hard on him. She leaned down to Maria's mother and kept as quiet as possible. "May I take a piece of your bread?"

"Of course. Let me get it for you."

"Stay with your daughter." She patted the woman's thin shoulder and made certain to take a modest piece of the loaf.

Once seated, she offered the bread to Enrique. "Given how little you ate at the gathering, you might get hungry."

His face lit up with such delight, she might as well have offered her heart rather than such meager sustenance. A thread of disquiet along with too much desire filled her. She warned herself not to let him believe he'd have what wasn't possible.

He broke the bread in two, giving her the largest portion. "You barely ate either."

His size, heat, and scent hadn't allowed her an appetite, the same as now. She warned herself to refuse his offer.

His warm smile defeated her. In taking the bread, their fingers brushed. She came alive instantly, in a way she hadn't before, her skin exquisitely sensitive to even the lightest touch, making her want more of whatever he could give. "Gracias."

He didn't seem to notice how her voice trembled. He ate his bread eagerly, like a man starved or one who'd never tasted anything better, marking this as one of the happiest moments of his life.

She'd never enjoyed an evening more.

They were losing control and Sancha wasn't certain how to remedy the matter. She couldn't ask him to leave when he'd been so kind and giving. Daunted, she nibbled her bread, unable to swallow a large bite.

"Would you like water?" He glanced around. "I can fetch some fresh."

"You have no idea where the well is."

"I can ask."

"Or I could gather my own. Some for you too."

"And leave your patient to do so?"

What was the matter with her, forgetting the child again? Maria still rested, eyes closed, breathing steady as her mamá stroked her hair. "I need nothing to drink."

"As you wish. If I may say so, I believe you will make a magnificent mother."

She grew hot, cold, then hot again. "What?"

Unfazed at how she'd blurted her question, he leaned close. "You knew what to say to Maria in order to calm her as much as circumstances allowed. You were kind yet strong, doing what you must. She trusted you."

"She wanted her mamá."

"Only because she had yet to spend enough time with you."

Sancha might have laughed at his outrageous praise but couldn't. Like most men, he had no idea how children felt or thought, forgetting the time he'd been small and helpless. "I could spend an eternity with the child and she would still prefer her mother, as I would mine. I miss her greatly and will never forgive myself for not being able to save her."

He glanced away for a moment then faced her again. "Fernando told me what your uncle had done to your parents. He never mentioned you ministering to your mamá."

She'd done everything possible to save her and had failed, the poison her uncle used unknown to her. There hadn't been enough time to prepare and experiment with her own remedies. "Mamá succumbed so quickly, I barely had the chance to do anything."

"How awful for you and your sisters." He touched her fingers. "I am so sorry."

Her throat tightened. She turned her hand to cup his, then stopped, worried he might misread her intentions. "No one was sorrier than I that my few skills were no match for Mamá's illness. I may not be a man with all the knowledge the world offers, but I will do what I can and more. Never again will I lose a person I love."

He stroked her thumb, then rested his hand on his thigh. "Where have you learned these things? Surely, someone other than those in the order taught you. The nuns I know have never been as skilled."

She lowered her face. If his words had come from another man, they would have sounded like an accusation of witchcraft. How she wished to live in a different world where women's lives weren't made unnecessarily difficult. Forcing them to hide their feelings, tell lies when truth would have served better, and to always wear fear as men did their sense of privilege.

Weary of having to pretend to be someone she wasn't, and to prove to Enrique why he shouldn't woo her, she faced him. "As the nuns know little and physicians would have been suspicious of any questions I might have had, I learned most of what I know from books."

"Books taught you this? Whose?"

"Mine." There were also the experiments she'd mentioned earlier.

He glanced quickly at the adults, then leaned closer to her. "Will you show your books to me? I can come to your castle whenever you find a visit convenient."

"The books are elsewhere."

"Oh. Do you bring them with you when you travel?"

She laughed softly. "Even the strongest man would have difficulty carrying dozens of volumes. A woman would have no chance."

"Where do you keep such a collection?"

She was afraid to say.

He sighed. "Do you trust me so little?"

She already believed in him too much, captivated by his integrity, the way he listened to her, and his presence. If there were such a thing as sorcery, he'd been working his spell on her from the moment they'd met.

She kept yearning to be closer to him, feel his heat, and enjoy the taste of his lips again. A stray crumb on the corner of his mouth fascinated her, urging her to lick the morsel away, feel his beginning stubble against her tongue, cheeks, and fingers.

She had to stop thinking such things. "Isabella's."

"Isabella's what?"

"She has my books at the castle."

"Fernando's? Why?"

She regarded the wrappings on her hands rather than him. "Should anyone question my actions and send the authorities for me, a search of my castle will yield them nothing, especially my books. Whatever happens—"

"Nothing will. Not to you."

She slumped. "The books will still be safe and available to another woman."

"Why are you always worried about everyone else rather than yourself?" He leaned toward her, gripping the seat of his chair. "Why do you insist on putting yourself in such danger?"

She gestured to Maria.

He fell silent. She did too, her fatigue too great to resist. Closing her eyes, she kept alert to any sounds Maria would make.

The girl was blessedly silent, allowing Sancha to recall the celebration, the thrill and worry of having Enrique next to her. Their moments on the balcony. His concern and kindness here, followed by his quick anger when he believed she was careless with her safety.

She had no choice. Death wouldn't wait for the world to grow fair for everyone. She had to do what she could while there was time. Endless people needed saving, their health and lives restored. She pictured her patients recovering only to grow ill once more. Inquisitors nearby, watching, waiting, ready to pounce.

A hand rested on her arm. She flinched and struggled to open her eyes, her lids gritty with sleep.

The child's uncles lay sprawled on the floor, one snoring loudly. Maria's mother still watched over her daughter, the child's face slack with slumber, no pain etching her features.

Sancha stifled a yawn.

"We should go." Enrique squeezed her arm gently. "You need real rest in a bed. Twice, I had to keep you from falling off your chair."

He had? "I feel fine now."

"Will the child heal faster if you force yourself to stay awake so you can watch her sleep?"

She refused to smile at his teasing. "You know she would not, though a vigil is comforting." She straightened and tried to shake off her fatigue. "Maria's uncles are clearly too tired to see me back to the castle. They need their rest. I have no intention of disturbing them."

"I agree. You and I can ride together on my horse."

"No." To have him pressed to her was more than she could allow.

"I see. Have you suddenly lost your desire to defy convention or was I correct that you trust me so little?"

She didn't trust herself. She'd proven how weak her flesh was when they'd been on the balcony. To have the excuse of riding behind him would prove too tempting, her hands roaming his chest, firm belly, thighs, the area between his legs.

She shook her head. "We both risk injury if you fall off your horse because you need sleep."

"I have never been more alert and will protect you."

He would undo her resolve as surely as the sun rose each morning.

Before Sancha could counter him, he left his chair and approached Maria's mother. "Will you be able to care for your child when she awakes?"

"Nothing will stop me." She turned to Sancha. "I remember everything you said I should do. If Maria needs you again, I promise to send word."

"Never speak of what happened here to anyone," Enrique said. "Do you understand?"

She drew back at his suddenly harsh tone. "I know what trouble gossip can bring, and so do the others in the village. They too may need help someday." She glanced at Sancha. "You saved my daughter's life. I owe you my own. No one will ever make me betray you."

After embracing the woman, Sancha checked the linen covering Maria's wound. Everything was as it should be. With naught to delay her, she followed Enrique outside, her heart pounding. The coming dawn tinted the horizon orange, pink, and pale blue, colors that seemed more vivid this morning than they had on any other day. A soft breeze shooed away the acrid smoke, replacing the stench with the scent of vegetation and Enrique's delightful fragrance.

Giddy with anxiety and excitement, she locked her knees to keep from swaying. He offered his hand.

She didn't slip her own inside. "If you mount first, you can easily help me up so I can ride behind you."

"And have you tumble off my steed if you fall asleep? What kind of a protector would I be to allow such a thing?" He dragged his hair off his forehead where the wind had blown it. "I can see to your safety far better if you ride in front of me. No arguments, as I gave you none during your time with Maria."

No wonder he'd been so agreeable, figuring he might use his actions to sway her at some future point. "Any protests you might have made would have angered the child's uncles and her mother."

"I fear no one's fury except yours. Especially if we reach the castle in full light with the guests seeing how we ride." He pointed at her shirt. "And how you dress."

Darkness was definitely her friend.

She allowed him to help her mount. He settled behind her, his muscular thighs pressed close, stiffened shaft nestled against her buttocks. She gripped the saddle horn to steady herself. Her pulse throbbed even harder.

With too much ease, he held her to him and left the village.

The men guarding the community lifted their pitchforks in farewell. Enrique bowed his head in acknowledgment, his heated breath skipping across her cheek.

She turned into him without thinking, reckless need racing through her until she curbed her feelings. Sitting straighter, with her back barely touching his chest, she searched for something to discuss. She sensed her experiments would hold his full interest and would open a flood of questions she wouldn't want to answer. Speaking about Maria seemed safe, until she considered him asking how many other times she'd stolen into a village to treat a peasant.

Better never to address the subject.

He settled his mouth on her ear, his lips heated and soft. "Are you comfortable?"

She was about to lose control. Her heart walloped, and perspiration ran down her spine. She dug her nails into the horn and willed herself not to ease closer to him, her desire and self-control battling with longing determined to win. She made a noise that sounded wanton to her.

He leaned over, his face close. "What did you say?"

"Why did you warn Maria's mother?"

"What? Warn her? When?"

His admonition to the woman had surprised Sancha and gave her something to speak of other than his thumb stroking the area directly beneath her breast. Her belly fluttered. "You told her never to mention my visit. Why would she? I helped her daughter."

"You exposed yourself to gossip."

She waved her hand. "A woman invites scandal if she breathes too deeply."

"Make light of this if you will, but did you ever consider how miraculous your healing appears to others?"

She twisted to look at him. Even in the wan light, his forelock stood out within his dark locks. His handsome features and hooded eyes seemed slightly dangerous, completely male. "My intent has never been to amaze anyone but to offer what relief I can."

"Your intent hardly matters. There are many who would insist your healing powers are so great you gained them from something other than the books you read. Namely, Satan. They would also suggest if you have the means to heal, you can also use your talent, power, or whatever you want to call it, to destroy."

Although she was well aware of how foolish and cruel people could be, having him state the matter made her belly cramp. "Do you think so of me?"

"You know I never will."

"Nor do the peasants."

"Until you fail them, which you will at some point, as you are hardly God. When one of them dies in your care, the others may begin to talk, accuse, and want revenge. Have you ever considered such an outcome?"

She'd been so intent on helping others, she hadn't considered the aftermath of failure. "If your intent is to dissuade me from healing—"

"I want you to understand the possible consequences of your actions. As a wealthy woman, you have much to lose to the inquisitors. All they need is a reason to confiscate what you own in the name of saving a sinner. Rumor says many innocents face accusation so the inquisitors can enrich themselves. Powerful men have gotten rid of their wives by claiming those women were witches. Nobles can easily dispose of rivals with false allegations. If the tribunal succeeded in accusing you, men would search every part of your body for witch marks and perhaps rape you in the process. Even if you lived through such horrors, death by strangulation or burning alive at the stake would be next. For what? To practice your healing?"

"To save others. Am I to live my life in fear or do what I must? If an enemy were to come to Spain and threaten her, what would you do? Flee to save your life or fight to spare others?"

He sighed. "The situations are hardly the same."

"They are precisely the same and you know it."

He lifted his face to the sky. The ridge in his throat bobbed with his hard swallow. "You and Isabella…"

"Me and Isabella what?"

He looked at her. "Never have I met women like you."

She inclined her head slightly to concede his point. "Now you understand why I said you must find another more in accord with your needs."

"I want no one but you."

"Enrique."

He'd cupped her face, his thumb skimming her bottom lip. Her mouth tingled. Her breath spilled out on a wanting sigh at the tenderness and desire in his expression.

He reined in his gelding and lowered his mouth to hers.

She couldn't fight him. Didn't want to. The night was perfect for love, their attraction too intense, his kiss soft and searching at first then filled with raw male need, his tongue slipping into her mouth.

Sancha sagged against him, suckling his tongue as though she'd been born for the task, loving his clean flavor, his strong caress.

With the reins in one hand, he eased his other beneath her shirt, fingertips grazing her skin, hand cupping her naked breast.

She should have pulled away, told him to stop. Trembling with unbearable need, she opened her mouth even more to his tongue, inviting him to invade her deeply, intoxicated by his scent and strength.

Emboldened by her willing surrender, he dragged his thumb over her nipple, making the tip even harder. She ached for him in a way she couldn't deny. All her life others had told her how sinful lust was. For her to avoid it at all cost. A woman's purity was worth more than love. Passion could fade in a moment. Chastity alone proved a female's honor the same as valor did with a man.

She'd never doubted those truths, having rarely thought of them until now.

Within Enrique's embrace, she was complete for the first time, even though they had no future. Somehow, this moment and a few others seemed enough. On some level, she knew her sentiments were wrong. A better woman would fight for what was right, denying herself and him.

She gripped Enrique's thigh, not wanting him to stop. Her touch seemed to excite him even more. He tore his mouth free and lifted her shirt, exposing her breasts to the ebbing moon and night air. The cool breeze skipped lightly against her feverish skin. His mouth was hot and damp on her throat. After he'd kissed her thoroughly there, he leaned over, straining to latch onto her nipple. Sancha faced him as much as she could, unable to deny what they both craved.

He claimed her breast, running his tongue over her areola and tip, suckling each.

The folds between her legs grew damp with obsessive need. All she could think about was lying with him, his chest nestled against her breasts, shaft buried deep within her belly, skin touching, breaths mingling.

She cupped the back of his head, her fingers buried in his thick, silky hair to keep him close.

He laved her nipple, drawing a sound from her that she didn't recognize. The noise sounded too base, raw with desire. She curled her toes and pushed into him, trying to get closer. He seized the opportunity to squeeze her other breast, using her thoroughly.

She allowed the pleasure, lost in his embrace, the lusty promise of his strength and heat. Forever wouldn't be enough to sate her passion. Another moment was out of the question. The horse shifted its weight again, impatient to move on.

Straightened, Enrique gulped air like a man saved from drowning. Sancha was so lightheaded she gripped his arm for support. Still panting, he kissed her cheek, ear, hair, shoulder.

"You should always wear a man's shirt." He stroked the fabric.

She laughed, surprising herself. "What if others see me do so?" She gestured to the horizon, sun spilling its first rays across the fields, groves, and forest.

He swore. "We should have left the hut earlier."

They shouldn't have stopped to enjoy each other. Rather than point out the obvious, she pulled the shirt over her breasts and settled properly on the saddle, surprised she hadn't fallen off during their passion.

She was doomed whenever they were close. He'd spoken of her having magical powers granted by the Devil. What of his? A woman had no hope of keeping her wits when faced with his seductive touch.

With the horse at a gentle speed, he slipped his hand beneath her shirt once more, enjoying her breasts as though they were his to do with as he pleased.

She had to stop this.

He rolled her nipples between his thumb and forefinger.

She released her weight into him. He eased the shirt from her neck and kissed her there, rewarding her carnal surrender.

She trembled with delight and more than a bit of worry. "People can see."

"What people? No one else is on the road."

"Ahead, at the castle." She lifted her hand to show him what she meant. He was so busy nuzzling her neck, he couldn't have noticed. Again, she drove her fingers through his hair, anchoring him to her.

Several moments passed before he lifted his face from her neck and rested his chin on her shoulder instead.

She smiled at the weight of his head, liking it.

"Who would be up at dawn when they drank and feasted throughout the night?" Before she could answer, he ran his tongue over her lobe, tickling her.

She giggled. "Stop it."

"Why?"

This was so wrong. She twisted around to tell him. Something moved in the corner of her eye. Facing the castle, she squinted, trying to see the balconies more clearly from this distance. They appeared empty now but she could have sworn someone had been on the one to the left, watching her and Enrique before moving away.

He tightened his arm around her waist. "Why?"

"Why what?"

"Should I stop kissing you?"

The fact they weren't betrothed or wed and would never be came to mind, though Sancha wasn't about to get into such a discussion now. "I saw someone."

Enrique pulled his hand from beneath her shirt. "Who?"

"Isabella?"

He leaned over her shoulder to see her face. "You seem uncertain."

"She moved before I could see her clearly. Who else would be up worrying about our return?"

"From what I can see, your sister's only worry is our never being together."

She chose to ignore his comment. "We need to get inside before full light."

On a loud sigh, he prodded his horse to a faster pace.

The stable boy and house servants pretended not to notice her odd attire. They bowed graciously, kept their tongues, and continued with their duties.

Knowing the castle design, she avoided any possible crowds by darting toward a back stairway that led to her bedchamber. Halfway down the hall, Enrique grabbed her hand.

She looked over. "What?"

"Show me your books."

"Now?"

"I want to see them."

Male and female voices drifted from another hall. Not wanting to find out if they belonged to servants or guests, she hurried down the corridor, gesturing for Enrique to follow.

She stopped at a hidden door. Colorful mosaics matched the rest of the wall, concealing this entrance, the same as the one she'd fled through last night. Before she pressed the seam to open the door, she removed two candles from their holders, lit the wicks, and handed the spare to Enrique.

The scant light turned the darkness a dismal brown as they descended a stairway cut into the earth. Here, packed dirt pressed close, smelling dank, cooling the air.

At the bottom of the steps, she pointed. "This way."

He grabbed her hand, mindful of the linen strips he'd wrapped around her fingers. "Take care not to hurt yourself again."

His concern was so genuine and unnecessary, she wanted to throw her arms around him, giving her all.

She nodded instead, leading him through a narrow passageway, the oppressive quiet broken by skittering sounds. Mice she had yet to catch. The creatures had served her well in the past, even though Isabella found any vermin appalling.

She'd argued against Sancha using this space for her books, thinking it too grim. Nonsense. The area was perfect, hidden from prying eyes. Even if something happened to her, the volumes would always be safe.

She stopped in a surprisingly large room, guessing the Moor who'd owned this castle had kept prisoners here. Rusted chairs rested on the floor. Bolts studded the walls at intervals sufficiently high to hold a man's arms above his head, low enough to shackle his feet.

Enrique bypassed those items, stopping at the lone chair and long table, her volumes stacked on top. She had so many the wood was no longer visible beneath her books.

He put his candle in a holder, picked up the first volume, and turned page after page, his handsome features slackening with shock. "This is in Arabic."

"Some are in Latin. I can read both languages."

"This volume is on Islamic medicine."

She put her candle into a holder. "All of them are."

He stared as if seeing her for the first time with the image not pleasing him. "This is heresy."

Her spirits fell. Although she hadn't expected him to understand fully or to grin in delight, she didn't want him to be so intolerant.

She joined him and stroked her books as she would a beloved child. "This is knowledge."

He rested his hands on her shoulders. "Sancha, listen to me. What you have here are from Spain's enemies."

"No." She pushed his hands off her. "Physicians penned these books centuries before our birth. How can they threaten you, me, or anyone else in this country?"

"I concede those men pose no menace now. However, their ancestors did and the generations that follow still do."

"Then hate them, not those who wrote the books. What they discovered is beyond compare and saved Fernando's life, arm, and leg. When his wounds infected, I learned how to treat them as I had Maria's in order to save both of them. Not because of Spain's physicians, the Church, religion, or custom. Because of Zakariya Razi. Rhazes to those who honor him."

She gestured to the great man's book. "Reading his work opened my eyes to so many possibilities. Men need not go lame, blind, or die needlessly if someone knows how to treat them. Rhazes's people established medicine far surpassing what we know. A famous tale relates how he determined where to build a hospital for the community. He had meat hung in various locations around Baghdad. The spot where the carcasses rotted the least was the one he chose, because he knew what caused illness."

She circled the table and lifted a cage with mice inside. Three fat ones eyed her, noses twitching. "I experiment on these creatures wherever I am, testing what my books claim. Thus far, all holds true. The potions and treatments these men discovered centuries ago help us now. How can that be wrong? Would you have preferred I let Fernando die?"

"Of course not." He threw up his hands. "But this…"

"This is the future. Spain may keep its people from knowing anything so miraculous but the rest of the world will never stand still. They will move forward as we mire ourselves in unending battles and for what? A piece of land? A castle? What about people? Do they have no value except for your family?"

He frowned. "You matter."

"Then try to understand why I do what I must. How important this is to me."

"I can see that. You rage like a madwoman."

"Perhaps I am." She turned away. "You should leave."

"Without you? Never."

She crossed to the other side of the room before he could reach her. "You have no claim on me."

"Not yet."

Frowning, she looked over.

"Study what you want." He made a sweeping gesture to take in all her books. "Experiment on whatever creature appeals to you. Heal when you will."

Surprised at his comment, she softened her stance. "Truly? You believe in what I do?"

"You give me no choice, and I give you none. From this moment forward whenever and wherever you heal, I intend to accompany you as your protector."

Chapter 4

She stepped back.

Didn't matter. No distance would keep her from him. He was resolute in what he required, no different from Sancha with her needs.

"No." She fisted her fingers but stopped quickly at the scrapes on her skin, pain tightening her features.

"Are you all right?"

"No." She planted her hands on her hips and lifted her chin.

What light there was sparkled in her eyes. They appeared ghostlike, belonging to an apparition rather than the angel he first thought upon seeing her at the celebration. In either case, she was breathtaking. "You said no twice. What was the first one for?"

"Everything. You have no right to make demands of me."

"I have every right and reason."

She advanced a step, her frown hard. "Because of a few kisses?"

"Hardly, though I enjoyed each, the same as you. Never deny your response. I. Was. There. I saw and felt your passion."

She glanced to the side, chest heaving with her rough breaths.

Even though the light was dim, it revealed her deepening color. Whether her blush resulted from anger, arousal, or both, he wasn't certain. At least she wasn't indifferent to him. As far as he was concerned, she'd always be a part of his blood, heart, the fabric of his being. Her secret had simply bound him to her even more.

Fernando had told Enrique how learned she was. He hadn't guessed her knowledge was so great. Most women would have despaired at learning Arabic, the writing symbols rather than words. For Sancha to have taught herself treatments and potions, then to have experimented on mice to test her theories was more than he could comprehend.

He'd always considered himself a scholarly man, having had no choice except to learn everything he could as the firstborn son. He'd worked hard and had excelled. Only science had proved challenging to him. From the little he'd read, the subjects in her books were unbelievably complicated. Yet, she'd mastered them. Given what she'd accomplished tonight and had said earlier, she seemed to absorb knowledge effortlessly, possibly making her more learned than him.

He wasn't certain what to think about that or how to feel.

"You believe my being a woman and you being a man gives you the right to tell me what to do?"

He'd have to be a lunatic to make such a claim and risk her wrath. Having her annoyed at him was bad enough. "Again, no. However, what you have already done to my brother not only gives me the right but the obligation to see no further harm comes to him because of you."

"What?" She dropped her hands to her sides and strode to him. Like a man. "How have I hurt Fernando? Have you forgotten I saved his life and spared his limbs?"

"With you reminding me repeatedly? I will be eternally grateful for your efforts, but I will not allow you to put him at risk with these." He gestured to her books. "What do you intend to do if the authorities come here to search? Tell them the volumes walked in on their own?"

Her frown dissolved into a surprised expression followed by concern. "That could never happen."

"Why not? Although Fernando's holdings are far less than yours, inquisitors would find them equally attractive. After all, wealth is wealth."

"Fernando served Spain bravely in his battles, proving his loyalty to the Crown and Church. No one would ever suspect him of heresy or witchery."

"They might be suspicious of you. As your brother-in-law, Fernando may have known the details of your alleged crimes and hidden them from the authorities at Isabella's request. Perhaps by keeping your books here."

Sancha backed away. Enrique followed. "Tell me, did Isabella inform my brother that you have the volumes hidden here? I won't bother to inquire whether she asked Fernando his opinion on the matter, seeking his dreaded permission first. Isabella does whatever she wants, the same as you. At least until now."

Sancha stopped pulling in her shoulders.

If she were preparing to do battle with him, she would never win.

"Finally, I understand your intent." She looked down her nose at him. "You mean to secure my obedience to your will by threatening me."

"Never, and you know so in your heart. I simply want you to see reason. You had no right to bring these books here and put my brother, his wife, and their coming child at risk. For a caring woman with the peasants, your behavior with your own family has been quite inconsiderate."

Her cheeks flushed darker than they had before. She pressed her fingers to her forehead.

He wanted to say something to make matters better but couldn't dismiss the gravity of her actions. She wasn't a foolish woman except when it came to healing.

"I was wrong to have done this." She dropped her hand. "Isabella only suggested the room because she knows I worry about saving this knowledge for future healers. I shall move the books at once."

"Where? Back to your castle?"

"No. Too many already know of my desire for knowledge and question why I would prefer books to parties. The convent is equally dangerous. None of the sisters would betray me, of course. They want to learn as I do. The *sacerdote* who oversees them is an arrogant man, wanting to keep women from knowing too much. He would readily contact the authorities." She strode back and forth, chewing on the edge of her thumb. "There has to be another place."

"There is. Mine."

She stopped. "Your castle? No. Never."

"Why? I have even more hiding places in mine than Fernando has here."

"And the same risk of discovery. You rail at me for putting him in danger, then offer to do the same for yourself?"

"My ties to Isabella and you are nowhere near as strong as his." Yet. "My suggestion is the perfect solution."

"For who? In addition to keeping my books safe, I need them at hand to study and perform my experiments."

"You can do whatever you need at my castle. If you require an entire wing and every mouse on the estate, you shall have both."

"No." She paced even faster. "What of the peasants I have seen to for years? If—"

"Years?" He regarded her clothing. "I thought last night was the first time you dressed as a boy."

"It was. I tended to the peasants at the convent, though not to the extent I would have liked."

"At my estate, freedom is yours."

"To do what? Decide which of your demands to obey first?"

Oh, this woman. Intractable. Maddening. And unfortunately, irresistible to him. "My only request is for you to remain safe."

"Under your protection."

"What else?"

She advanced so quickly, he instinctively stepped back.

"Under your protection as what? Your wife?"

He grinned. "Say the word and we shall wed."

"If I remain silent on the matter?"

His smile faded at how she persisted in wounding him, though he didn't believe she did so intentionally. Her response to his caress and kisses told him what was in her heart. Her trust, however, was another matter. She seemed convinced he'd shackle her will and spirit if they married.

He'd expect some obedience, of course. What man wouldn't? But he'd never demand she agree with everything he said and wanted. He needed a woman to stand by his side, not behind or in front of him, as she seemed determined to do. "Your response to me on the ride here said more than words ever could."

She sighed. "Enrique."

"No. Nothing you say will change my mind on the matter. I offer you my home and protection, while also allowing you to do whatever you want, within reason. Few men would be as permissive."

"With *my* life, *my* desires, and within whatever you consider reasonable. Very well, allow me to be as permissive with you as you want to be with me. Anyone can clearly see your lust is getting in the way of your good sense. You and I would make a horrible match. To spare you a lifetime of misery at my side, the answer is no."

He opened his mouth to retort.

She held up her hand. "Never suggest I live with you without a chaperone as tongues would wag at my unwed state. Before you enlist Isabella for the position, know this: she will never leave Fernando's side to watch over my virtue."

"Lust is only part of what I feel for you, as you well know. You could live at my castle undetected. We have no reason to announce you staying there."

"What of your servants? Are they blind and mute? Or do you hope none of them will gossip?"

"Each of them and their offspring has been with my family for years and are as loyal to me as I will always be to them. You have two choices. Find a place to store your books on your own, travel alone to villages to heal, not knowing what dangers you face, or accept what I offer. A safe place for you and your books, a chance for you to continue healing."

"With you always at my side."

She made the prospect sound more horrible than the worst marriage. He should have stormed out but couldn't, refusing to let her thoughtless words deter him. "I will be at your side on the ride to the villages and our return to the castle. If you prefer I not witness your treatments, I can always remain outside the huts and wait until you finish."

"How is that fair to you?" She flapped her hands. "You deserve more."

Indeed, he did and hoped to win her over with his endless patience and restraint. Given what she'd just said, Enrique sensed he was already making some progress. "I need your answer."

She wrapped her arms around herself.

He wished he knew the words to convince her that with him nothing bad would happen, only good. Their growing bond, understanding rather than uncertainty, unparalleled love. A future at each other's side, sons and daughters, a family.

He could only hope her indecision wouldn't last so long they'd both be too old to have children.

She exhaled loudly, seeming to shrink with the loss of air. "Very well."

His pulse ticked up. "Very well what?"

"I will move my books to your castle."

He suppressed a grin, not wanting to appear too happy. "Will you move yourself with them?"

She lifted her face to the ceiling. "You may not like what you see when I heal others."

"Will you promise to treat me if I swoon?"

Her laughter pealed through the space, capturing another piece of his heart. Her subsequent sigh threatened words that might wound him again.

"Do we leave now?" she asked.

Although Enrique wanted nothing more, he shook his head. "The guests might see us and wonder what we do. We best wait until everyone departs. During the delay, I can send for one of my carriages. You can use the transport to take your books to my estate."

She looked at them longingly, almost as much as she had him.

"I assure you, your volumes will be safe."

She searched his face and nodded finally. "I should tell Isabella my plans. If anyone asks about me, she can always say I left the convent to stay with her and Fernando. When friends visit, she can claim illness has kept me in bed or that I returned to the convent."

"You have no reason for concern." He'd never allow gossip to force her into a marriage she claimed not to want but also seemed drawn to. When he made her his, the moment would be because she couldn't endure the thought of anything less. "I promise, no one will find out you and I are living together."

She took her candle. "We should go back to our bedchambers before anyone misses us."

"Dressed as you are? Tell me where your room is. After I bring your clothing, you can change down here, then leave."

She bit her lip.

"I promise to be careful."

"You had better. My chamber is on the second level, the last on the right with a large wardrobe. My gowns, kirtles—"

"I promise to bring one of each." Enrique was well aware what women wore. He'd undressed enough of them. "Swear to stay here until I return."

"How long will you be?"

With guests possibly milling about, who knew? "Please stay here."

She hesitated then nodded.

After taking a candle, he considered kissing her farewell, but he didn't want to press his good fortune. Swiftly, he crossed the passageway and climbed the steps to the hidden door. With his ear pressed against the wood, he listened for footfalls or voices but heard nothing more than his blood rushing in his ears.

His pulse hammered at the promise of being near Sancha from dawn to dusk, smelling her sweet fragrance, feeling her heat, drowning in her gentle smile that could turn wanton in a moment. He'd witnessed the transformation and longed to have her behave the same again, impetuous and unashamed.

He opened the door a crack. No one on the left. The right was also empty. After making certain he'd sealed the passage entrance, he put the candle in its holder, then rushed down this corridor to the next and reached the stairs in scant minutes.

Halfway up the flight, footfalls rang out behind him. "Enrique."

Luscinda.

Poised to run, he nevertheless forced himself to face her.

She'd dressed in bright blue silk. The corners of her lush mouth turned up wantonly. "*Buenos días.*"

"Señorita."

His cool greeting did nothing to diminish or extinguish her smile.

Not wanting to drag out the moment, he inclined his head. "Please excuse me."

"Did you have a pleasant night?" She climbed the stairs, taking him in. "Did you sleep at all?"

He frowned at her intrusive questions.

"You seem tired." She studied every part of him. "You haven't changed your clothes from yesterday. Your doublet and robe are such a beautiful blue I decided to wear the same color today." She laughed softly. "We match."

Not in any way.

Before he could move from her, she was on the same step as his and rested her hand on his arm. "Accompany me to breakfast."

"Your mamá can." He pulled his arm away. "Please ask her, as I have no appetite."

"Perhaps not, but during my repast you can tell me what you were doing at dawn. How strange to see you riding about in the shadows, holding on to what appeared to be a boy."

Bile rose to his throat. "You surely saw another man. At dawn, I was in my chamber."

"How curious. Is that where your clothes became so dusty?"

He glanced at the whitish streaks on his sleeves from the secret room.

She touched one quite daintily. "If you were in your bedchamber, why did you fail to answer my knock?"

He stared. "Why would you come to my door?"

"Why not?" She stroked his arm.

He backed away until the railing stopped him.

She blocked him from leaving, her hand trailing down the buttons on his doublet. "Who was the boy? Why were you with him instead of a woman? Unless he was a woman." She tilted her head, studying him. "Tell me and I promise to keep your secret."

"There is none." He pushed her hand away.

She ignored the insult, her smile as shameless as ever. "Spend time with me today and I will make you forget everyone, man or—"

"Enough." He brushed past and went down several steps before he faced her. "Stay away from me."

Her smile finally faded into a ruthless glare. "Spurn me at your peril, Señor Don Enrique."

He laughed. "Are you actually threatening me?"

"Advising. No man rejects Señorita Doña Luscinda."

He'd been wrong about her. She, not her mamá, was the one to take care with. "Perhaps the time has come to meet the first man immune to your charms. Stay away. I warn you."

He climbed the stairs two at a time, giving her no chance to retort. Luckily, guests who hadn't drunk themselves senseless flowed down the staircase, greeting him and her, serving as a buffer and barrier. With so many about, he found it difficult to move more than a few feet before old friends and new acquaintances greeted him with a hearty good day, gaining his promise to visit their estates to hunt, fish, and discuss the political situation, including the Inquisition.

"Mark my words," an outspoken young man said. "If the tribunal can confiscate merchant treasures, they will surely come for the nobility next."

An older fellow scoffed, portly from too many years of fine food. "No one dares touch us."

Enrique said little, barely following the converse before finding a chance to excuse himself. Upon reaching Sancha's floor, he had to wait at the other end of the hall for two señoras to pass. They smiled sweetly at him. He offered a small bow in return. The moment their footfalls faded, he rushed to the chamber.

The room smelled of Sancha's light fragrance.

He selected her undergarments and a pale yellow gown that would complement her coloring beautifully. With the clothing in hand, he searched the area for a satchel or sack. Failing, he pulled the blanket from her bed, dropped her things in the center, including shoes, then tied the ends to carry the lot.

Now all he had to do was dash through the corridors without running into anyone who might wonder what he was doing or ask if the blanket contained items for the boy he'd ridden with last night.

Of all the rotten luck to have Luscinda see what no one should. He didn't want to consider what she might say to the others. None of them would believe he preferred males as some men did. His friends knew his appetite for women, having seen him make moves on countless señoritas. However, they might speculate on who the boy was and perhaps wonder where Sancha had been while he'd also been gone.

He'd yet to share one minute with her at his estate and already their time together seemed threatened.

With the way clear, he recalled the tour Isabella had given him, the castle having seemed like a maze at the time. After a few false starts, he finally found the back way to the hidden door. Muted voices sounded in the next hall with this one still empty. Taking no chance on anyone seeing him, he pressed the seam quickly and slipped inside total darkness.

Too late to return for a candle now and risk discovery.

Feeling his way down the steps took far too long. At length, black brightened to murky brown, candlelight guiding him to the room where he'd left Sancha.

"Forgive me for the delay." He paused to catch a breath. "With everyone milling about wanting to speak, I had to—"

He stopped and turned a complete circle. "Sancha?"

She wasn't in the shadows. He checked the other side of the table, thinking she might be on the chair, head down, fast asleep.

Not there either, nor on the floor.

"Sancha!"

He searched everywhere, finding no hidden corridors other than the one he'd come down. She'd promised to stay here until he returned. Or had she? He thought back, realizing she'd nodded but hadn't actually offered her word.

He lifted his face to the ceiling and thought of the areas above filled with guests, Luscinda, her mamá. Sancha dressed as a boy, possibly surrounded by everyone, while she tried to dodge their questions.

* * * *

Isabella held up her green gown adorned with tiny pearls. "This should do nicely. Fernando gave it to me the day we wed when he thought I was you."

Sancha sat on the edge of Isabella's mattress, sack hat in hand. Her tangled hair flowed over her shirt streaked with Maria's blood and dust from the secret room.

Isabella regarded her closely. "Did your treatment go well?"

Sancha didn't answer, concerned what she had to tell her sister.

Isabella sucked in a breath. "Oh no. The child died?"

"No. Not at all. I…"

"What?" Isabella joined her on the bed. "Tell me."

She covered her eyes with her hand. "After your guests leave, Enrique plans to move my books and me to his castle."

"Wonderful!" She hugged Sancha heartily, rocking her back and forth.

Isabella's *galgo*, Diego, pushed his narrow snout between them.

"Diego." She tried to be firm but was soon caressing the dog that licked her cheeks and chin. "You must give your mamá some peace. Go over there and wait." She pointed to a bed of soft blankets created for the greyhound.

Once he'd obeyed her, she blew him a kiss. "Good boy." She faced Sancha. "I knew Enrique would win you over. When do you plan to wed?"

She leaned away. "Never. I want no man ruling me, as you well know."

Isabella made a face. "How can you live with Enrique if you refuse to wed him? A betrothal will never stop gossip."

"There will be no betrothal either."

"What—why? Wait." Isabella shook her head. "As much as I love you, I could never leave Fernando to serve as chaperone for days, months, possibly years on end. My duty is here with him."

"Mine is to protect both of you. Enrique pointed out how inconsiderate I was to bring my books here, exposing Fernando, you, and your unborn child to the Inquisition."

Isabella sniffed. "No one would ever suspect me of witchcraft. I have no idea how to take care of any illness nor do I wish to learn. As to Fernando, why would anyone suspect such a great warrior, a knight with no equal?"

"Because of me. My thirst for knowledge and healing taints the entire family."

She took Sancha's hands and stared at the linen wrappings. "Why did you tell Enrique anything?"

"Confession was never my intent. He followed me to the village and saw what I do. You must have a word with Fernando about the peasants. They lack adequate food."

"The village belongs to the noble who owns the adjacent estate."

"Then Fernando must have a word with him."

"Your worry about the peasants' food led you to confess everything to Enrique?"

"No. One thing led to another and before I knew it, I was showing him my books in the secret room."

Isabella grew thoughtful, nodding finally. "Did he kiss you?"

Sancha pulled her hands away. "Do you think of nothing but romance?"

"Someone has to. You surely give the matter no thought."

"We kissed quite shamelessly."

"I knew it." Hands over her heart, she sighed. "Was it the most glorious moment in your life?"

Far better than that and best not repeated. Sancha rubbed her forehead wondering how she could avoid Enrique's mouth, hands, passion, and her own when they were under the same roof with servants who would turn a blind eye even if he stripped her bare and took her on every available surface.

She held back a moan. "More thrilling than I ever imagined."

"Wait till you lie with him."

She rolled her eyes.

"You will." Isabella wagged her finger. "From the moment Fernando kissed me, I found myself falling hopelessly in love, even though he belonged to you."

"I never wanted him. Splendid warrior that he is."

"Then everything worked out as it should. You and Enrique were meant to be together."

She feared Isabella was right. Circumstances kept pushing them close as though fate wanted her to be a wife and mother rather than a healer. She should have been able to do both with none of her dreams so needlessly complicated and dangerous.

A sharp rap rattled the door. She flinched.

Grimacing, Isabella pushed to her feet. Sancha grabbed her hand. "Are you feeling all right? Is the infant giving you trouble?"

"Only when I awake. Afterward, I could battle any puto who dared threaten me or Fernando."

"Best not to let your husband hear you utter that word."

"He always forgives my indiscretions." Isabella grinned. "As I said, we play games. If you only knew..."

Sancha hoped she never would, afraid Isabella's tales might give her ideas when it came to Enrique. "Are you going to answer your door?" Whoever was on the other side had rapped again.

"I fear it may be Luscinda. She came here earlier looking for Enrique."

"Why?"

"She has her eye on him. You best catch him while you can."

At the rate their relationship was progressing, within a day or two they'd be so entwined and moaning merrily, no one would be able to separate them. Not even Luscinda.

Sancha had seen the young woman eye Enrique at the gathering. She remembered the cutting comments about her returning to the convent, how lucky she was not having to keep up with her appearance. She could become even uglier than she already was and no one would care.

She dug her nails more deeply into her palms. "If she gives you any trouble, leave her to me."

"Aha, you do want Enrique."

Of course she did, no matter how foolhardy her feelings were.

Isabella opened the door and growled. "Whatever do you want this time—Enrique?"

"You expected someone else?"

"Ah, no. Sancha is over there." She pointed.

He stormed to her.

Sancha stood and backed away.

"Why did you leave the room?" He gestured wildly. "I looked everywhere for you."

"You never returned. I had no choice but to leave."

"Dressed as you are?" He lifted her blanket. "When I brought you this to wear?"

"Wait." Isabella held up her hand. "You expect her to put on bedding when you rail about what she has on now?"

He looked over. "Do you mind? Your sister and I would like to be alone."

"In Isabella's room?" Sancha asked.

"You give me no choice. You fled before I could come back as I promised."

"What kept you?" Isabella eyed the blanket. "Did you have trouble pulling the sheets off the bed?"

"How you jest." He gave her a sour look. "Sancha's gown and other items are inside. I came upon so many guests before I could get to your sister's room, the greetings and converse nearly did me in."

Sancha could imagine. "Was one of those guests Luscinda? Isabella said she came here asking where you were."

His face went white.

Isabella didn't see. She had her back to him as she closed the door. "Luscinda appears to want you quite badly. Of course, we know she has no chance for your heart."

A faint blush tinted his cheeks, though not enough to restore his color.

Sancha's stomach hurt. "What is it?"

"Luscinda stopped me on the stairway. She was the one on the balcony earlier, not Isabella. She saw you with me."

Isabella joined them. "What are you talking about? What were you doing?"

"Riding his horse." Sancha spoke to him. "What did you say?"

"What else? I denied everything and left as quickly as I could." He glanced at Isabella. "You may hear rumors. I trust you to handle them quickly."

"Of course. If Luscinda says anything untoward concerning either of you, she will have to deal with me."

"Not only her, everyone. Should anyone ask about Sancha in the coming days, tell them she stays here but is too ill to leave her bed. After a time, if questions arise again, say she remains at the convent."

Isabella regarded Sancha. "How long are you planning to stay with him?"

"For as long as she wants," Enrique said. "Forever, if things come to that. She always has my protection."

Isabella exchanged a glance with her. Sancha chose not to comment.

After pulling apart the knots in the blanket, he gestured to the clothing inside. "Everything you require should be there for today's journey. No need to take anything other than what you brought here, including your books. Once at my estate, tell me what you want and the item is yours."

Including freedom to do as she willed without consulting him first?

"Give us a moment." Isabella ushered him to the door.

He didn't open it. "I want a promise neither of you will take off, forcing Fernando and me to chase after you."

Isabella smiled dreamily. Sancha expected her sister to regale Enrique with those times she and Fernando had played the game.

At last, Isabella nodded. "Of course."

"Yours too."

Sancha inclined her head in agreement. "You have my word."

"Wait till you see my castle. The grounds, the rooms. Everything will enchant you."

She didn't doubt his claim. She'd sat happily with him in a hovel that offered the barest necessities. When splendor surrounded them at his estate, those moments would certainly seem enchanting. Clearly, her resolve had to be strong.

"We can pack your books after everyone leaves. I promise to take care and will tell my servants to follow your directives in regards to them."

His kindness was too much, threatening to weaken her determination. Although she had to fight her feelings, she couldn't deny him a smile or her gratitude. "Gracias, Enrique."

He gave her a pleased grin and left.

She took Isabella's hands. "If anyone in the village requires me, tell Juanita to send word. I trust her completely."

"Of course. Will you send word to Rupert?" He'd been the trusted manservant to their late father.

"I will. If those in the villages surrounding my estate need me, Rupert knows what to do."

"Will you now help those near Enrique's castle?"

"Nothing will stop me. I made him well aware of my intent and calling. Should he fail me in any way, I shall take my leave."

"Take care not to fail him."

She shook her head. "How?"

"He loves you greatly and would die if you came to harm. Do be careful of the world lying beyond a castle's walls. When I traveled with Fernando, I saw things that would have horrified you."

"What goes on within these walls is oftentimes as bad. Nobles can turn as ruthless as the poorest man. Sometimes more so, as they have much to lose."

"Perhaps you and I can make the world a safer place. Me with Fernando's sword, you with your healing."

Laughing, Sancha embraced her sister. "I will miss you during these next days."

"Prepare for a much longer time. Your future."

Chapter 5

Enrique's castle sprawled over the highest hill in the area, the white stone tower seeming to touch the sky. Because of the impregnable location, there wasn't a need to keep the windows narrow, scarcely letting in air or light.

Arched openings three times the height of Spain's tallest men graced the upper floors, offering an astounding view of the valley. As far as the eye could see rows of vineyards, olive groves, rich pastures, and grazing cattle competed for attention.

To him, the lake was his property's most magnificent feature, its water a startling blue beneath a flawless sky. The pond closer to his castle was far smaller but more accessible and as inviting.

Sancha noticed none of the splendor today or on any other. As always, she had her head bent to a volume, reading intently.

Late afternoon light poured into the room, setting fire to her hair. Her silk gown shimmered each time she breathed or shifted her weight, the coppery color as rich as her dark eyes. Her long lashes cast shadows on her cheeks.

A surge of warmth settled in his groin, thickening his shaft.

He willed her to look at him.

She'd toiled enough this day, no different from the others these last weeks. He'd provided her one of his largest rooms, as promised, its ceiling high, space airy, affording enough brightness throughout the daylight hours that she never needed to use candles or oil lamps. During the evening, the room blazed with flickering flames while she read ceaselessly or experimented endlessly, pacing at times, often frowning, always pondering.

He craved to have her notice him.

She had during the ride to his estate. With her seated on one side of his carriage, him on the other, they'd had no choice except to gaze at each other or the moon-washed land passing by.

Sancha had chosen to study him.

Given the darkness, he hadn't been certain if she scrutinized him because she believed he couldn't see her actions. He'd smiled to see what she'd do.

She offered her own smile in return.

His doubt had vanished, heart soaring. Of course, she hadn't grinned as broadly as he had, but then Sancha seemed determined to resist their growing closeness.

She'd gently refused most of his invitations to dine together. During the few times she had accepted, she'd glimpsed at him while he greeted each glance with renewed wonder. As though she'd offered to share their future. She'd asked about his day, the same as a wife would, listening carefully, delighting in his success with accounts, servants, cattle, which made him boast even more.

Not once did she call him on his foolish behavior. She cared about his feelings.

He wanted nothing more than to make her happy and see her fulfilled. However, her healing had begun to take precedent over everything else, even their scant time together.

At first, he sensed she'd buried herself in this room or her books to avoid the servants and him. He soon realized she also seemed to be fighting time. There never seemed to be enough, discovery always out of reach as the inquisitors edged closer, prepared to take away her dreams and hope.

He'd fight to the death before allowing such a thing.

She flipped a page, turned to another volume on the long table, and stopped, seeing him at last. Surprise rushed over her lovely features and then her gaze softened.

His legs went watery.

They regarded each other in silence. Words weren't necessary, the moment growing charged between them.

Sun spilled into the room. Particles of dust danced in the beams that touched her hair and gown. Again, she seemed a vision from on high yet also of this world. A woman with needs as great as his.

His chest tightened with desire, every part of him hungry for her. His sex responded most, the length fully erect, weighty sac tight, the feeling pleasant and torturous.

Color stained Sancha's cheeks, proving how his presence affected her. She seemed to want to turn away, the same as she had at other times when she'd caught him watching her.

This moment was different.

She ignored her books to take him in, lifting her eyebrows slightly at his clothes. A long linen shirt, leather belt, hose, and shoes, no doublet or robe. She lingered on his thighs and groin before glancing at his chest then to the basket he carried, a cloth draped on top, hiding the contents.

She regarded his casual attire again. "Have you been hunting mice?"

He chuckled. Cages already littered this room, each one holding one or more of the creatures. If he'd brought her any more, she'd spend all her time feeding them.

He lifted the basket. "This holds food. You missed the midday meal and rushed through breakfast."

"I have much to do."

"Remember what you told Maria's mother about eating enough to stay in good health? You should follow your own advice."

Sancha gave him a sheepish smile, until she regarded her books, notes, and other items taking up every part of her table. "Give me a moment to clear things."

"No need. We can eat outside. Never has there been a lovelier afternoon. Come." He held out his hand.

She didn't run to him as he'd hoped and throw her arms around his shoulders or kiss him wantonly. Regrettably, she didn't move at all.

"Would you deny me food?" he asked. "Do you want me to starve?"

She smiled. "You require my presence in order to eat?"

"I prefer you at my side as I enjoy every morsel, with you sharing news of your work. Too many days have passed since you told me of your progress."

Her shoulders slumped. "There is none. The mice are horribly well."

He tried to make sense of what she'd said but couldn't. "I thought that was your intent. To heal the creatures, then use what you learned on humans." An odd notion, to be sure, but one she embraced.

"My intent now is to experiment to make them ill."

"With poison? Are they beginning to annoy you so much?"

She laughed. "No and no. This has nothing to do with poison. At least not in the way you mean. The mystery involves what causes a certain illness."

"You must tell me everything whilst we eat." He wiggled his fingers.

She joined him, slipping her hand inside his.

Her soft touch sent a current of pleasure racing through him. He laced their fingers, taking care not to hold her too tightly or pull her close. His fantasies of her pressed to him, his shaft inside her tight, heated sheath already consumed too much time. Her scent always sent him reeling with images of her velvety flesh, lavish breasts, tightened nipples, the curly thatch between her legs, those delicate hairs surely reddish.

He had to lock his knees to keep steady.

She gave him a questioning look. "Where are you taking me?"

If he could, he would have chosen his chamber and bed for months on end, not allowing her to ever wear clothes again or leave his side except to bathe and eat. Given his vow to woo her with unending patience, he put that dream on hold for the moment. "To the pond. I noticed how much you liked the spot when you first toured the grounds."

Her face had already lit up. "I do."

"Then we should check to see if anything about it has changed."

"It had better not. I need no more disappointments this day."

She'd have none as long as she was with him. Outside the room, he released her hand long enough to grab the wool blanket he'd left on a side table. With the soft fabric slung over his shoulder, he captured her hand once more and kissed her knuckles, the skin slightly red from her previous injuries. "You healed well."

"Because of your tender care."

He liked her words and obvious desire to be with him. She seemed unable to dam up her feelings a moment longer, matching his passion.

On his orders, no servants roamed the areas of the castle they passed. He wanted no one spoiling this day. The grounds were the same. The men who usually worked here toiled on another part of the estate, tending to a project he'd given them earlier. This spot, these moments, belonged to no one save him and Sancha.

Even at this hour, the day was still heated, though not unbearably so, the coming night promising softness and continued warmth.

She lifted her face to the caressing breeze. They walked past colorful flowers perfuming the air and a series of trees until they came to a cleared space. She grinned at the ducks on the pond. A papá, mamá, and their brood, paddling happily, the male bird ever alert to danger. As he should be. His family was his world, his mate making each day worthwhile.

A matter Enrique had never considered for himself until he'd met her.

With the basket on the ground, he spread their blanket over a soft cushion of grass beneath the wide canopy of an olive tree. A surge of wind threatened to blow the blanket away. He secured the corners with rocks. Finished, he offered Sancha his hand.

She accepted his help without hesitation, sank to the blanket, and smoothed her skirt. Once he'd brought the basket over, she threw back the covering and smiled. Cold pork and beef, a *bota* of wine, olives, cheese, freshly baked bread, figs, and oranges awaited them. "You packed a veritable feast."

His cook had done so. He'd rewarded the woman with a hearty "Well done" and a *real*. Seated next to Sancha, legs crossed, he handed her a napkin. Their fingers touched. She didn't pull away, and nor did he, the moment wonderfully intimate.

A duck honked.

She flinched. Laughing self-consciously, she tore off a piece of bread and threw it into the pond.

Father, mother, and offspring hurried to the morsel.

"What delightful creatures." She clapped. "The babies are precious."

"Good thing." He eased her face to his and teased the seam of her mouth with a slice of pork.

She parted her lips, accepting what he offered, focused on him to the exclusion of everything. Her delicate nostrils flared slightly.

He understood her struggle to get enough air, dizzy from his lack of breath.

She chewed and swallowed. "Why is it a good thing I find the ducklings precious?" She fed him a slice of beef.

Before she could lower her hand, he captured her wrist and licked her fingers, enjoying her skin's slight saltiness. "If the ducks resembled mice, you would have them in a cage within seconds, even the smallest ones."

Blushing, she took an orange and glanced at him. "Do you find me cruel for experimenting on the creatures?"

"When they eat my grain, nibble everything in sight, and are nothing but a nuisance? Hardly."

"Good. I want to duplicate Holy Fire in them."

He stopped breaking apart his bread, not having expected her to work on an illness so difficult or obscure, unless she meant something other than what he was thinking. "Are you referring to the burning disease of France and England?"

"Spain too in the tenth century. My books relate instances of horrible sores and limbs growing black. Even when physicians cut off their patients' arms and legs to save their lives, many still died."

He parted his lips to the orange slice she fed him, again licking her fingers. "Many would say the illness is God's punishment for sinners."

"Do you believe it is?"

Not being a devout man, he'd never given religious subjects much consideration. Uncertain what her feelings were on the matter, he lifted his shoulders.

She finished a fig. "It seems curious to me God's displeasure would still affect other nations but not Spain. Has everyone here been so good these past centuries to have kept us in His favor?"

Enrique knew of ruthless thieves and murderous nobles who would kill their own mothers to gain even the smallest advantage over everyone else. Sancha's uncle had murdered her parents to steal her inheritance and would have slaughtered her, Isabella, and the rest of their sisters to get what he'd wanted. "Not at all. Have you any idea what might cause the malady?"

She sighed. "Something each of the countries has in common, otherwise the illness could never thrive in such diverse areas. England and France are far rainier than Spain. What we eat is somewhat similar to their fare in terms of bread, meat, and fruits, though none of it matches their diet exactly. What's more, the literature notes how patients grew better when they made pilgrimages to holy sites."

"Are you saying a miracle saved them?"

"No, though the Church believes so. Clearly, none of those in the hierarchy has read my books. After the patients from long ago returned to their homes, they grew ill again in the same manner. Something in their surroundings must have made them sick. Nothing else makes sense. At first, I thought the problem might be their poor nutrition. Throughout history, the illness never affects nobles, only peasants and the poor. Upon further reflection, I wondered if uncleanliness might be the cause."

Her comment sparked a memory in him. "You washed your hands before tending to Maria. You burned the blade and needle prior to using them."

She nodded. "The men who wrote the books stressed how a physician should have clean hands and implements. Although I searched the text for some means to fight Holy Fire, there was none. At one point, I did think the answer could be in tainted water." She made a face. "No matter how I spoiled what the mice drank, they never developed the same symptoms in my volumes. They simply stopped breathing and died."

Enrique warned himself not to smile or laugh at how casually she discussed these matters. He tried to imagine Luscinda talking about blackened limbs, how she dirtied water, and watched vermin die to discover the cause. "Weariness could be keeping you from an answer. You work too hard."

"I have no choice. What if the illness returns to Spain?"

"I will do everything in my power to protect you, our families, and those in the villages to spare you from having to tend the lot of us. I know you would try."

She laughed softly. "I can barely recall a time when I thought of naught but rest."

"Take this moment to do so."

He offered her the bota. After she took a long drink of wine, he fed her olives, a generous portion of cheese and bread, then more meat, running his finger over her bottom lip, brushing away crumbs.

At last, she caught his wrist and licked his forefinger.

Her damp heat registered in his belly, groin, and shaft, his sex painful with impossible need.

He eased his free hand into her silken hair and lowered her to the blanket, wanting to take her in every way, fill her with his child. Which would bind her to him forever, forcing her into a marriage she would find confining, killing the joy he'd seen in her today. Her willingness to share her thoughts, dreams, and concerns.

He wanted Sancha more than life itself, though not in such a way.

Although he reined in his feelings, he couldn't stop all his desire. "Allow me to pleasure you without compromising your virginity. No one is near, nor will they be."

Alarm didn't cross her features. She drank him in as he did with her. "What of you?" She touched his cheek, running her fingers to his jawline.

Stunning warmth and need coursed through him at her gentle touch. A wanton one would surely undo him. "Pleasing you is all I want."

"You deserve more. Allow me to pleasure you in the same manner."

He stared, not certain he'd heard her correctly. However, he must have. Her eyes were bright with passion, features softened with surrender. Perhaps she hadn't considered her words. "Have you any idea what you said?"

She nodded.

Far too casually for his taste, though her hand gliding down his throat to his chest was a touch straight from heaven. Even so, he needed to ask her what any man would. "How could you possibly know such things?"

"Isabella."

Of course. His brother was an incredibly lucky man to have met such a woman, though not as blessed as he was with Sancha beneath him.

With his weight and strength imprisoning her, he kissed her deeply, demanding she mold her mouth to his.

She did better than he'd hoped. Their tongues danced. She slid her hands up his chest and past his shoulders to his back, clinging to him as he did her as though some horrible tragedy would separate them in a moment and they had no time to lose. Noises poured from them, the kind only lovers make. A wanton moan, a lewd groan, growls and sighs. Music for the soul, sounds a man could build a future on.

He cradled her breast, frustrated by her clothing, layer upon layer keeping him from her heated flesh. He pulled his mouth free and pressed his face to her neck, his breath skimming her skin. "I want you naked."

With her hands cupping his head, she forced him to ease away and look at her. He dreaded doing so, not wanting to hear that she'd changed her mind about this and intended to return to her studies.

She regarded him solemnly.

He couldn't stand the suspense. "What?"

"I want the same of you. Fully naked."

Astounded and pleased, he grinned.

"You must take care with my virginity though. I may lose my resolve. You cannot."

He wanted to laugh, bellow his frustration, beg her to reconsider and agree to wed him, with their betrothal solving everything.

"Please." She touched his cheek lightly.

His heart stalled, then raced out of control, but he nodded, determined to honor her request. Getting them out of their clothes wasn't an opportunity he'd pass up, though the matter soon proved far more daunting than he planned. He wasn't a stranger to buttons and laces on a woman's garments. However, hers seemed made to defeat him.

Biting back oath after oath, he forced himself not to rend the fabric in his haste to uncover her. At last, her gown lay on the blanket, followed by her kirtle, farthingale, and chemise.

After placing her shoes to the side, Sancha faced him.

The sun had gone behind the trees, the last of its light streaming across her nudity. The finest cream couldn't have competed with the smooth texture of her skin, its flawless white flushed with pink. Her nipples were rosy and aroused, tips erect, the curls between her legs fiery, the same as her hair.

She looked too perfect to be real. His mouth watered.

She tugged on his shirt. "How does this come off? Why are you still wearing it?"

"I thought you were a woman with endless patience."

"I have been in the past when I had to see to my own restraint. Now I have you to protect me from myself."

Yes, there was that. He held back a sigh at what he'd promised, wondering if such denial would kill a man. Good sense told him to turn away, order her to dress, return to the castle, and drink himself into a stupor.

His heart wouldn't allow defeat, urging him to woo her to his side, prove she could trust him not to clip her wings as she did with him.

Before either of them changed their minds, he tossed his shoes aside, pulled off his belt, shirt, hose, and braies, dropping everything into a messy pile. At last, he was naked and fully aroused.

* * * *

She studied him as one would a celebrated painting or a brilliant sunset, speechless at its beauty.

His arms were muscular, and his chest, torso, and the rest of him so perfect she'd never understand how anyone could consider a man's nudity wrong. To her, his male beauty was miraculous.

Dark hair dusted his powerful calves and thighs. His sex was pendulous, the root of his shaft nestled in a nest of thick, dark curls. Veins dashed up the erect column, his crown scarlet with passion. A bead of clear fluid escaped the small slit at the top.

She longed to touch and taste the pearl of moisture but still had far too much to see. His sac was lightly furred, the two halves plump to make a perfect whole. Yearning and curiosity encouraged her to touch and explore him as a blind woman might, caressing every part until she'd had her fill.

She never would.

She'd guessed his intent about these moments when he'd come to her room with his basket. Yet, she hadn't stopped him. Didn't want to. She'd been in agony these last weeks with him so close, every look, word, unexpected touch tormenting her. Hours would go by with her reading the same passage dozens of times understanding none of the words. Her mind kept drifting to him. She'd listened for his footfalls, waited to hear his deep voice as he spoke to a servant, smiled when he laughed, wondering what had made him happy.

Avoiding Enrique hadn't caused her to forget him. Her longing had merely deepened, driving her mad with desire. She still feared succumbing to their basest needs, though not because it was wrong. Sancha couldn't imagine anything more sacred than a man and a woman coming together, or a matter more frightening than marriage when it came to her freedom.

She'd come to treasure her days and nights of undisturbed study, not wanting to lose the peace she had. If only the quiet moments would stop killing her with an incessant desire to be with him.

They both had known this day of reckoning would come. The only solution to their attraction was pleasuring each other without jeopardizing her virginity. At least for today. She didn't want to consider what might happen tomorrow or in the coming moments.

He eased her to the blanket, hair tumbling over his forehead, his forelock enthralling her as much as the rest of him. The balmy air caressed, tightening her nipples, skimming across the dampness between her legs. Proof she wanted this moment and him. She wreathed her arms around his neck and held him close, reveling in his naked flesh pressed to hers. His skin was delightfully hot, chest, groin, and legs roughened with hair she found incredibly masculine and seductive.

He kissed her thoroughly, his tongue slipping deep. A poor substitute for his rigid shaft burrowed within her channel as she gave his thickened member a home.

She raised her hips to meet his, part instinct, part need.

He eased back, denying her, controlling his passion because she couldn't manage to do the same with hers, proving his honor. She clung to him, wanting nothing more than to know the full extent of his desire and would have given anything for those moments, even her soul. But not her freedom to do with her life as she willed.

Any other man might have left her frustrated and wanting. Not him. He trailed kisses from her cheek to her throat and chest, at last cupping her breast, confining the soft globe in his palm. At the stroke of his thumb, her nipple tightened, the tip begging for his mouth.

He brushed his lips over that part of her, then tongued her flesh. A shock of delight raced through Sancha. He suckled her nipple as a babe would, loving her with the strength of a man.

He groaned throatily. She cradled his head to keep him at his task and ran her fingers down his back then his arms, desperate to touch each part of him, saddened she couldn't as yet.

He latched onto her left breast and trailed his hand down her belly to her triangle of hair, exploring her at his leisure.

Currents of pleasure dashed through her, building relentlessly at him touching the fur between her legs, dipping his fingers to her damp folds. She trembled.

He stilled his hand and licked her nipple instead, biting the tip gently before he suckled once more.

Adoring his touch, needing him close, she pushed her leg to the side and exposed her sex, proving she wanted him to know every part of her.

He fitted his mouth to hers again, his desire scarcely controlled. Deep, uncivilized sounds rumbled from him that would have frightened her if they'd come from another man. His excitement stoked hers. She lifted her hips, giving him what he wanted, eager for all she'd yet to experience.

He eased his fingers down her cleft, slick with her desire. His groan sounded pleased. He touched her nub, the kernel hard and sensitive.

Jolts of heat and aching need sped through her. She gasped around his tongue.

He kissed her more deeply and stroked, increasing the delight. A curious tension coiled within her, begging for freedom. She squirmed, wanting release, yet she also fought its arrival, the delicious ache between her legs maddening, thrilling, too much for any woman to bear.

Cry after cry flowed from her, muted by his tongue.

She dug her fingers into his arm. He stroked more slowly and finally stopped to rest his hand on her thigh.

No. This couldn't be the sum of his passion and her pleasure. When she and Isabella had spoken, her sister claimed the feeling should burst and flood to every part of her. The thrilling pressure between Sancha's legs had already dulled and began to fade.

She pulled her mouth from Enrique's to question him.

He rubbed her once more, harder and faster than earlier, not stopping this time, bringing her to a place she'd never been. Pleasure so intense, she could barely endure the feelings and cried loudly.

A bird squawked and took wing, rustling leaves, the same as the light wind. She gasped and gulped air in her struggle to catch her breath. Impossible. A pulse ticked deep within her channel. Swells of heat bombarded her, followed by delicious weakness, the moment more astonishing than what Isabella had claimed.

Sancha clasped Enrique with the little strength she had left, her cheek against his shoulder. "Gracias."

"You enjoyed my touch, no?"

She would crave him until time ended. Possibly beyond. "Sí. As soon as I catch my breath, I must see to your pleasure."

"I have yet to finish with you." He slid down to kiss her torso, belly, and finally her delicate curls.

Her cheeks stung.

"Open your legs." He pushed against them gently. "Part them for me."

She wanted to obey but needed a moment. Having him stare at her most intimate area gave her pause.

He asked no more. With his palms on the insides of her thighs, he spread her widely and positioned the soles of her feet on the blanket to display and expose her sex to him.

Her face burned. The breeze did nothing to cool her, seeming to blow nowhere except the folds between her legs drenched with moisture.

He ran his fingers up and down her slit.

She stared at the sky, the leaves, a bird on a branch far above her. Enrique touched her nub and stroked slowly. The glorious tension mounted within her again, her mouth sagging open, breaths faltering. He pulled his hand away. No! She lifted her hips, frantic for his touch, demanding he continue. He didn't.

She struggled to her elbows. He smiled broadly. She had no idea why when he hadn't given her relief. "Touch me again."

He rested his fingers on her mound and stroked her hard kernel.

Moaning crudely, she dropped to the blanket and kept moving into his hand, her body acting independently of her thoughts. The logic she'd always employed evaporating beneath his skilled touch. Her sole goal now was to experience this moment fully.

She lifted her hips. He withdrew his hand. She growled. "Touch me."

"In time."

"Now."

"Later."

Oh, this man. "Have you forgotten how to finish the task? Do you need me to remind you?"

He laughed. "Never. My hands are hardly the only way I can offer pleasure."

He slid his palms beneath her, lifted her buttocks, and lowered his mouth to her cleft.

She moaned, the sound wanton and passionate, speaking of her desire for a man among men.

He tasted her folds, grunting softly, growling too, his pleasure noisy and obvious. He seemed uncertain whether to lick her, tongue her nub, or bury his face in her curls, trying to do all three simultaneously. His appetite for her sex appeared as endless as her hunger for him. He paid no heed to her bawdy cries, except to squeeze her cheeks, keeping her still and close to him.

Nothing would have made her move away. Not the servants return or an inquisitor's presence. If she was damned, she wanted this act to be her last before facing an eternity without him.

He kissed the inside of her thigh, giving Sancha a brief respite from the wonder he stirred, then held her nub carefully between his teeth and licked relentlessly.

A tempest of delight battered her, more intense than what he'd done earlier. She dug her nails into the blanket for some measure of control. He slid his thumb down the furrow between her cheeks and touched her tightest opening.

The pressure between her legs broke free, relief rolling in from all directions, lifting her to heights she'd never known. She seemed to reach the sky, spin wildly, then drift back down. Exactly as Isabella had claimed when she'd said this act allowed a woman to soar.

In the aftermath, Sancha could scarcely breathe. Perspiration coated her throat, a drop sliding between her breasts. Her legs wobbled, her limbs too heavy for her to lift, body spent.

Enrique grinned, his hands still on her.

Never would she complain about his touch. She smiled as well as she could, craving sleep but denying herself any rest. "Now, I see to you."

Chapter 6

How could he refuse her giving and lusty suggestion?

She looked like a cross between an angel and temptress, her hair mussed from his passion, several tresses spilled over her shoulders to graze her breasts. A most seductive and shameless image. He'd used her nipples well, their tint slightly darker than their natural state, the halos around the tips pebbling at his scrutiny.

They and her soft folds had tasted more delicious than the finest foods he'd known, her response equal to his desire. Sancha wanted him.

She may have decided it was best for him to protect her virtue, but in time she had to see the wisdom of their coupling and wedding, or their marriage first before full intimacy. As far as he was concerned the order of events hardly mattered.

She was his for a lifetime. Their union a done deal.

Pity he didn't have her full acceptance and compliance now. Sighing in stark need, he dropped to the blanket, arms and legs flung out, hiding nothing. His member was so rigid it lay on his belly, the crown pointing at his chest. No matter how many breaths he took, none seemed sufficient. "I accept your offer."

Her laughter filled the pleasant air, dusk beginning to settle on them. No matter. Tonight the moon would be fat, allowing her to peruse his nudity while he did the same with hers.

At his side, she glided her fingers over his throat and down his chest, her touch light yet powerful enough to stir a dead man to life. She circled the flat discs of his nipples, making the tiny tips stand erect.

His shaft grew longer and harder, the skin stretched painfully. He feared his flesh might split if relief didn't come soon.

She ran her fingers through the crisp curls on his chest and swept her tongue over his nipple, generating heat that had his toes curling and his sex demanding its due immediately. Even a short wait might do him in.

Unmoved by his turmoil, she suckled his nipple and stroked the hair in his armpits.

"Enough." He wiggled. "There are other parts of me requiring your ardent attention."

"As you wish."

She curled her fingers around his thickened shaft, her thumb on the small slit. With the moisture from the opening, she lubricated his cap and ran her thumb over the plump head to the uneven skin on the back.

An eruption of pleasure tore through him, stealing his breath. He lifted his hips, seeking her marvelous touch.

She stopped stroking the spot to work her sweet fingers up and down his shaft instead, mirroring what her channel would do.

A riot of feelings bombarded him. He shuddered. Her strokes grew harder, faster. He tensed, driven closer to the edge.

She slid down him, reaching his tangle of curls and rubbed her nose against his thatch, inhaling deeply of his fragrance.

Their musk already perfumed the air, driving him past restraint.

He panted, barely able to keep still at her stroking the back of his crown. A squall of heat and unrelieved passion battered him. He held his breath, trying to stave off the whirlwind, wanting to prolong the act. No good. His lungs burned so badly, he lost what air he had on an explosive sigh.

She tongued the base of his shaft.

He gritted his teeth hard enough to make his jaw hurt. One more lick… no. What she was doing was too much. He cupped her head. "Enough."

"Are you quite certain? You haven't reached the most pleasurable part. Nothing has happened."

She couldn't be serious. "What are you doing? Do you intend to take me in your mouth?"

"If you allow me."

He'd wanted nothing more from the other women he'd known. The well-bred ladies had never suggested or offered their mouths in such a brazen fashion. Only harlots had given him unrestrained delight. "Is this more of Isabella's doing?"

"My sister likes to talk. Because I love her dearly, I am obliged to listen."

His laughter sounded slightly frantic to him. "You two…"

"My sister and I are no different from you or any other man."

Sobering, he lifted his head, taking in her breasts and the delightful hair above her cleft. "I beg to differ."

"Do what you must, but in our needs we are quite the same. Why should I deny myself your amazing body, surely the most wondrous of any man, when you never hesitated a whit when it came to mine?"

She had a point. He slumped to the blanket, hands still on her head. "Do what you must."

Her soft laughter sounded amused. "You will not regret this."

How could he? She drew her tongue down his shaft and cupped his sac in her palm, running her thumbnail over the ruddy skin. The slight rasp registered at the top of his head, the back of his throat, the tips of his fingers and toes. He groaned lustily.

She dipped her tongue into the small opening in his crown.

Never had another señorita savored this part of him as she did, not even the ones paid to deliver pleasure. To them, sex was work with an ample reward if they performed well. To a lady, coupling with a man was part of her duty as a wife and mother, not a delight she couldn't live without.

To Sancha, enjoying the man he was seemed enough for her without any hidden or unhidden motives. As though she'd been born to pleasure him in the most intimate acts as he did the same with her.

He released her head and ground the heels of his hands into his eyes. She slipped his crown into her mouth, its heat warmer than the sun, her tongue sweeping, licking, loving.

He couldn't stay still. He stiffened, relaxed, then grew rigid once more, all feeling centered in his groin, his passion threatening to consume him. Desperate to keep from reaching his peak and having this end, he tugged on his hair.

She slipped another inch of his member into her mouth, followed by more until she finally reached the end, her nose pressed against his hairy groin.

His mouth hung open, words beyond him, noises his only means to communicate. He growled and groaned like a wild creature. She eased back, allowing his shaft to slip out except for the head that she imprisoned between her lips. He never realized anyone's mouth could be so hot and wet. She took his full length back inside, running her lips up and down him, creating the same heat and friction her channel would.

Perhaps better. Her tongue added a dimension to the erotic play her sheath never could.

He bellowed his delight. Before the sound had faded, he shouted again, his seed spurting before he could warn her to move away.

She remained, her mouth still around his sex as she swallowed.

Overwhelmed and humbled, he cradled the back of her head to let her know she'd honored him. He was still too weary to speak.

Once she'd finished, she let his shaft slip from her mouth and tongued his sac.

His hair stood on end. He cupped her head. "No. Enough. I cannot...."

She stopped tonguing him. "It is true."

"What is?"

She rested her chin on his hipbone and circled his navel with her finger. "A man can endure most anything: the prick of a sword, hunger, thirst, intense heat, unbearable cold, but not a woman's tongue on him after he spills his seed."

Heat flooded his cheeks. This was too much. She'd actually put him to the blush. "Would that be another of Isabella's tales?"

"Not a tale, the truth. With you, I proved what she said."

"It would be wise for you to stop listening to your sister."

"That would be rude."

He lifted his head to look at her. She laughed quite gaily. "Would you prefer me to be less bold?"

Such a request would be like asking the sun not to shine, the wind to stop blowing, rain not to fall. That would be a tragedy of the greatest order. "Never change. Stay precisely as you are. Except I want you up here, near me, rather than so far away."

She settled in his arms, her hand on his chest. He gathered her even closer and draped his calf over hers. She slid her other leg across his until her knee reached his groin, his shaft warmed by her heated flesh. "Comfortable?"

He stroked her hair. "I am. You?"

She nodded.

He finished his yawn. "We must do this again."

Her breasts wiggled against his chest with her soft laughter. "Indeed."

Happier than he'd ever been, he stroked her silky back, his movements dulled by spent pleasure. At last, he had to rest his hand on her hip, unable to do more.

She nestled closer. "Sleep."

"Not long. Promise to wake me within a minute."

"I fear the time you speak of has already passed."

"Two then. No more. I want your pledge."

She rubbed his chest in answer and snuggled closer, delighting him to the point he forgot what to say next and surrendered to fatigue.

* * * *

His quiet breathing was more comforting to Sancha than anything she'd ever heard. Within the protection of his caress, she knew contentment. How right Isabella had been on the wonder of sharing intimate moments with a lover.

As long as he was the right man, of course.

She couldn't imagine giving herself to anyone other than Enrique. He seemed created for her, her for him, everything fitting, nothing at odds. The notion should have made her leap with joy and run headlong into a life with him.

Having witnessed other women's lives tempered her joy. To the outside world, her mamá and papá had the perfect union. Sancha had never known a couple more devoted to each other. Her mamá had always been willing to give her life for her husband, with him feeling the same about her. He denied her nothing except decisions, a voice, a goal of her own.

Her mother had craved knowledge on potions and poultices, the same as Sancha, only she'd denied her needs in favor of her husband's.

Her mamá hadn't been unhappy, but she'd never been truly fulfilled. She knew of Sancha's dreams and encouraged her, without her husband's knowledge, of course. She'd listened with interest to everything Sancha had learned, her expression hungry for converse that didn't involve children or her husband's pursuits and victories.

Sancha hoped she'd given her mamá a part of life she'd missed.

For her to have come this far and to have risked so much only to surrender everything to Enrique would go against what she believed in. Worse, if she submitted fully to his needs and neglected her own, she might grow to resent him one day, even though none of her pain would be his fault.

He simply behaved as men did, raised to anticipate obedience from women. He demanded nothing now, because he couldn't. If they wed and had children, he'd expect her to devote her life to them and him to the exclusion of everything else. A role everyone demanded women to fill, no matter how unfair and foolish.

Men waged wars, built cities, expanded their estates, advanced science, painted, sculpted, made the world a better or worse place and still sired children. No one said they couldn't because of their other, more important duties of husband and father.

Would there ever be a time when women were equal to men?

Fearing not, she sighed deeply. At the same moment, Enrique loosened his hold on her and rolled to his back.

A more resolute woman would have seized the opportunity to return to the castle alone, no longer wanting pleasure, looking forward to studies and experiments.

Sancha wanted those things, but she craved Enrique too. She propped herself on one elbow, loving how peaceful and innocent he looked in sleep, like a little boy. The son he would surely want.

He wasn't going to give up his notion of wedding her. She'd have to leave his side first, their moments together counted in weeks, not decades, the passage of this day reducing their time even more.

He'd wanted her to give him only a few minutes to sleep. She'd promised nothing, allowing him full rest.

A plump moon finally hung in the inky sky. Stars winked. The ducks had departed long ago, their honks replaced by insect chirps. A bird flapped its wings, adding to the night sounds, along with animal noises in the distance, and Enrique's faint snores.

She turned to him, her heart catching at how wonderful he looked, the pleasure she found in lying at his side. The time had already passed for her to avoid love. She was falling more deeply with each second, the events of this evening serving to feed her desire and foolish hope that he could be different from other men, allowing her full latitude in everything she did. He knew she wasn't a fool who would bring either of them harm or ruin. How splendid if he could also trust her opinions and decisions, or at least discuss them, before he demanded she do as he wanted.

Picturing such a paradise, she smiled.

He snored loudly and jerked at the sound, his expression confused as to what had awakened him.

One look at the sky revealed how long he'd slept. He pushed to a sitting position and frowned. "You promised to wake me."

"I did no such thing." She sat up as he had. "I stroked your chest and you accepted that as my answer."

"Fool that I am." The corners of his mouth turned down. "Look at what time it is. The day nearly over."

As far as she was concerned, the night still stretched before them. She wasn't going to speculate what might happen on the morrow. After pushing to her feet, she offered her hand. "Come."

He regarded her nudity bathed in moonlight, his attention tarrying most on her nipples and mound. Her sheath was still so damp from their passion the moisture must have sparkled in the silvery rays. Enrique seemed incapable of looking anywhere else.

She finally wiggled her fingers at him as he had earlier with her.

He didn't accept the bait. "Where do you intend to lead me?"

She inclined her head to the left.

"The pond?"

She longed to go there before leaving this spot. When she was growing up, her father had never allowed her, Isabella, or their sisters to enjoy themselves in a stream or pond. Water was for bath times, always in their chambers, behind closed doors, with female servants attending them.

Her male cousins had frolicked in whatever water they found, always nude. Isabella had repeatedly dragged Sancha with her to spy on the spectacle, giggling madly as she watched.

She leaned down to Enrique. "Do you know how to swim?"

"Of course."

"Will you teach me?" Isabella had learned on her own, away from their father's prying gaze. No surprise. She'd always been outspoken, a warrior, when Sancha preferred to handle things quietly. Pretending to be demure had caused her far less trouble and notice.

Enrique pushed to his feet, his brow furrowed. "Why do you want to learn?"

He made her request sound as though she planned to swim to another continent, no doubt to escape the shackles of marriage. "Why did you?"

"I had no say in the matter. When I was four, my father brought me to a stream, tossed me in and shouted, 'Swim or drown!'"

"Oh no. What an awful thing to do to a child."

He shrugged. "I learned not to drown. Do you fear coming upon a body of water when you visit the peasants?"

"No. I thought swimming might be fun. Is it?"

"Indeed. Come, let me show you." With her fingers entwined in his, he led her to the pond.

She held back suddenly, recalling what he'd said earlier. "If you plan to throw me in and expect me to survive, you may be surprised that I drown."

"I am not my father." He pulled her forward. "Take care, though, the water might be colder than you like."

She welcomed anything to cool her fevered skin and desire. All Enrique had to do was hold her hand and she forgot her resolve.

The sweep of water against her calves and thighs was lovely. If she'd been a man and lived here the rest of her days, she'd come to this spot each night to dig her toes in the mud and sink into the water's refreshing embrace. "What now?"

He cupped her face and kissed her.

Sancha slumped against him, powerless against his needs, with hers as pressing. Once he'd finished and eased his mouth from hers, she didn't move away. "Was that my first lesson?"

He laughed. "No. My passion. Take a deep breath." He demonstrated how. "Hold it then lie back in the water. Face up."

Of course. Face down would be foolish. Still, she wrinkled her nose. "And go under?"

"Not with my hands beneath you until you feel confident. The air you took in helps to keep you from sinking, allowing you to float."

She recalled when she and Isabella had spied on their cousins. If memory served her, the boys had floated on their backs.

"Allow no fear," Enrique said. "Anyone who becomes alarmed and thrashes about sinks like a stone."

"If I do, will you save me?"

He gave her a tender smile. "Always. Now do what I say."

She lifted one eyebrow.

"Whenever you feel you can."

She liked when he afforded her the same consideration he would a man. Preparing herself mentally, she pulled in as much air as she could, held it, scrunched her face, and fisted her fingers.

He pointed. "You still need to go into the water."

She fell back into the pond, sank faster than a stone, and flailed her arms, trying to right herself.

He pulled her to her feet. "I said lie back in the water, not fall."

She coughed and gasped. "I did precisely as you instructed."

"Very well, but do so more slowly this time."

She clawed wet hair from her face. After taking another deep breath, she inched toward the water, bending back as far as possible without falling in.

His shoulders trembled with quiet laughter. "A trifle faster, if you please."

Tensed, Sancha did as well as she could.

As promised, he kept one hand beneath her buttocks, the other under her back. To her amazement, she didn't sink, though her lungs ached.

"Sancha."

She nodded.

"You can let out your breath and take another."

She did, grinning as she stayed on the surface, floating effortlessly. "What happens when you remove your hands?"

"I fear telling you."

His laughter said otherwise. "Release me. I want to find out."

"Very well." He pulled back his hands.

She folded at the waist, her buttocks dragging her to the bottom. She flailed again.

"Be still." He slid his hands to where they had been and lifted her. "What did I say about thrashing?"

"To accept my fate and drown with dignity?"

He laughed loudly. "We shall keep at this until you perform to my standards."

Such dedication could take the remainder of the night. A heady and delightful prospect.

He instructed her calmly while she did nothing but panic. At last, she grew so weary and annoyed she didn't care what occurred. Her new outlook resulted in success. She floated on her own, gliding her arms and legs through the water while staring at the starry sky. "This is marvelous. You must teach me to swim."

"During your next lesson."

"When?"

"Tomorrow evening. Surely you must want to rest now."

She'd never experienced such energy or power, having conquered her fear and succeeded at a skill he had. Once he taught her to swim, they could challenge each other. He'd win, of course, being larger and stronger, but she'd show him she was as good as any man.

Hopefully, he would then believe in her ability to run her own life, removing an obstacle to their relationship. Possibly giving them a chance for a future together.

"Are you famished?" she asked. "I am."

Out of the water, she ran toward the blanket. He passed her easily and settled first, handing over the bread, cheese, and meat. She offered him half of everything and gobbled her share greedily. They ate, drank, and smiled until the food and wine made them sluggish.

She stifled a yawn. "I wish we could stay out here forever."

Finishing the last of the olives, he took in her breasts and the reddish curls between her legs. "Dawn may make you change your mind."

His servants certainly would. She smiled. "Tomorrow evening it is. Give me your oath not to forget."

"To keep you from drowning?"

Laughing, she threw the last of her bread at him. The piece bounced off his chest and fell to the blanket.

He scowled playfully. "How dare you treat a noble lord in such a manner."

"I shall behave whatever way I feel."

"Is that so?"

"It most certainly—Enrique! Stop."

He straddled her and tickled until she gagged, unable to laugh or breathe. At last, she lay limp beneath him.

He grinned broadly. "Remember this lesson well."

How could she forget? This night was the most captivating she'd ever spent. Surely, the coming ones couldn't be better.

They kissed until they needed a full breath, then enjoyed each other again. He suckled her breasts once more and buried his face between her legs. She licked his sac and shaft, bringing him to completion a second time, wanting him as happy as she was.

After he peaked, he refused to rest. "Time for bed. Both of us need sleep, especially you." Once he'd tended to her laces and buttons, he pulled on his garments, gathered the basket, and threw the blanket over his shoulder.

Hand in hand, they strolled back to the castle, their hair slightly damp from the pond, clothes wrinkled, neither of them caring how they looked. Her sighs and his were content, movements unhurried.

Upon reaching the rear entrance, he took the long way to her chamber, a delay to their eventual parting. They entered an unused area, seemingly reserved for storage.

Scuffling noises broke out.

Enrique looked over. So did she.

Two of his guards supported a third man between them, his clothes filthy and quite odd, nothing like what an ordinary Spaniard wore, not even peasants. Rather than hose, the garment covering his legs was as voluminous as a woman's skirt or a robe, his shirt the same, belted with a sash. He sported a beard, his complexion swarthy, expression dazed. Blood stained his arm and torso.

Sancha pressed her hand to her throat.

"What goes on?" Enrique strode to the group.

The taller of his guards, a burly man who appeared no more than twenty, spoke first. "Forgive the intrusion, *patrón*. The men you sent to the other side of the estate found this savage hiding in your fields. He must have been with the Moors tonight and became separated from them. They raided the village to the west, taking what they willed, wounding some of the people."

Chapter 7

"Wait here for my return," Enrique said to his men. With his hand on Sancha's arm, he led her past them.

She resisted and pressed her mouth to his ear. "We must go to the village."

"What—why?"

"You heard what your guard said. The people there are injured. I can treat them. After I tend to your prisoner, we can leave."

"No." He tightened his grip. "The only place you go tonight is your room."

"By force?"

He held back a sigh and loosened his hold.

She immediately pulled her arm free and rubbed the spot where he'd held her. "I am not going to my room."

He warned himself not to say something he'd regret and spoke to his guards instead. "Take him away."

The man couldn't match their quick pace. They dragged him.

Alone with Sancha, Enrique turned to her. "How dare you question my authority in front of my men."

"Forgive me, but you gave me no choice. The people need my skills and I intend to go to them."

"You will not." He kept his voice as low as she had. "I would never allow you to put yourself in danger to save anyone, not even me."

She frowned. "How can you say such a thing? When you invited me to stay here, you said I could heal and you would serve as my protector. When the time comes to do so, you want to keep me here. Did you lie to me before?"

"No. I said within reason. I never promised to accompany you to a village the Moors just attacked where there are more hazards than I care to consider."

"How could the danger persist? Your guard said the Moors took what they willed in the raid. The man they captured was hiding in the fields. That land is to the east, the same as Granada, where he and the others were surely heading before losing each other. I suspect his friends are back on their land and in their homes, not giving any of us a thought."

He made a face at her damnable logic. Of course, the Moors were gone, not that their absence changed anything. "I am not taking you to the village."

"Very well. Your guards can."

"Never."

"Then I shall go alone."

He blocked her before she could get around him. "How do you intend to get there without a horse? Walk?"

"If I have no other choice. The people need me."

What of him? Did his love for her and his worry over her safety mean nothing? Even if she cared naught about his devotion, he was master of this estate. He, not she, made the decisions concerning the land and people under his authority. He crossed his arms over his chest.

She didn't back down. "You cannot stand in my way on this."

He could. Being stronger, he'd succeed and lose her heart, as Isabella had warned. He wanted to shout his frustration and pain. Already, he'd tightened his shoulders to the point they ached. Why did she have to be so headstrong? Simple compliance to good sense was what he wanted and wouldn't get.

With her willfulness, they could be at odds for days. Never had he been as weary, not wanting to fight, only to love. Perhaps even compromise. "I can send my men to the village. They can collect the injured and bring them here for you to treat."

"How? Slung over a horse if the man or woman has fainted? What if they bleed heavily? They could die before I could do anything to help. The only solution is for me to go to them and save as many as I can."

"And risk injury or worse in another attack."

"You know the danger is past, otherwise you would never have offered to put your men in harm's way."

"Their duty is to face danger."

"The same as your brothers Tomás and Pedro, both soldiers. When they accompanied Isabella and Fernando to my castle, she said they boasted of past deeds, including how they bested the Moors during raids such as the one tonight. As I recall her tale, your brothers and the other men rode to the scenes as quickly as they could, defending the peasants, then fanned out to make certain other communities in the area faced no threat. I would think Tomás and Pedro would be particularly brave in protecting land under your authority and the route leading to your castle."

He dug his nails into his arms. "My brothers and their men have a surgeon available. They can use him to treat anyone who needs care."

"With the surgeon putting the wounded at further risk should he lack good skills. How many soldiers have died of injuries similar to Fernando's because the man charged with their care lacked the knowledge I have in my books?"

Too many, though their deaths weren't his concern. She was.

"I know you worry about me." She touched his arm. "I feel the same about you."

He searched her face and saw sincerity despite her stubbornness. Lost as to how he could make her listen to reason, he uncrossed his arms and covered her hand. "I have yet to do anything to cause you pain."

"You would if you felt you had no choice in doing what was right. I have no desire to hurt you in any way. I simply want to heal those in need, and I do promise to take care."

Until she risked even more to provide the outcome she wanted. At times like this, Sancha was as bad as a man. Worse. He cursed nature for not having made her cautious and compliant like other women. Knowing her, she'd walk to the village alone, potions and instruments in hand.

Weary, he held back a sigh. "Before we leave, you need to change."

"Gladly." She hugged him harder than she had after they'd enjoyed each other by the pond.

What a fool he'd been to have fallen in love with her, though he couldn't change the matter now. She was his life.

"What should I change into? One of your guard's clothing?"

He rolled his eyes. "One of the servant's."

"Male?"

He eased back to see if she were jesting. Her expression remained sober. "Do you prefer to wear men's garments?" Would that be another trial she'd put him through?

"No. I thought my dressing as a man would make the journey safer in your mind."

His, not hers. "Having you stay in your room would accomplish the goal."

She stepped back. "Will you bring me the clothing or should I find the garments on my own? Or, I could wear what I already have on."

"And call attention to your station and wealth? I think not. Go to your room. I can see to the items you need."

She didn't move. "What of the Moor? I should tend to his injuries."

Enrique clenched his jaw. "No. I don't want you touching any part of the filthy beast."

"You say that now, but when he heals and lives, your men could question him on the Moors' plans. Should he die, a great opportunity could be lost."

"Come with me." He took her arm.

"Wait—where do we go?"

"The Moor. Make fast work of tending him. Every minute at his side is less help for our people."

"I need my materials first."

"Gather them as I gain the clothes you need. Meet me here."

"I shall." After she'd given him another quick hug, she bolted down the hall, her footfalls fading quickly.

He dragged to the servants' quarters, pondering his future with her, questioning whether he could withstand many more moments like this, or if he could ever become accustomed to them. Images filled his mind of her heavy with his son, mounting a horse, galloping away, hair and the ends of her gown flying as she raced to village after village, intent on taking care of its inhabitants.

He pictured her turning the castle into a hospital with the ill everywhere, her darting from bed to bed, seeing to her charges and neglecting him.

He frowned at the awful scene and sought out Hortensia, an older woman in charge of the female staff. She'd been with his family for years, having known him as a willful little boy.

He found her near the castle entrance. "Señora."

"Patrón." Despite him holding her hands and smiling, she still bowed her head in deference to his station. Afterward, she winked. "What do you need?"

Sancha to love and obey him, what else? "Clothing for the señorita to blend in with other woman in the village." He wasn't about to explain further.

Hortensia nodded. "As you wish. I shall return in a moment."

"Tell the girl whose clothes you take I shall replace them and give her a reward for assisting me."

She smiled and hurried away.

He had the homespun garments within minutes, a long gown of dull red with a sleeveless tunic in brown. The girl had no shoes of her own, other than what he provided for her to work in. What Sancha usually wore would have to do.

He returned to where they'd spoken. She wasn't there. Turning a fast circle, he scanned the area, not seeing her. He was ready to go to where she studied when he had another idea.

Within the storage area were a few empty rooms, the ideal place for his guards to take the Moor.

The puto lay on the stone floor of an empty chamber without a window. Light came from two torches propped in holders on the walls. The Moor's chest was bare, his eyes closed. Sancha leaned over him, studying the slashes on his arm and torso. Enrique's guards stood to the side.

He stomped into the room. "I told you to wait for me."

She turned to him, a swatch of linen in one hand, a container of vinegar in the other. "He moaned so loudly, I feared he might die if I failed to tend him. Alive, he will be of great use to you. Dead, he is not."

Enrique motioned to his guards. "Out."

They closed the door behind them.

"Never challenge me in front of my men."

Her cheeks reddened. "I was merely giving you my reason for not waiting."

"Do not disobey me again either."

She regarded him. Quietly and coldly.

He didn't stand down.

She sighed. "I know you mean well. However, I am not your child to order about. You can offer a request, and I will consider the matter, then make my own decision how to proceed. The same as you would expect from me if I ever asked you to do anything."

Ever? "You have asked for so much I lost count of your endless requests. What I demand of you is not done to prove my authority but to keep you safe."

"I faced no danger in this room. Your men were close by protecting me."

He tightened his jaw.

She softened her stance. "I should have waited. Forgive me?"

He wasn't ready to but finally shrugged, then nodded.

She smiled. "Thank you for agreeing to take me to the village and allowing me to treat this man."

He stepped closer. "Did he swoon?"

"Not from his injuries. An earlier blow to his head." She eased his dark hair aside. Above his forehead was a knot the size of a goose egg, blood matted around the injury.

"Will he survive? His wounds seem less ghastly than Maria's."

"They are. I cleaned them as much as I could to avoid infection. Give me a moment to cover each with clean linen, then we can leave."

As disturbing as Enrique found the scene, he preferred her healing a Moor in the safety of his castle rather than riding to the village. Not that he feared a new attack. What she'd said was true. Soldiers raced to the scene of trouble, fighting, then guarding the besieged village along with others in the vicinity. Tomás and Pedro were surely out tonight. Seeing his brothers again would be a pleasure. Exposing her healing skills to even more peasants was not. Any one of them might gossip without meaning to, bringing her to the authorities' attention.

He'd known as much when he'd encouraged her to stay at his estate. He simply hadn't believed he'd face the problem this quickly, hoping everyone in the villages would remain healthy, along with her becoming so besotted with him, her healing would fall into the background.

If anything, she seemed more obsessed with her work each day.

She kept glancing at him, but finished with the Moor faster than Enrique had expected. "I can change in the empty room next to this one." After taking the servant's garments from him, she brushed her lips over his. "Then we can leave."

* * * *

Given the hour, she should have been tired. Concern over the wounded, anticipation of what she'd face at the village, and Enrique's dark mood kept her from rest as they travelled past a seemingly endless expanse of fields and pastures.

Dressed in the servant's clothing, she rode in front of him as she had the night at Fernando's castle. Enrique would hear of nothing else, even though she was capable of riding a horse. One of the few physical activities her papá had allowed his daughters to learn.

She recalled the wonderful swimming lesson she and Enrique had shared, a bright and promising moment between them. Gone now. Wanting to ease the tension, she turned to speak softly so the guards wouldn't overhear. His men were at a distance but still surrounded them, affording her further protection. "I look forward to our next night at the pond."

Enrique made a sound acknowledging her comment. A response greater than a grunt seemed beyond his capabilities.

She'd angered him at the castle, wounded him too with her behavior in front of his men. She would have done anything to avoid such confrontations if she'd known what the solution might be, other than submitting fully like a dutiful child. Deep inside, she sensed he didn't want her to behave as though she hadn't a mind or spirit. He enjoyed her fire.

To a point.

Missing his converse, she surrendered first. "Are you never going to speak to me again?"

He shifted slightly. His shaft pressed against her buttocks, growing thick and hard as it had when he'd first mounted. "Did you speak?"

His tone was far cooler than his other reaction to her. "Only of our pond. And my swimming."

"You floated. Barely."

She released her weight into him, stirred by his deep voice, teasing, and the way his arm tightened to hold her closer. "I shall prove myself in the coming days."

He grunted.

She sighed. They were back to him making noises rather than talking to her. "Are you tired of teaching me? Am I such a poor student? I request your answer please, not grunts, groans, or moans, no matter how much you intend to wound me with what you say."

"Wound you?" He pressed his mouth to her ear. "Every journey you make to these villages, every man, woman, or child you treat exposes your healing further."

So, they were back to that. She had hoped they'd moved beyond it. "These people are as loyal to you as your servants and guards are, no?" She spoke as quietly as he had. "You behave honorably with the peasants too, seeing to their welfare?"

"Of course. However, they are not at my castle where I can make certain they keep their tongues, saying nothing untoward. Who knows what the peasants might discuss after we leave? Gossiping about events is natural, even if they intend no harm."

He was right, of course. What had seemed a chance for her to help and learn appeared foolish now. She should have considered his feelings, chiding herself for not doing so. "Allow me to ride with the guards so you can return to the castle. That way, none of the peasants will see you with me. You can escape harm."

"What? No." He held her closer. "My concern is for your safety, not mine."

"If I come under suspicion, you will too, as I told you the day you offered your protection. The only answer is for no one to see us together outside your castle. In fact, I never should have agreed to stay there. Doing so was as thoughtless as keeping my books at Fernando's."

Enrique huffed. "Where do you intend to go? No place in Spain is safe from the Inquisition. The wisest course is to do nothing to bring attention to yourself."

She didn't comment.

"I will not let you go to any village without me. Even if you return to your castle, Fernando's, or someone else's, you have my protection whether you want it or not. And I do mean to see to your well-being if I have to threaten the peasants to keep their tongues concerning your work. If they fail to do so, I promise them a fate worse than any Moor could bring."

She looked over. "I never meant to bring you such anguish."

"Something to keep in mind when you treat your patients. Make certain they know to keep silent on the matter. I will see to everyone else. We approach."

A band of men on horseback blocked the road. Torches illuminated the helmeted soldiers in their distinctive red hose, boots, and upper-body armor. All carried crossbows, short swords, and long pikes. One man even had an arquebus.

The one in the lead held up his hand to the others, gesturing them to stay where they were. He, alone, rode to meet them, sword drawn, his attention on the guards, her, and finally Enrique.

Even in the faint light, Sancha recognized the man's handsome features.

"Brother, how good to see you." Tomás grinned. "How surprising too, considering…" He directed his horse closer, taking her in, before he smiled warmly. "Sancha."

Enrique sniffed. "Señorita Doña Sancha to you." He drew her closer, quite obviously and possessively.

Tomás gave her one of his winning grins. "Fair maiden, enchanting goddess, exquisite temptress, wondrous—"

"Tomás, as you know, loves to talk." Enrique stroked her hip. "You must ignore him."

Scowling, Tomás removed his helmet, revealing his surprisingly blond hair, thick and wavy.

She smiled at what a beautiful man he was.

With the helmet under his arm, he lifted her hand and kissed her fingertips. "How have you been since we spoke at the convent?"

"Well. Fernando is too. And Isabella. She mentions you and Pedro often."

Tomás rested one arm on his saddle's horn and leaned toward her, his expression playful. "In the most favorable way, I trust."

Sancha laughed softly. Isabella had said he could charm even the dourest woman. How right she was. "She has only the best to say on the de Zayas brothers."

Tomás arched one eyebrow, which was surprisingly dark, the same as his stubble, given his light hair. "Surely, she never included Enrique in her praise. Tell me, how did you come to be with him this evening? Did he snatch you from those you truly want to be with? If so, say the word and I will run him through."

Enrique knocked Tomás's hand away from hers. "The moment you can best me, little brother, is the day I take to my bed."

"You are quite old."

She smiled at their banter and the way they clasped forearms, greeting each other, affection and loyalty on their faces.

"What damage did the Moors do?" Enrique asked.

Tomás glanced at the guards.

Enrique spoke to his men. "Join the soldiers."

Once they rode away, Tomás turned to her. "Have you come here to heal?"

"Sí."

"Two of the men are past hope. They were at the entrance to the village, guarding the others. Fire burned one poor fellow before anyone was able to put out the flames. Some of the others have wounds on their arms, legs, and torsos, though none seems deadly. For the most part, the women and children are safe, having run into the forest, hiding there when the raid began."

She didn't understand. "What do you mean for the most part?"

"One young woman is heavy with child. The events caused the babe to want to come earlier than he should."

"Has she had the infant?"

"She was still in the birthing process shortly before you arrived."

Enrique glanced around. "Is the surgeon here?"

"He saw what was needed, did all he could, and said he was returning to the *fortaleza*. If anyone new required his skills, we could send for him again."

She suspected the man had done little, hardly knowing any better, blaming his botched treatments on his patients' poor health or God's will. "What of the women who usually tend to the ill in this village?"

Tomás lifted his shoulders. "No one came forward to help the worst of the lot. Many of the women are too busy taking care of their own husbands and others in their families to worry about anyone else."

"May I see the wounded?"

He exchanged a glance with Enrique, seeking his permission to grant what she'd asked. Her cheeks burned at him affording Enrique the right of a husband over her, but she kept her tongue. Neither man meant harm. They were simply behaving as males did in regards to women.

Enrique blew out a sigh but finally nodded. "Show us."

After a short ride, they reached the community. The area stank of smoke as most villages seemed to, only this stench was far worse. The Moors had set fire to the roofs of several huts. Black smoke and steam billowed upward. The villagers and soldiers worked feverishly to quench the flames, saving as much as they could. Pens that had probably been tidy and well-tended were now in disarray, the animals gone or killed. A pig's carcass lay to the left, the wound in the animal's side bloody and gaping. Someone had nearly beheaded a mule. The creature's body had fallen on a mongrel, also dead.

A lone chicken flapped its wings, running wildly to the left and the right, not seeming to know where to go. Blood drenched its feathers.

Enrique helped her to dismount and held her sack of supplies beneath his arm. She leaned in. "Can you see if the young woman needs help birthing?"

He stared. "Me? Why?"

"I want to help the man who was burned." She took her sack from him. "I fear he may need my treatment in order to survive. If the young woman is in distress, I will assist her without delay."

Enrique pushed his fingers through his hair.

"Please?"

He gestured Tomás over. "Will you show Sancha where the man with the burn is and stay with her to make certain nothing untoward happens?"

"Pedro can." Tomás lifted his hand to a group of men nearby and called. "Pedro. Over here."

He ran to them. Slightly shorter than Tomás, he had the same dark hair as Enrique, though he had no white forelock, and a charming smile identical to his other brothers'. "Sancha, how good to see you again." He took her hand. "What brings you here, and with Enrique no less? Has he finally convinced you to allow his courtship?"

Even in the gloom, Enrique's cheeks darkened with embarrassment. He glared at his brother.

Pedro smiled. "If not, may I offer my interest?"

"Fool." Tomás pushed Pedro's hand from hers. "Sancha is here to heal."

He nodded gravely. "The birthing is over there." He pointed toward the sound of high shrieks and wails. "Given the mother's continued agony, I suspect the babe will take his good time in coming."

She made no move toward the woman. "I need to see the man who was burned."

He made a face. "Are you certain? He was screaming quite piteously until he swooned. No wonder. His skin hangs from the side of his face in shreds, like pieces of ruined linen. The odor is more than anyone could possibly endure, smelling worse than—"

"Enough." Enrique's high color had faded, replaced by an ashy pallor, the same as Tomás's. "Show her and remain at her side."

"Of course." After grabbing a torch, Pedro offered his arm to Sancha, keeping his peace until they were out of earshot. "If you swoon, should I call Enrique or wait until you recover on your own?"

She smiled at his sweet guilelessness and allowing her, rather than anyone else, to make the decision. "I shall do my best not to cause any trouble."

"You?" He shook his head. "If Enrique gives you a moment's difficulty, I will beat him to within an inch of his life."

He'd have to wait for Tomás to run him through first. She wondered if all brothers spoke so casually about harming each other. The worst she and her sisters had done was stop talking after they'd finished screaming. As the eldest, she'd made the least amount of noise. Carmen and Concepcion, the two youngest, were the worst, known to pull each other's hair and leave bite marks. With them at court, under the Queen's tutelage, such activities had surely ceased.

Pedro led her past the ruins of huts, gardens, and lives. Many women sat on the ground rocking their children, most weeping softly. Her heart ached. They'd had so little to begin with and now lost everything. "We must do something to help them rebuild."

"Enrique will see to matters. He always does."

"Do these raids happen frequently?"

"More so now than in previous years, as the Crown wants Granada. The Moors grow increasingly desperate with each day."

Before she could feel sorry for those who'd attacked, Pedro brought her to the edge of the forest. Beneath one of the trees, a man sprawled on the ground, in a deep swoon, his face in shadows. Next to him sat a young boy.

"Who are you?" the child asked, eyeing her suspiciously. Soot smudged his face. His clothes were equally filthy, feet unshod, hair uncombed.

"I came here to help." She took a small loaf of bread from her sack. "Will you take this? You look hungry."

He snatched the loaf and pushed it beneath his grimy shirt.

"Is he your father or brother?" She gestured to the man.

"Cousin. Will he die?"

She wanted to assure the child everything would be all right, but lies wouldn't help. In the world in which he lived, hard reality was a constant with no sweet tales of fairies who showered children with sweets or knights who made everyone happy and rich. Those bedtime stories were for noble offspring who eventually learned boys would go to war and die, while the girls would wed men they neither knew nor loved in order to secure estates.

It seemed no one in this world had hope for constant happiness, though she'd try to ease this boy's burden. "I will do all I can for him."

Pedro brought the torch closer. She held back a gasp. Despite his horrifying description, the man's injury was far worse. His right cheek appeared to have melted away, his ear gone, neck blistered, parts of the exposed flesh raw and oozing a clear fluid or colored a dark brown, the skin charred.

As Pedro had said, the stench was horrific. Nothing smelled like burned flesh, not even death.

She sank to her knees, grateful the man was oblivious to pain at this point. There would be more than enough once he woke. She cleaned the wound with vinegar, wishing she'd brought maggots to eat away the ruined flesh. Thankfully, she did have pieces of linen to work with but needed more materials. She looked around hopelessly for the additional items.

Pedro leaned down. "What do you need?"

"Honey and animal fat." She couldn't recall if she'd need both, not having studied burn treatment fully. Being thorough couldn't hurt. "As quickly as possible."

"For the wound?"

"Sí." Honey would keep the burns from infecting, animal grease would also serve as a deterrent, while linen would provide a clean cover to aid healing.

Pedro used several rocks to keep the torch from toppling over and ran to the first intact hut.

Tomás strode up, glancing over at his brother. "Where is he off to?"

"To bring me honey and fat, though it should be fresh. Did you see the dead pig near the village entrance?"

"No, but I can look for the thing, then haul the carcass here if you want."

She smiled at how gracious he was. "I need several pieces of its fat, sliced thin. Not the entire pig, mind you."

"The fat shall be yours in a moment."

"I have the honey!" Pedro shouted. He ran to her, a cup in his hand.

"Well done." She beamed at him beaming at her. Tomás clamped Pedro on the shoulder, then took off for the fat.

The boy inched closer, eyes wide at what she did.

By the time Tomás returned, she'd already poured honey on the burn, covering the wound completely. She melted the fat with the lit torch. Once the substance had cooled, she applied the grease, then laid numerous pieces of linen over everything, at last tying two of the longest strips together. These she wound around the man's head, to beneath his chin, then tied the ends to keep the dressing in place.

She turned to the boy. "Is your cousin's mamá around?"

"Dead."

"Does he have a wife or someone to care for him?"

"Only me and Papá."

"You must tell your father to check your cousin's wound tomorrow to see how he heals." After wiping her hands, she gave the child several pieces of fresh linen, along with the remaining fat and honey. "Your papá needs to keep your cousin's wound clean, changing the linen, using new honey and fat. Can you tell him so for me?"

The boy shrugged.

She glanced at Tomás.

He smiled. "Pedro will have a word with the man, won't you?"

"Of course. Whatever Sancha needs. What a remarkable treatment. Did the nuns teach you this?"

Rather than tell the truth, she nodded instead, protecting everyone with a lie.

"Off you go." Tomás waved Pedro and the boy away. "Find the man's uncle. Sancha is needed elsewhere."

On her feet, she looked over. Enrique strode toward them, a bundle in his arms, the newborn's cries reedy. What a night to begin life.

"Here." He practically shoved the infant at her.

She took the child. "Does the mother know you have her baby?"

Tomás laughed. Enrique shot him a look. "Of course. No women were around to see to the infant's health. They have their own children and families to tend to. When the girl asked me if her child was sound, I had no idea what to say. Is he?"

Sancha lifted the threadbare blanket. The newborn was pink as dawn, face scrunched and red from shrieking, tiny fingers tightened into fists, arms flailing. "She is. A girl, you know."

Enrique stared at the man on the ground. "Will he be all right?"

"I hope so, though nothing is ever assured."

"Sancha was magnificent," Tomás said. "You should have been here. Our surgeon too. The old fool would have learned something."

Not if Enrique could help it. He seemed to have aged greatly tonight. She touched his hand. "Everything went well. And will."

"Even though nothing is ever assured?" The sadness and longing on his face begged an answer.

Tomás made a dismissive sound to his brother and gave her a smile. "No cause for concern. None of my soldiers knows of your healing nor will they. I kept them well away from you and busy with other matters. Enrique and I also spoke to the village elders, warning them not to mention your visit tonight. They promised no one would say a word. Enrique was quite the brute."

She could imagine and gave him a grateful smile.

His expression remained haunted. "Take care, please. I never want to lose you."

Chapter 8

Enrique stood at Sancha's side, watching, protecting while she treated those in need until well past dawn. He saw her weariness. Her movements painfully slow, speech halting at times. At last, she seemed to realize she couldn't tend to every person and finally instructed the women on how to cleanse and treat wounds to avoid infection.

Through it all, he worried what the peasants might say concerning her healing. They appeared grateful now for her help, but what of tomorrow and the next days? Favorable opinion could turn to distrust, envy, and hatred in an instant. The peasants might come to blame him for the raid because he hadn't offered enough protection against the Moors. None of them would care how impossible he'd find the task with so much land to cover and enemy plans unknown. If the peasants weren't able to take out their frustrations and anger on him, their noble lord, they could make her a convenient target.

Repeatedly, he checked the peasants' worn faces, trying to discern their concerns and suspicions, hoping to ward off trouble. As he'd said to Sancha, he couldn't lose her.

"Here you are." Tomás joined him. "Still worried, I see."

He ignored his brother's mocking tone to watch Sancha teach three young women how to stitch a wound using thread and needle. Her students looked repulsed, yet desperate for anything to heal their men, giving Sancha their rapt attention.

Tomás leaned toward him. "Everything will be fine."

"Easy for you to say."

"Not at all. Given your scowl and sour attitude, I worried greatly about bothering you, but decided to do so anyway."

"Lucky me." He spoke as quietly as Tomás had. "Wait till you fall in love and everything changes. Trust me, I intend to be there to hound you and make your life even more miserable."

"After watching you succumb to your feelings for Sancha, and Fernando to his with Isabella, I have no plan to join either of you in losing my heart to any woman."

Enrique smiled. "As though you have a choice." He sobered. "Men become fools when the right woman enters the scene. Your day will come."

"You sound pleased at my future downfall." He wiggled his eyebrows. "Tell you what. Before I face a woman as beauteous as Sancha and Isabella, one as devoted and loving, soft yet strong, brave, willing to stand at my side—"

"Do you have a point? If so, get to it."

Tomás grinned. "Be grateful for what you have and let the future take care of itself. Enjoy Sancha. If you can."

If he could? Tomás's eyes would have popped out if he'd known about her swimming lesson and their time on the blanket. How she pleasured him and the numerous times he'd delighted her before this scene had called them here.

The village was quieter now, many asleep, not seeing the destruction in full light. Ruined huts, animals and crops destroyed, personal items strewn across the road from peasants and soldiers trying to save what they could before fire consumed everything.

Wisps of smoke still rose from various areas charred beyond recognition. Children avoided those spots, playing beneath the brilliant blue sky and heavy sun. What had happened last night had nothing to do with them. Their future would take care of itself.

Enrique wished he could be as untroubled as they were and as resigned to fate as Tomás. Life and love would certainly be easier.

Finished with her lesson and treatments, Sancha stared at something in the distance, her lids heavy.

Children's excited shouts caught her attention and his. At last, his guards and the soldiers had returned with food from the castle, along with chickens, goats, cattle, and pigs from his estate. With the guards' help, rebuilding the huts would be an easy matter, the community soon returned to normal.

Tomás strode to his men, voice and hands raised, directing them.

Sancha joined Enrique, her clothes dirtied with blood, hair in disarray, soot on her cheeks from when she'd pushed stray tendrils aside.

Never had he seen her more beautiful.

She leaned against him, smiling at men delivering bread, cheese, oranges, and meat, small children chasing chickens and pigs, acquainting the animals with their new home. "What a good man you are to do this."

Her praise made him smile. "You seem tired."

She'd pressed her face against his sleeve to quiet her yawn. Her warm breath caused his heart to turn over, igniting his passion.

She shook her head. "I have never been better."

He slipped his arm around her waist to keep her from dropping to the ground. She'd already slumped against him, fast asleep.

Pedro ran up. "Is Sancha all right?"

"Tired." He swept her into his arms. She curled into him as though they'd done this many times in the past, her head on his shoulder, hand on his chest. "Bring her sack to my horse."

"Are you taking her to her castle?"

He was bringing her to his home, or rather theirs. He wouldn't consider her ever leaving his side.

At his gelding, she woke long enough to protest. "Why are we here? I need to check on my patients."

"If they need you, their families will send word. Time for you to rest."

"I have never been…ah, been…" She inhaled deeply and frowned.

"You have never been better. Which will be true once you sleep."

He helped her to mount and joined her quickly before she fell off his horse. Her head hung between her shoulders, hands dangling loosely at her sides. He eased her into him, arm around her waist, and motioned his guards to accompany them.

With Sancha asleep, he had to keep his gelding at a slower pace to avoid disturbing her or risk having her fall from the saddle. She was dead weight against him, arms flopping, feet bumping his ankles. What should have been trying delighted him. He couldn't stop smiling at having her close and finally relaxed, for the most part.

Halfway to the castle, she awoke. "Where are we?"

"Numerous leagues from home."

"Why?"

"Because we have yet to arrive there."

She fell back asleep.

He held her close, burning these moments into his memory. The air smelled fresher today, grass and wheat sweeter. A chirping bird seemed miraculous somehow when he'd scarcely noticed the noise before. Being with her heightened his senses, making him grateful to be alive, humbled that she was with him.

He recalled what Tomás had said about worrying too much, to take things as they came, enjoying what he had.

For once, his brother seemed to be right. If Enrique filled his life with fear about events he couldn't predict, he'd drive himself mad and push her away. She worried over him, as much as he had with her, and was willing to leave his castle to keep him safe.

He tightened his hold. Not enough for her to notice, to comfort himself. If he had to use all his power, will, and wealth to assure her place at his side, he would. Until they drew their last breaths. A man in love had no other choice.

He ordered himself to look forward to pleasant times. Her next swimming lesson, them pleasuring each other, her wedding him, them coupling, his first son, followed by a daughter, then four more sons, and another daughter or two, the children's pranks, their schooling, marriages, their own infants.

He couldn't recall a time he'd smiled so much. A few guards noticed. Enrique stared in return. They made certain not to glance at him again. Good thing. He refused to allow them or the lengthy ride to ruin his mood.

At last, they arrived at his castle. He woke Sancha gently. Once she was off the horse and in his arms, she snuggled into him. He carried her to his room where she belonged.

She regarded the sumptuous walls hangings depicting scenes from his estate and his bed with a canopy draped in red silk. The fabric cascaded down the posts. His mattress was wide enough for three men, perfect for a man and woman, the counterpane scarlet, sheets white as milk.

As he unlaced her garments, she watched, eyes still hooded with fatigue. "Do I tend to you next?"

He kissed the top of her head. "You need to sleep."

She pressed her hand to her mouth, hardly quieting her noisy yawn. "I have never been better."

He tossed her gown and tunic on the floor, made quick work of her chemise, then carried her to the mattress.

She sank to the featherbed, head against the pillow and sighed softly. "Join me?" She lifted her hand.

He kissed her fingers. After using a damp cloth to wash her hands and face, then his, he undressed quickly, though not fast enough. By the time he was nude, she was asleep.

He gathered her into his arms, her face against his chest, hand on his flat belly, leg draped over his. Stirred by her heat and softness, his carnal hunger battled with his fatigue.

Weariness won. They had decades to live their lives, to love as a man and a woman should. Trusting his newfound hope, he fell asleep moments after she had.

* * * *

Sancha awoke on her belly, her hand on Enrique's thigh.

She smiled. How wonderful his skin was, incredibly warm, his leg roughened with short dark hairs. She stroked them and spied the scene, not remembering how she came to be in here. He hadn't taken her. That, she would never forget.

He sprawled across most of the rather enormous bed, leaving her a sliver of mattress on her side. Another inch to the left and she'd land on the floor. That wouldn't do.

On her hands and knees, she crawled to Enrique then straddled him, her back to his front.

He grunted softly before going quiet and still. She turned as much as she could to see him.

He stared.

She grinned. "Buenos días. Did you sleep well? I did."

He regarded her buttocks poised above his navel and rested his hands on her hips, his expression hot with passion. "What are you doing?"

His voice was so deep his words rasped. Her belly fluttered. "What does it look like?"

He laughed. "I have no idea—wait. Is this something else you learned from Isabella? If so, you need to tell her a woman and man face each other to seek pleasure."

"Not always." She backed over him until her cleft was above his face, hers in line with his shaft. His member blossomed quickly, growing thick and hard, precisely as she wanted. She cupped his sac and smiled. "Do you now understand what we do?"

He laughed, growled, and grabbed her hips, bringing her mound to his mouth. "Not one more sound from you, only pleasure."

Was there any other way?

She cradled his shaft and lapped his crown, tasting the fluid that seeped from the tiny slit. The flavor was as wicked and enticing as the first time, his musky scent exhilarating.

He tensed his legs, long toes splaying then curling. Twice he stopped licking her soft folds, groaning softly from what she did to him.

Pleased with her effect, she eased his shaft aside and licked his sac.

"Ah." He squirmed.

Surely, he could do better than that. Wanting him to bellow in joy, she took his right testicle into her mouth.

He cried out then made more noises, crude and uncontrolled.

Her lips caressed the wrinkly skin on this part of him, her tongue learning the contours of his sac, stroking him lazily, mouth suckling.

He bellowed at last. "Holy mother. Are you trying to kill me?"

She released him. "Do you want me to stop?"

His chest heaved with his labored breaths. "You already have. Why? Did I tell you to do so?"

At times, he was impossible to please. "Forgive me. I shall continue."

She eased his left testicle into her mouth, then ran her hand up and down his shaft, taking charge of him finally.

He gasped and moaned. After panting an oath, he gripped her hips, brought her down to him and licked her nub.

A heavenly ache built within her, making her forget his pleasure. His sigh, possibly pleased or arrogant at what he'd accomplished with her, reminded Sancha of her power. She flicked her tongue over his testicle, licking the short hairs, liking their roughness on her tongue.

He growled an oath, lapped her folds and nub, finally settling there, stroking, teasing, trying to deliver ecstasy quickly.

She wasn't about to allow herself release until he reached his peak at least three times.

He'd risked so much for her last night, giving all he could in spite of his concerns. She had to make these moments the best he'd ever had. Not only because she was grateful for his kindness. She loved him, always would. She'd tried to talk herself out of the truth but her heart wouldn't listen, wanting him so badly she ached with tenderness and need.

He swept his tongue over her nub.

Whimpering, she steeled herself against further arousal and eased his testicle from her mouth, taking his shaft inside to its root.

He groaned louder than any time before.

She kept him as deep as she could, a matter she wouldn't have believed possible if not for Isabella explaining how women accomplished such a goal. She'd have to thank her sister for speaking freely. With his member in her mouth, his sac in her palm, and her tongue lavishing him with undivided attention, Sancha was determined to give him her best. As soon as she could deny her own pleasure.

He suckled her thigh, ran his thumb over her nub, and dragged his other hand down the furrow between her cheeks, pausing on her tightest opening. The spate of pleasure he'd stirred threatened to overcome her.

Determined to resist, she tongued the back of his crown and slid his member in and out of her mouth quickly, only to slow, stop, then begin anew, sensing his delight fading with each pause. The same as hers had when he'd repeatedly pulled his hand from between her legs.

His growl said he didn't like her doing to him what he'd done to her. He settled his mouth on her sex and licked her nub fervently.

Sounds of delight filled the room from her and him, both racing toward release, their competition forgotten in favor of shared joy. She knew bliss first, the towering delight that was too much to deny or resist, her cries muffled by his shaft still in her mouth.

His seed soon glided over her tongue, creamy and rich, the flavor faintly salty and unique in the best possible way. As she'd done at the pond, she swallowed the proof of his satisfaction, pleased to have given him such joy.

Gulping air, he lay sprawled worse than he had earlier, taking even more of the bed.

She rested her forehead on the mattress between his legs. "Do you want me to sleep on the floor?"

"What—no—what?"

She fell over his leg, one foot planted on the bed, the other on his sex, chin lifted to the canopy. The lovely red silk shimmered in a thread of light spilling past a separation in the velvet drapes. "You have most of the mattress. I did notice a soft carpet over there."

She gestured toward the window, then dropped her hand, finding it too heavy to keep up.

He finished his yawn. "After the pleasure I gave you, you still complain?" He sniffed. "Very well, come here."

Despite his fatigue, his strength remained. He pulled her into his arms easily and ran his hand down her hair and back while planting light kisses on her temple and cheek.

She stroked his jawline, liking his stubble. "I did not. And I did the same to you."

His hand stalled on her back. "What?"

"I never complained, and I also gave you pleasure. Never deny it. I. Was. There."

He laughed at her parroting his words from weeks before. "Indeed you did, and I thank you."

His gratitude was wonderful, but what she truly wanted was that he never leave her.

She tensed at the sudden truth of what her heart craved, even though she feared what it would mean for her freedom and healing.

"What is it?" He loosened his arm. "Was I holding you too tightly?"

She buried her face in his neck, not willing to get into her feelings. "No. I twisted my foot the wrong way."

"Are you all right now?"

No. She'd fallen too deeply for him and didn't know which direction to take. Going back to loneliness didn't seem possible. Moving forward with him was equally daunting. Although their shared lust was more than she'd dreamed of, what they'd done together wasn't enough. She needed full completion as he did, if their passion wouldn't mean ruin.

Lying with him one time could prove disastrous, resulting in a babe. They'd wed, as he wanted and she was beginning to desire, but what of her healing? Another woman might have been able to ignore outside interests, no matter how passionate she was about them, as long as love, home, a husband, and family were within reach.

Sancha couldn't. Poultices, potions, experiments, and healing were in her blood. Without those things, a part of her would die, leaving her empty and wanting no matter how much he and their children loved her. She needed more for fulfillment, as men did. A purpose to strive toward other than a husband using her to produce heirs.

"Sancha, are you in pain?"

The worst kind, not easily solved by any healer no matter how skilled. She looked over. Her worry faded more quickly than she would have guessed, a smile replacing her gloom. His hair stuck out on each side and stood straight up on top of his head. Shadows ringed his eyes from lingering fatigue. Stubble darkened his chin, cheeks, and upper lip. Despite his clean face, soot dirtied his throat.

He was so beautiful tears filled her eyes.

"Show me where you hurt." He sat up. "I may be able to help."

She pushed him back down and leaned over him, her hair gliding across his chest. "You have soot on your jaw."

"So did you until I washed it off."

"You should have told me how awful I looked."

"Never has there been a lovelier woman." He kissed the tip of her nose. "In any event, would you have cared if I had told you about the state of your face and dress?"

No. Her appearance, gowns, jewels, what other ladies craved had never meant anything to Sancha. She adored books, learning, knowledge. "Thank you for being so wonderful at the village."

"I did naught but watch you."

Without interference or complaint. "You saw to the people's needs, kept order, and not once did you become ill, even when I cleaned the most hideous wounds."

"I saw hope on the villagers' faces. What you did was remarkable and brave."

She hugged him fiercely. "I want naught these next days except to be happy. Can you join me?"

He rolled them over until he was on top, his forehead against hers. "No books?"

"None. Nor experiments. The mice deserve a rest and so do we. I want to learn to swim. We can walk your estate hand in hand beneath the moon." She cupped his face. "We can pleasure each other greatly near the pond, in the fields, within the stable, in all the hiding places the castle holds."

His shoulders shook with quiet laughter. "I fear the servants may see or hear."

"Send them away."

He sobered, growing as serious as she had. "Do you still want me to protect your virtue?"

She didn't, but there was no other choice. Until he pledged not to stand in the way of her healing, no matter a union, children, or the Inquisition, she could never lie with him. Most men would have called her mad for attaching such a requirement to love. She hoped one day Enrique would be up to the task and would stand by her side in everything she wanted as she did the same with him.

She stroked his jaw. "Please."

He sighed deeply but nodded. "Do we begin our happiness today?"

"Immediately, beginning with food. Cheese, bread, meat, eggs, olives, oranges, figs, and whatever else your cook can provide. Neither of us has eaten for hours."

"Closer to a full day. Do you mind sharing your food?"

"With you? Never. Why would you even ask?"

"I never did. I meant with my brothers and the other soldiers. I invited them here to feast as much and as long as they wanted as a way to thank them for their service."

"I have no qualms as long as they leave me a morsel or two. Come." She rolled off the bed, stopped at her clothes, and made a face. "You should have told me how filthy I was."

He came up behind her and wrapped his arms around her waist, pulling her into his stiffened member. The wonder of his heat, strength, and masculinity had her moaning wantonly.

He rested his chin on her shoulder. "Would you have cared?"

"About what?"

"How filthy your garments were?"

"No. Though I do now. I need my own clothes, a basin of water, and a comb." She turned into him. "I will not shame you in front of your guests."

"I doubt you could if you tried." He kissed her deeply, his love obvious to her. He'd proven himself repeatedly, dispelling most of her doubt, leaving one last hurdle to clear. She hoped these next days would give her the courage to discuss their future, secure their oaths to each other, and move on with a life satisfying to both.

Growling in delight, he finished their kiss and pulled his mouth free. "Wait here. And I do mean here, nowhere else. Upon my return, you shall have water, clothes, a comb, and whatever else you need."

* * * *

For once, Sancha obeyed him, offering a broad smile as though he'd returned from several years at war, rather than taking a few minutes to gather needed items in her bedchamber. After she'd scrubbed herself, combed her hair, and dressed with his help, she folded her hands in front, rather than lacing her fingers through his, so they could go to the dining hall together.

He didn't want to guess why she hadn't. "Have you changed your mind about the meal?"

"No. But we should arrive separately to avoid talk."

He remembered how Fernando had brought Isabella to the fortaleza dressed as a boy with their nuptials happening a short time later, the soldiers in attendance. To the best of Enrique's knowledge, none of those men had dared gossip, fearful of Fernando's sword. "As you wish."

He left her in his room, praying she would come down rather than burying herself in her books, her desire to be happy with him already a distant consideration.

She entered the dining hall, as promised. He sat at the head of a long table, capable of accommodating fifty, the same as the rest of the tables. Enrique pushed to his feet immediately, as did Tomás, Pedro, and the others.

She paled a bit at the attention but still held herself like a queen, her beauty unrivaled, hair falling to her waist in soft waves, the color vibrant, threads of gold making the auburn tint seem even deeper. Pink bloomed in her cheeks. Her sapphire-blue gown was simple yet elegant, complementing her perfect form.

He held out a chair for her next to his. "Did you sleep well?"

"I did. You?"

"Very much."

He wasn't certain if their act fooled anyone. Tomás and Pedro appeared skeptical, smiling slightly.

Once she'd sat, the men resumed eating with abandon.

Pedro smiled sweetly at her. "Guillermo asked me to give you his thanks."

She stopped reaching for the pork. "Guillermo?"

"The boy you gave your bread to. He said every bite was delicious."

She smiled. "How wonderful."

Enrique offered the cheese to her. She didn't notice, her attention still on Pedro, expression worried. "How is his cousin?"

"The man you—"

"Pedro, hand me the eggs." Enrique wiggled his fingers for them.

His brother looked at the ones near him then those closer to Sancha. "You have some over—"

"So we do. Has anyone questioned the Moor I have in my storage room?"

"I did." Tomás finished his goblet of wine and wiped his mouth off with the back of his hand. "He told me nothing. Once we return to the fortaleza, I intend to keep at him until he does."

"As you should," Enrique said. "Using a napkin rather than your hand would also be nice."

Tomás scowled.

Enrique asked Pedro questions about the attack, followed by more questions for the other men, keeping them occupied. He hardly wanted Sancha to discuss her healing in front of the soldiers.

She seemed to have realized his concern, no longer staring at him as though he'd grown another head.

Once Tomás finished what was on his plate, he stood. His men shot to their feet.

Tomás offered a gallant bow. "Your hospitality is sublime, but we need to return to our duties. Brother, beauteous Sancha"—he inclined his head to both—"I hope we can see each other again soon."

"Certainly not because of a raid," Pedro said.

Tomás arched one eyebrow.

"Adios." Enrique dismissed them with an impatient gesture. "Be certain to take the Moor with you. Tomás, a word?"

His brother leaned down to him.

Enrique whispered, "Tell Pedro to be quiet about Sancha's healing."

"I had already planned to."

The moment the men's footfalls had faded, she touched Enrique's hand. "Forgive me."

"For what?"

"Worrying whether they would gossip if you and I had come in here together but not once thinking to keep quiet about my work."

"No harm done." He wrapped his fingers around hers. "I kept them occupied on other matters as Tomás had at the village, so none saw what you did."

"I should be more careful."

"Agreed."

She lowered her face.

"You need not quit. Just be more careful."

"I will."

He smiled as she did and kissed her fingertips. "Have you had your fill of food?"

"I have."

"Come." He caressed her fingers. "I have something to show you."

He brought her to the kennels. Since she'd moved here, he'd instructed his servants to keep the dogs away from the castle, fearing the animals would disturb her studies or frighten her.

At the first yip, she pulled her hand from his and hurried into the building, as airy and clean as her rooms. By the time he entered, she was on her knees, holding a galgo pup to her cheek.

"How could you keep her from me?" She pushed out her bottom lip. "How dare you."

He laughed. "If you love her so much, you can tend to her all you want. The pup is newly weaned and yours."

She kissed the dog's long snout. "She will surely miss her mamá."

"Make her forget. Make her happy."

The pup licked her neck. She giggled. "What should I call her? Wait—I have it. Rosa."

Perfect. The dog's name matched Sancha's wonderful fragrance. He instructed his servants to place a blanket in a basket for the pup so she could take Rosa with them as they enjoyed their first hours of pursuing happiness.

* * * *

Enrique wasn't certain what was best: their long walks, her interest in his work with the estate, or their pleasant meals on the balcony, in the garden, and several times near the edge of the hill, where they had an unrestricted view of his property.

There were so many things to do and for him to show her that they didn't end up at the pond until three days later, near midnight.

With her nudity pressed to his, she suckled his throat.

He grinned so hard, his cheeks hurt. "Are you certain you want to go into the water?" He was perfectly happy to stay on the blanket within each other's arms.

"Can you teach me to swim here?"

He laughed. "No."

"The water it is." She pushed to her feet. "I challenge you to a race."

He propped himself on one elbow and looked over. She'd offered her challenge when she was already steps from him. "Go on, keep running. Even if you fly, I will best you."

She curled her upper lip.

He sprinted, catching her before she reached the pond, and lifted her into his arms. She squealed.

"Now, you learn to swim." He entered the water.

"No." She buried her face in his chest. "If you throw me in as your papá did with you, I will surely drown."

Not likely. She was strong enough to teach a man how to be brave. Someday, she would be his in every way. Smiling, he lowered her into the water and had her float first to ease her fear.

After several minutes, she frowned. "I tire of this. Challenge me."

He became the stern taskmaster, putting Sancha through her paces until she swam on her own. Not well, but skill would come on the other days where they sought to be naught but happy.

After eating their late meal, they sauntered back to the castle. Rosa was in her basket, asleep, at the bottom of the grand stairway. The servant who'd tended her bowed slightly and left for bed, given the hour.

Sancha stroked the galgo's head.

A letter lay on a cabinet to the side, left there without the servants telling him. His fault, not theirs. He'd given them stern instructions not to disturb him and Sancha. The missive had Fernando's seal on the back, Sancha's name scrawled on the front.

"For you." He handed her the unopened letter.

She stepped into the candlelight, head bent as she read, complexion draining of color.

"What is it?" He prayed Fernando hadn't take a bad turn from his previous injuries or that Isabella had lost the baby.

Sancha looked past him at a horror only she could see.

He touched her arm. "What happened?"

She handed him the letter. He regarded her for a moment, then read the missive.

> *My dearest Sancha,*
>
> *You are my sweet sister, my best friend, without you I would die.*
>
> *My greatest hope had always been to send you naught but good tidings about my coming child, a son if God will, and of Fernando's and my great happiness.*
>
> *I am pained to have to tell you this. Rumors are flying about you. Foul words as to you not wedding, refusing to have children as a woman should, you lying about being at the convent (someone inquired and found you have not been there in some time).*
>
> *Some are saying only a witch would shun marriage and children, as she has already wed the Devil to do his work.*
>
> *Fernando is trying to learn who is spreading these horrible lies. He promises to run them through when he learns their names.*
>
> *Sancha, I fear for your safety. Please, you must protect yourself without delay.*
>
> *I am so sorry to have to tell you any of this.*
>
> *Your loving sister,*
> *Isabella*

Chapter 9

Sancha sank to the stairs, unable to stop trembling. Although the evening was mild, a deep chill settled into her.

Enrique sat close and slipped his arm around her shoulders. "All is not lost."

She looked at him, knowing their time together had ended.

"I promise to protect you."

How? He was one man against how many faceless accusers. To say anything in her defense would put him at risk. She pulled away, unable to allow him to endanger himself.

"Sancha, please." He gathered her to him, his caress gentle yet firm, not allowing her to escape.

She dug her fingers into his shirt. "I only wanted to help others, to learn what I could. How could anything so innocent be wrong? How could anyone say such horrible things about…" She was unable to breathe suddenly. Lightheaded, she clung to him.

He brushed his lips over her ear. "We should speak in my room, lest the servants overhear us."

With them spreading more lies. Nowhere was safe, free of fear and the reprisals of others who would claim what she'd said or had done was wrong. She wanted to run from the castle and never stop but couldn't move, her legs leaden, thoughts too scattered to make any plan.

She feared what would happen now, if soldiers were already on their way to arrest her. She had no idea where the Inquisition kept its prisoners. Or whether anyone would listen to the truth concerning her healing, how she'd done nothing more than help others. No matter what she claimed, the inquisitors wouldn't listen or care.

She shivered again.

The galgo yipped.

"Rosa." Sancha cleared her throat, surprised at how odd she sounded, as though she'd been crying. She touched her face, damp with tears, not understanding when she'd started to weep. "I have to talk care of the pup."

On her feet, she stopped at the cabinet where Enrique had found Isabella's letter. A new fear gripped Sancha as to whether her sister and the babe she carried were safe.

Enrique slipped the missive in his belt and rested his hand on her arm. "We need to go upstairs."

"I have to get Rosa." She had to hide her before the authorities harmed the gentle pup, claiming she was also evil because her owner was a witch.

"Once I have you in my room, I can return for her." He swept Sancha into his arms.

She twisted his shirt in her fist. "Make certain no one harms her."

He gave her an odd look. "No one will, I assure you." He carried her to his chamber and lowered her to the mattress. Candlelight shone from every part of the room as he always ordered. "We can talk as soon as I return." He gave her the letter.

She grabbed his sleeve before he could leave her side. "Isabella cannot come to harm. She behaves as a warrior, believing she can fight everyone. You have to stop her before she also meets ruin."

"No one will harm her or you. I give you my word, as Fernando will. Stay here."

He left for the pup.

She crushed the letter in her fist. A few hours before, happiness had seemed within reach, laughter and joy filling her day. How quickly life could change, dreams ruined, hope denied.

On the word of another. Who? Why? She'd never harmed anyone in her life, making certain to be kind and giving.

Outrage raced through her, pushing away her desperation and fear. She left the mattress and gripped the bedpost hurriedly at the room swaying. She lowered her head to stave off dizziness.

Enrique returned. After putting Rosa on the floor, he closed the chamber door.

She backed away from him. "I have to leave."

"No." He sat on the bed and pulled her onto his lap, keeping her close. "Running will change nothing."

"My worry is for you, not me. If the authorities learn I was here, they will come for you next. Even if I claim to have bewitched you, they—"

"No one is going to do anything to me or you. The solution is simple and right before us." He touched Isabella's letter. "The rumors involve you not being at the convent. How could you be there when you were with me? No one can be two places at once, except a witch with dark powers, with this proving you are nothing of the kind."

He'd gone mad. "You intend to tell the authorities I was here? Have you not heard anything I said?"

"I refuse to hear any plans that take you from me. You being here makes perfect sense when we simply tell everyone we wed."

"No." She pushed off his lap.

He pulled her back down. "Why? Because you find me so repulsive?"

"How can you say such a thing after what we shared? You are a man among men. I would be a fool to think otherwise."

"I know naught of what goes on in your mind until you tell me. I adore you, Sancha. I fell in love the first moment I saw you at the convent. My feelings have only grown deeper since you came here. What of yours? Is lust all you feel, or can I someday hope to win your heart?"

She cried, "You have my love. I have never wanted a man as I do you, but—"

"No." He rested his finger against her lips. "I know what you mean to say and I can finish for you. You fear marriage, having any man shackle you, taking away your books and healing. If I could replace your desire for knowledge with my love, in order to keep you safe, I would. However, I am no fool. At the village, I saw what healing means to you. If I were to hinder you in anyway, you would hate me forever."

She shook her head, her throat so tight she could barely speak. "I would protest and resist. Never would I hate you."

"I would hope not, but I also have no intention of finding out. Wed me and keep to your healing. Not in the villages, though. Not right away. You need to let the rumors die down and behave as other women do, at least around everyone save me. Here, in my castle, you can continue as you have been—learning, experimenting. Your work will be our secret."

He was giving her the world, his future, and safety without a thought for himself. She couldn't allow such a thing. "What of your servants knowing what I do here? I know you say they remain loyal, however—"

"They are loyal, but they know nothing of what you do, save for the few guards who accompanied us to the village. In the castle, Hortensia is the only one who has ever been in the room you use. She cleans the chamber, no one else. She has known me since I was a headstrong boy. When Mamá died, Hortensia did everything she could to comfort my sister, my brothers, and me. She will not betray you or us."

"You offer too much."

"Only my heart. Will you take it?"

Weeping, she threw her arms around him. "You deserve a woman who would never bring you pain."

"I want you because of the joy you give me. Tell me you accept my offer."

She hugged him as hard as she could. "How could I ever refuse you?"

He kissed her deeply, finally broke free, and smiled. "Do you truly expect me to tell you how to refuse me?"

She laughed then froze. "Wait. What of the banns? The ceremony?"

"We need to wed in haste and in secret like our King and Queen."

"What do you mean?"

He eased back until he could see her face. "Given the rumors and what we must say to disavow them, that you were here with me as my new wife, not consorting with the Devil, we need to keep our nuptials a secret."

"No. I mean, what were you referring to when you mentioned the monarchs?"

"Oh. They wed in secret, after having known each other for only a few days and kept their marriage hidden for years with the Queen's father disinheriting her when he found out. Years ago, Papá told me of the scandal, which he found quite amusing. You and I will surely not be the first or the last nobles to wed thusly."

Although the news was a surprise, the sovereigns' past didn't change matters for her and Enrique. "Without banns, someone could accuse us of trying to hide an impediment to the marriage, my being a witch for one. The Inquisition wasn't established in Spain when the monarchs wed. What sacerdote will join us now without notice to the community? Surely, not the same man who wed Fernando and Isabella. She told me how he threatened her when he learned she wasn't me."

"The man is a fool and will not preside over our union, not even if he agreed to do so for a bribe."

She frowned. "Would he actually ask for one?"

"That or food, since he likes to eat. Many priests have accepted payments to forgive a sin or ignore a rule. Why do you think no one ever holds nobles accountable for their misdeeds? Heresy and witchcraft may be the exception, but other crimes are not. Power and wealth put us above ordinary people who must be circumspect in their dealings. Dominico, a boyhood friend of mine, is a sacerdote, given to the Church by his parents despite his protests. He wanted to be a knight and understands what a heart needs. He will be more than happy to perform and bless our union. Tomás and Pedro can be our witnesses." He held her chin between his thumb and forefinger. "I know you would prefer to have Isabella at your side, but we have no time to wait for her and Fernando to travel here."

New tears welled in her eyes.

His expression grew pained. "Will you miss her so much or are you concerned about wedding me?"

"No. Yes. No." She showered him with kisses on his neck, cheeks, and eyebrows. "I will miss having Isabella here but look forward to our union. One day I hope to deserve you."

Before he could speak, she claimed his mouth, slipping her tongue inside, tasting him and her tears.

He stilled for a moment, then pulled her against him, his hand on the back of her head to keep her close.

She never wanted to leave his side.

He took command of their kiss as a noble lord should, filling her mouth with his tongue, possessing her with tenderness, need, passion. She pulled at his garments as he did hers. Soon, they lay naked on the bed, both breathing hard.

Across the room, Rosa yipped, sounding curious rather than distressed.

Concentrating on Enrique, Sancha held his face in her palms.

His smile was slow and seductive, filled with carnal sin. "Does your virtue still need protecting?"

"Not from you. My body and heart are yours to take for as long as you wish."

"Until our last breaths."

And beyond, as far as she was concerned. She would need him for eternity. "Fill me."

He swooped down and captured her mouth once more, hand between her legs. Already, her folds were damp with her desire for him, her channel prepared for his rigid shaft. He pressed closer, his member hot and hard against her thigh, moisture from the slit in his crown dampening her leg.

An unrestrained moan rushed from her, a sound born of love. She drove her fingers through his hair, her mouth hard against his, their kiss desperate as they each tried to get closer, reach deeper.

If they'd been at this a thousand years, she sensed neither of them would have been satisfied until they were a part of each other's heart and blood.

With his mouth still on hers, he guided Sancha to part her legs. She did even better, drawing her knees back so he could finally, and easily, reach her core.

He thrust his tongue more deeply into her mouth, his fingers gliding over her nub, the movements deceptively slow, decidedly possessive. The familiar ache returned, growing more intense than the other times, more powerful than hate, fear, sadness.

She lifted her hips, delivering herself, wanting Enrique to take her with the right she'd given him.

He controlled himself far more than she had, not rushing, even though he'd waited a long time for these moments.

She'd been searching for him before realizing he existed, finding him at last, and now worried about how long they'd be together or if anyone had a right to the happiness they knew. Dread swept through her with such force, she clutched his upper arms.

He pulled his mouth free. His hair hung over his forehead, his forelock hidden within the other locks. "You have no need to fear this. There will be some discomfort, but it will pass quickly."

Moved by his concern, she ran her thumb over his bristly chin. "I fear nothing from you. Fill me, please. Keep me from loneliness and sorrow."

"Always. What good am I if I cannot do something so simple?"

She loved his boasts and teasing. "Then why do you wait?" She feigned confusion. "You are aware of what to do with a woman, no?"

He arched one eyebrow at her impertinent question. "We shall see."

"Seeing is not what I seek. I want you within me."

"As you wish." He lifted his shaft and ran the crown down her cleft. Warmth settled in her cheeks, throat, and chest, born of excitement, not shame. She pitied women who found this act indecent or loathsome. If they had loved the men they were with, those women would have forbidden nothing, wanting what she did now. A thick, hard shaft inside her, filling her emptiness, making her whole.

Returning her smile, he eased the tip of his member into her opening, the pressure unusual and arousing.

With his shoulders bunched and face reddened, he panted as one would after running a league or more. "Are you ready for me?"

For a lifetime. "I love you."

Yearning, tenderness, lust radiated from him. He entered her in one hard thrust, breaking through her virginal barrier.

A sharp sting cut through her.

He sank down, propping himself on his elbows. "Are you all right?"

She was better than that, the discomfort unimportant, the width and length of his shaft stretching her sheath, demanding she accommodate his size. How could she ever do anything less? "Although you filled me near to bursting, I believe I will live."

He laughed. "I still have a bit to go."

"Proceed, please."

"Are you certain?"

She lifted her hips, eager to have all of him inside her.

Taking over, he plunged deeper until their bodies touched, his throat bobbing with his swallow.

She snatched a breath and tightened her inner muscles around him, squeezing his shaft as her hand would. Perhaps better, given his sharp intake of air.

"No—stop." He groaned. "I need a moment."

Of course he did. Isabella had told her what to expect when a woman lay with a man. Again, her words had proven true. "Forgive me."

"No need." He cleared his throat. "Shall we continue?" He stroked her nub.

She moaned brazenly. He pumped. The easy slide of his shaft within her sheath fed her passion. Her channel was glutted, achy with unrelieved desire.

Rather than seek his own relief, he measured his thrusts and strokes, working her with skill and love. She yielded, a curious combination of arousal and surrender filling her, leaving her fully vulnerable to him.

He quickened his pace. The bedframe groaned with his powerful thrusts, his sac tapping her buttocks each time their bodies came together. The faint smack of skin against skin the most glorious sound she'd ever heard.

He brushed her nub quicker, harder, forcing her toward the peak.

No. She needed to hold onto these enchanting moments as long as she could, sensing he also battled release. Perspiration dampened his chest and throat, his complexion darkened, features grew strained. He seemed caught between rapture and agony with her the cause.

She'd never been as proud or had dreamed a man could want her this much. He loved her even after all she'd put him through, and what they had yet to face. She prayed they'd find more good than bad in their future, wanting nothing more than to bring him happiness.

To that end, she squeezed her inner muscles around his shaft. He trembled then growled, growing more intent in his determination to delight her.

The wonder of his thrusts was soon more than she could resist, his strokes on her nub as needed as air, food, water. She tensed at the carnal storm swirling within her, the pleasure so extraordinary it had nowhere to go and needed to break free. She fought the end helplessly, crying her release, unmindful of who might hear. Her only concern was the glory of his heat, scent, strength, so many emotions and feelings pummeling her she was too weak to move, her channel pulsing around his shaft.

His member was still hard, thicker than she recalled, straining against the walls of her sheath. He hadn't peaked as she had. With a tight smile, he thrust again.

* * * *

She was his at last, which made him want her still more, his shaft inside of her for hours, days, months at a time. He never wanted to separate himself from her. Her channel was deliciously hot, smooth and damp, giving his member a home, a safe harbor he could always count on.

She loved him.

He wanted to roar with joy but could barely draw a full breath. Sweat ran into his eyes, the sting not nearly as bad as the dull ache in his sac and shaft, his sex begging for relief.

He ignored his desires, his mind and soul needing the act to continue indefinitely until he'd had enough of her.

He never would.

His fierce kisses had bruised her lips, leaving them puffy and red. A deep flush colored her face and throat. She seemed unable to keep her lids open for long, though she didn't sleep. She stroked his arms lightly, speaking with touch rather than words.

Nothing she could say would make this moment more singular, a slice of paradise he would fight to keep. No one would ever take her from him.

Battling his overwhelming need, he thrust faster and stroked her nub once more.

A wail burst from her. "No. You must stop."

He panted. "Before I have my due?"

"No. Yes. I mean—are you trying to kill me?"

He grinned at her using his earlier words, and then he struggled for more air. "If I am, what a pleasant way to die, no?"

"No." She pushed his hand away.

He touched her nub again. "You must take the bad with the good."

She stopped turning her head from side to side. "How right you are." She tightened her sheath around his shaft, her movements timed so she was at her narrowest as he nearly pulled out of her before he thrust back inside.

His head fell forward. The friction between them was more than even he could bear. He ground his teeth so hard they hurt. "Stop. No more of what you do."

"As you wish." She reached down and cupped his sac.

He gasped and shoved her hand from him. Again, she tightened her channel around his member.

He gave up, unable to tame her. "Do what you must."

"I am." She worked her muscles around his shaft *and* ran her fingertips over his sac.

Every part of him shrieked for relief. He fought the release he had to have and rubbed her nub once more.

She cried wantonly.

He pumped for all he was worth.

She tumbled over the edge and moaned with abandon, forgetting to torment him in return.

He was past control. The snugness of her sheath, inner warmth, and loving touch had already done him in. On a wild cry, he pushed into her a final time. His arms and legs tensed, then trembled with the force of his delight.

The room whirled.

Too dizzy and weak to catch up, he sagged down and held onto to her as she did with him. Their chests bumped on each ragged breath.

She kissed his cheek and ear. "Will you live?"

He laughed faintly. "Will you?"

"For a second, I thought I had died. Everything went white, black, and white again."

He rested his forehead on her shoulder, savoring her fragrance. She smelled of sweet flowers, him, sex, love. "Sounds as though you were blinking, no?"

She slapped his arm.

"Have it your way. You were doing something other than blinking?"

"Be serious." She kissed the part she'd smacked. "I was trying to praise you for performing so well."

As though he could ever do anything less. With what little strength he had left, he pushed to his elbows and looked at her. "Did Isabella say these moments would be otherwise?"

Had she boasted about Fernando's endurance? Surely, his brother's stamina wasn't as great as his own.

"No." She brushed his hair off his forehead. "I intend to tell her how wonderful you are whenever you take me. I plan to make her quite jealous."

Laughter bubbled in his throat, followed by tenderness so deep, his eyes stung. "You are a wonder."

"I am a woman now. Gracias."

Grinning, he rolled them over until she was on top with his shaft still inside her channel. She molded to him without pause, her weight a wonderful burden, their forms fitting perfectly.

She ran her fingertip around his nipple. "Will you sleep now?"

He wanted nothing more than to take her again. Sensing she wanted to talk, he shook his head and stifled a yawn. "Would you like to discuss our plans?"

"In part, though something else too."

"Which first?"

"Our plans. Will we wed tomorrow? That is, today?"

"As soon as I send word to Pedro, Tomás, and Dominico. None is too far from here. By this evening, you and I will be husband and wife. Can you withstand the wait?"

She stopped licking his nipple to bite the flat disk instead.

He yelped. "Now you draw blood?"

"I barely touched you. Will you be able to endure the time before you can wed me?"

"You know I cannot." He squeezed her buttocks. "Any other questions concerning my desire for you?"

"No. I trust I have your heart. Who do you think started the rumors about me? Do you think it was the sacerdote who wed Fernando and Isabella?"

"Why would he have anything against you?"

"He was at the convent when I was healing Fernando. I made certain he never saw anything I did, but he seemed surprised, maybe suspicious, when Fernando survived."

Enrique frowned. "Why would he have wanted my brother to die?"

"He anointed him in preparation for death. Fernando's return to good health disproved what the sacerdote had expected. He was already angry with Isabella for lying about the betrothal and tricking everyone. After thinking on the matter, he might have come to believe I had done the work of the Devil in saving Fernando."

"You said the sacerdote had no idea what you did."

"Does it matter? During my time with Fernando, he grew better."

He considered her suspicions and shook his head. "The priest hardly thinks of anything except his next meal. He had no problem railing at Isabella. If he thought you had done anything wrong, he would have told you. Starting rumors takes cunning and cowardice. Luscinda is probably behind this."

Sancha pushed off him.

He caught her wrist before she could move too far away. "If I thought mentioning her would make you leave me, I would have kept my tongue."

"This is no time to make light of matters. Why would she hate me so much to start rumors about—oh no, she wants you."

"She wants what my position and wealth can give her. You, and my contempt, stand in the way." He shrugged. "My feelings are the least of her worries."

"Do you think she knew I was the one with you that morning?"

"For certain? No. However, she did see how I looked at you at the gathering. Any fool would know I wanted you." He pushed up. "I am so sorry. This is my fault. I should never have spoken to her as sharply as I did. If I had only—"

"Shhh." She placed her fingers on his lips. "How were you to know what she might do? We have no proof she was the one."

He recalled Luscinda's fury and wouldn't have put murder past her to get what she wanted. "If she was, our union will prove her rumors wrong about you hating marriage, men, and anyone but the Devil." He left the bed.

"Where are you going?"

"I need to compose my missives to Tomás and Dominico for my servants to deliver." Although tired, he pulled on his braies and hose, determined to set things straight so he and Sancha could begin their union in joy not fear. "The sooner my friend and brothers arrive, the faster we can put this behind us." With his shirt, belt, and shoes in hand, he kissed her deeply. "Sleep. I promise to give you no rest once we wed."

She smiled. "I would hope not."

* * * *

Enrique made fast work of his letters, his words cryptic enough not to feed old rumors or start new ones should the missives fall into the wrong hands. He'd simply told the truth about his love for Sancha and their desire to wed immediately, without fanfare. Given the raid at the village, who knew what danger guests would face if they came to his castle for a celebration? The Moors might slaughter them all.

Satisfied with what he'd written, he sent two servants to deliver the items. After telling his cook to prepare for three more guests during the main meal, he caught up with Hortensia.

"I have news."

She nodded patiently but still seemed alarmed.

She'd yet to forget the constant trouble he'd given her as a boy. Hopefully, she'd find this newest disclosure more pleasant. "Tonight, I wed."

Her expression brightened. "About time—if I may say so."

He laughed. "You already have."

"Señorita Doña Sancha is lovely. You are wedding her, no?"

"Who else?"

Hortensia hugged him. "I am so happy for you."

"Take care to keep the other servants out of her study room."

"I always will."

He hugged her with gratitude and left to check on Sancha.

She'd brought Rosa to bed with her. The galgo explored the tangled linens, pillows, and counterpane. Sancha lay on her side asleep, hands to her heart as though in prayer, pleading that no one would harm them with the rumors.

Torn between sorrow and anger, he finally sighed. If he'd had proof Luscinda was the one who'd gossiped, he would have seen her pay in a moment. Without evidence, he'd only make matters worse by confronting her. Who knew what she'd do then?

After gathering fresh clothes, he closed the chamber door and chose another room to prepare for his wedding.

* * * *

Dominico arrived first, shortly after sunset. He was more rawboned than Enrique recalled, nothing but arms and legs, his lanky body swallowed by the drab robe of his order.

"Look at you." Enrique's sweeping gesture took in all of the man. "Has the Church stopped feeding its priests?"

"I stopped eating. Their food is terrible." He smiled. "I hope to get better fare tonight."

"My cook will stuff you until you burst. She loves to take in strays."

"Is she comely too? If so, I may fall in love with her."

Laughing, Enrique embraced his friend, both trying to outdo each other on how hard they squeezed.

"Enough." Dominico pulled away. "Tell me about this woman you want to wed. Is she very beautiful?"

"Should a man in your position be asking such a crude thing?"

"Surely not, if the poor girl is plain. Knowing you, my guess is she makes every other woman ugly in comparison."

And then some. "Come to my study." Enrique glanced around the entrance hall, making certain the servants weren't nearby. "We can talk there."

"How serious you become." Dominico frowned. "Is something the matter?"

"Not at all." He forced a smile. "There are chairs and wine in my study. None out here."

Once inside the room, he closed the door and turned to his friend. "I need your promise never to repeat what I tell you."

"You want to make a confession?"

"I want information. Sit. Please." He gestured to a leather chair, its wood engraved with his coat of arms. "I shall have your wine in a moment."

He filled a goblet, gave it to Dominico, then sat across from him. "Have you heard what the Inquisition is doing in this area? Who they might be targeting?"

Dominico finished his sip and lowered his goblet. "I only hear what others do. My work is different than the tribunal's."

"Have you heard rumors about the inquisitors focusing on a young noblewoman? The daughter of a grandee and duke."

Dominico lifted his eyebrows, a light brown shade, the same as his hair. "No. Have you?"

"Would I be asking you if I had? Have you heard the nobles discussing this?"

"This what? The girl? Why are you being so secretive? Who is she?"

Enrique hesitated a moment then relented. He had no other choice. "The woman I speak of is the one I plan to wed tonight. Sancha Lopéz de Lara." He huddled near, telling Dominico about the encounter with Luscinda, her jealousy and threat, the subsequent rumors.

Finished, he gripped the arms of his chair. "Will the Church take this talk seriously?"

"How can they? Granted, the Church is suspicious of unmarried women who refuse to wed and bear children as nature intended. Tonight Sancha will be yours. Nine months from now, she will surely bear your son."

He expelled the breath he'd been holding and sagged into his chair. "Gracias."

"For what? Telling you what you already know?" Dominico regarded him closely. "Is there something about Sancha you have yet to reveal?"

Chapter 10

Cautious of questions from a priest, Sancha waited until the last possible moment to meet Dominico.

The second she entered Enrique's study, unannounced, both men pushed to their feet. She closed the door, clearly not planning to leave. Not the best behavior for a soon-to-be wife, but she hardly cared about custom. She feared for her and Enrique's future.

He seemed pensive, not alarmed, and looked astonishingly handsome. His doublet and robe were a dark green, like the heavy forests on his estate. One leg of his hose was white, the other had alternating stripes of black and a pale rose. The pinkish tint reminded her of a new sunrise. With combed hair and a fresh shave, he presented an image of the powerful noble he was. His forelock seemed to mark him even further as being superior to others.

What an image of male authority and beauty he presented, though Sancha preferred his hair tousled, face shadowed with whiskers, muscular body naked. How wanton she'd become in such a short time, wanting the formalities of their union at an end, guests departed, leaving her and Enrique to their bed.

She suppressed a sigh and smiled instead, hoping she appeared cordial rather than yearning or pained.

Enrique joined her. After kissing her cheek, he pressed his mouth to her ear. "You look exquisite."

She'd worn one of the few grand gowns she brought to Fernando's castle before coming here. A gift from Isabella who'd always said her eldest sister dressed too simply. Of the finest red silk, the garment had a gold embroidered kirtle and jeweled undersleeves.

She would have preferred a maid's clothing and an evening at the pond with Enrique after a hard day studying or tending the ill.

She squeezed his hands, his warm, hers icy, and spoke in his ear. "Is all well?"

"We have nothing to fear. Trust me."

She searched his eyes, hoping he wasn't trying to spare her new worry or grief.

He met her gaze honestly, longing mingled with determination. The kind a man has when preparing himself for a battle he intends to win.

She hoped the fight now wasn't between him and Dominico. She pressed her cheek to Enrique's to keep the priest from overhearing. "How much have you told him?"

"Merely of Luscinda's jealousy and your reluctance to wed until you met me. Nothing else. I will protect you to my dying breath."

His assurance brought tears to her eyes. Her secret was theirs to face together, not hers alone. With those words, he'd fully delivered his heart and future to her. At another time, she would have been reckless with joy. Not tonight. She worried about Dominico. He may have been Enrique's dear friend, but he was still a priest.

And quite homely.

Poor man.

He had not an ounce of fat on his tall, scrawny frame. His nose was large, teeth long, hair thin and already balding. However, his smile was warm and quite beautiful, enhanced by two dimples as Enrique brought her over to meet him.

"My dear," Dominico said before anyone else could speak. "You must be the señorita who enchanted Enrique."

Her smile froze at his word choice. Enchanted, as in spells and witchcraft. Thankfully, she recovered before he noticed her distress. "I hope I am." She regarded Enrique, feigning confusion. "Would there be another woman you intend to wed, leaving me to plot her end so I might have you?"

Dominico laughed heartily. "Your señorita has spirit, Enrique. How wonderful." He spoke to her. "Sancha, no?"

Rather than take her hand, he gave her an enthusiastic hug. Her hands floated in air before she embraced him in return, thankful he hadn't had an opportunity to kiss her fingers and notice how icy they were.

Dominico released her and turned to Enrique. "Leave us."

He stared. "What?"

"I need to hear Sancha's confession, then yours before the nuptials. Go on. I will hear hers first." He gestured Enrique to the door.

Sancha's stomach fell.

Enrique didn't move. "She has nothing to confess. No woman has ever been as perfect. Giving. Loving."

Dominico smiled at Sancha. "You sound delightful."

She wasn't certain whether to laugh or flee.

Enrique crossed his arms over his chest. "Confession is not a requirement of you joining us. Why do you seek to delay me in wedding this magnificent woman? Are you jealous of what I have?"

Dominico leaned toward Sancha. "Enrique has changed greatly since we were young boys. Is he always so disagreeable now?" He smacked Enrique's chest. "Have you done something that will shock me if you confess?" He grinned. "Your secret is safe with me."

Enrique offered Sancha his hand. "He wants to brighten his dull life. Come. Neither of us is telling him anything of our love."

"Pity." Dominico bounced gently on his heels. "I hoped to enjoy myself tonight."

"Get as drunk as you want, eat until you burst, chase after the servant girls, take the lot of them to one of the rooms to—"

"What?" Sancha looked from one man to the other.

Dominico's gaunt face had already turned bright red. "Enrique jests."

She hoped so. Although she knew some priests were married or had mistresses, overall the Church hardly tolerated holy men chasing women.

Enrique touched her hand. "Forgive me for getting carried away."

He hadn't though, because that wasn't like him, and she suddenly realized as much. Masterfully, he'd changed the subject from confession to Dominico's sexual appetite, moving the attention off himself and her to his friend.

How brilliant he was.

The men bantered without stop. Enrique goaded the worst, moving the converse further from her until he and Dominico seemed to have forgotten she was in the same room. They spoke of childhood antics, fishing, riding, and no end of male pursuits. Sancha listened happily, ignored, and relaxed at last.

The door flew open. In strode Tomás and Pedro, both grinning.

Enrique scowled at Tomás. "Have you ever heard of knocking before invading a man's private domain? No, wait. What a foolish question. You have yet to learn to use a napkin at your meals, rather than your hand or sleeve."

Tomás crossed the room to Sancha and took her hand. "You are exquisite. Brighter than the sun, more breathtaking than the moon, fresher than the—"

"Enough." Enrique pushed his youngest brother aside and slipped his arm around her waist. "None of us want to waste the rest of our lives listening to you babble."

"I do." Dominico glanced at everyone. "I was hoping to hear what Sancha was fresher than."

Tomás threw his arms open in a grand gesture. "The very air we breathe. She is—"

"Laughing at you," Pedro said.

All eyes turned to her. Her face flushed hot with laughter and embarrassment. Sobering quickly, she cleared her throat. "Forgive me." Her shoulders trembled with new giggles she found difficult to suppress. She wasn't certain if relief, lingering anxiety, or joy at having the chance to spend her life with Enrique caused her emotions. "I enjoy how you tease each other."

"We like you too." Tomás pulled her from Enrique's embrace so he could hug her. "Best wishes on your marriage to my brother. You will need them."

She laughed throatily.

Pedro embraced her next, less forcefully than Tomás had, and added a chaste kiss on her cheek. "How lovely you are. Are you very happy?"

So much, she found speech difficult. She nodded.

Tomás smiled. "My brothers are dropping like flies when it comes to matrimony. Poor fools."

"Take care." Enrique offered a smug smile. "Your turn may be next."

"Tomás would have to settle on one girl first." Pedro shrugged. "He has so many."

Sancha snickered, unable to help herself.

Blushing, Tomás gestured to everyone. "Is this the extent of the wedding party?"

"We could always invite the servants if you want a crowd," Enrique said.

Tomás inclined his head to Dominico. "And have this one scare the prettiest girls away?" He hugged the man, both grinning.

Pedro also gave the priest a fervent welcome.

"Someday," Tomás said, "we need to have these ceremonies when Isabella and Sancha are both in attendance." He gave her a stern look. "You keep missing each other's nuptials."

She laughed despite her disappointment that Isabella couldn't be here. Sancha had spent the day writing a long letter to her sister, explaining events, promising they would visit soon. She'd also penned a missive to her sisters at court and Rupert, telling him of her nuptials, new home with Enrique, and that her husband would now handle all matters at her estate. Taking care with her phrasing, she'd also asked Rupert to send word if anyone needed her. He'd know she meant the peasants she'd sworn to treat.

How she'd continue to do so until the rumors died down, she had no idea. Nor did she know how long she'd have to wait for matters to return to normal, allowing her to visit the villages freely again. She hoped the delay wouldn't be more than a few weeks, possibly a month or two. Surely, not years. So many could die or suffer permanent injuries without her care.

Enrique must have sensed her renewed foreboding and sadness. He slung his arm around her shoulders and kissed the top of her head. "We are well on our way to a grand future."

"As soon as we get to the chapel." Dominico glanced at the group. "Shall we proceed with this?"

Enrique led the way, his hand firmly around hers, offering comfort and protection, the same as the small room they entered.

The chapel boasted stained glass windows, several pews, a simple altar, the crucifix and statues of the holy mother Mary and saints. To the side were votive candles, each lit and shining brightly.

Dominico's eyes rounded at the flames. "Someone has been praying mightily, petitioning God for His good favor." He glanced from Enrique to Sancha.

She wasn't about to confess. Hopefully, God would answer her entreaties. She'd begged for His mercy before she'd joined Dominico and Enrique in the study.

Enrique leveled his gaze on his friend. "Make fast work of this. No need to go through all the pomp."

Tomás and Pedro chuckled.

Dominico folded his hands in front. "Allow me to tend to my duties, and I shall allow you to tend to yours." He glanced at Sancha.

She blushed to the roots of her hair and studiously avoided his gaze through the ceremony. What little there was.

Enrique kept hurrying the man along until Dominico came to the part where the intended husband pledged himself to his future wife. Enrique took both her hands and kissed her fingertips. He looked at her so long and tenderly, Pedro cleared his throat.

Tomás clamped Enrique's shoulder. "Until you speak, none of us can enjoy the wine or food. Say what you must, we beg of you."

Enrique shrugged him off and gave Sancha a smile filled with hope and promise of their days ahead. A good marriage, children, her work, his earnest attention to their safety.

"I have never loved anyone as I do you." Joy lit his features, making him more handsome than she believed possible. "For the rest of my days, I promise you my all and give myself to be thy husband."

Pedro clapped.

Enrique shot him a look. Dominico continued with the ceremony, pausing when the time came for Sancha to give her pledge.

Enrique still faced her, both of them entranced with the other's presence, as though no one else existed.

"Sí." She eased closer, wanting to kiss him. "Most certainly."

Dominico laughed. She and Enrique looked over.

The priest rubbed his fingers over his mouth, sobering quickly. "What you said was lovely, my dear, especially since having any woman love Enrique is a miracle, but I need the answer the holy mother Church requires."

Of course. Despite her embarrassment, she behaved with dignity, speaking the words that would forever change her life. "I give myself to be thy wife."

Tomás and Pedro cheered.

"Well done." Tomás pivoted. "Now we feast."

"My blessing on the marriage first." Dominico recited the words, followed by a wink to Enrique and Sancha. "You are joined forever. Now Mass."

Everyone stared at him.

Tomás strode to the door. "Pedro and I shall see the rest of you in the dining hall once Mass is over." He gestured for his brother to follow him to the food.

"Have it your way." Dominico trailed after them. "Someday you may regret your decision."

"Never," Enrique called to his friend, then slipped his hand beneath Sancha's chin and lifted her face to his. "Happy?"

She wrapped her arms around his torso. "Dangerously so."

"You intend to lead me into carnal sin this night?"

"Until the following morning and afternoon, if you can keep up with me." He laughed. "We shall see."

* * * *

They had to wait through an interminably long meal with Dominico, Tomás, and Pedro's appetites too hearty, their converse endless.

Enrique wanted to throw them out.

They must have sensed his intolerance. Each man ignored him during the feast, concentrating on besting each other in imagined deeds or peppering Sancha with questions on who she thought was the better man.

She waved her hands in front of herself repeatedly, refusing to take sides. "I leave the decision to you."

Beneath the table, her foot played with his. She'd slipped off her shoe and slid her toes up his leg. Minutes earlier, she'd settled the ball of her foot on his groin. He'd swallowed his wine too quickly and coughed until he couldn't breathe. Still wheezing, he'd assured everyone he was well. Pity he'd reacted as he had. Sancha didn't put her foot on his shaft and sac again.

She did eat with zeal, either because she believed the worst was behind them or wanted to fortify herself for their marital bed.

She reached for more beef.

Pedro handed her the tray. "With you wed now, will your servants be coming here?" He glanced at Enrique. "What do you intend to do with the castle where she used to live and all the others from her inheritance?"

"I know what I would do." She slid a thick slice of beef on her plate. "I would turn the grandest into a hospital."

Dominico paused mid-chew, staring at her.

She grew quite pale and looked at Enrique.

He shrugged to dismiss any suspicions about her words. "We almost lost Fernando several months ago. Two knaves stabbed him repeatedly while he was protecting Sancha and Isabella. Tomás, Pedro, and I brought him to the convent, where I met her. She was there praying." He gave her a smile then concentrated on Dominico once more. "Fernando nearly died during the journey. If a hospital had stood near the castle where she used to live, the far shorter distance would have spared us what might have been unspeakable grief."

"All turned out well," Tomás said. "I believe Sancha has an excellent idea for her former home."

Dominico dumped another helping of pork and cheese on his plate. "Enrique's first-born son may think otherwise. Sancha's castle would be part of his inheritance. Just as Enrique's father gave him this estate until he inherits all."

"Seven castles from Papá." Tomás sighed wistfully. "Countless acres of land, villages."

Pedro leaned toward Enrique. "It may take you the rest of your life to visit everything you have." He smiled at Sancha. "You too."

"None of it means anything to me."

Dominico finished his sip of wine. "You say that now. If you were forced to live in a hut in one of the villages, rather than this splendor, I trust you would feel quite differently."

"So would the peasants." She frowned. "None of us had a choice where we were born. None of this is right."

He shook his head. "Not having a choice in where one is born?"

"No." She gestured to the dining hall. "Is this estate not grand or large enough for one family? How much more do we need when those around us have so little? When most children die before their second year because they lack food and skilled heal—"

She'd stopped so abruptly, her pause seemed to intrigue Dominico more than her earlier words.

Enrique wrapped his fingers around hers and squeezed gently. "What a wonder she is." He grinned at Dominico. "Did I not tell you she was loving and giving?"

"You did." After working his tongue around his mouth, he pointed his knife at her. "Make certain not to be too giving. You have your own family to worry about. Listen to your husband on this."

"Like you do the directives of the Church?" Enrique asked.

Dominico scowled, and detailed what a stellar priest he was, unknowingly taking attention off her.

Relived, Enrique tapped her foot with his. After a moment, she tapped back, quite sluggishly, her gaze lowered, shoulders slumped. He wasn't certain if she felt badly for talking too much or not being able to say what was on her mind as men always did.

With him, she could. Trying to lighten her mood, he wound his foot around her leg and tugged. She slid her gaze to him and tugged back. Before long, they were snickering with him wanting an end to this play and the start of her naked in his bed.

He pushed back his chair and stood. "I thank all of you for helping me celebrate this wondrous day. However—"

"There is always a however," Tomás said. "Are you tired of us already?"

"I reached that state hours ago and can barely stomach your ugly faces a second more. I want to be alone with my bride." He offered Sancha his hand, which she took readily.

He spoke to the men. "Stay as long as you like. I know you will anyway. None of you have manners."

Tomás finished wiping his mouth off with the back of his hand, Dominico belched once more, and Pedro scratched beneath his arm.

Sancha smiled. "But we love you anyway."

Led by Tomás, each man offered her a hug and a wish for a long, prosperous marriage, then returned to their food and converse.

At the bottom of the grand stairway, she hiked up her skirt and bolted up the staircase. "I challenge you to a race."

She made it halfway up the steps when Enrique passed and waited for her at the top.

Winded, she joined him. "A moment."

"You want me to wait again after you put me off for so long? No." Bent at the waist, he slung her over his shoulder.

She squealed.

"Quiet." He carried her to their chamber.

Earlier, he'd instructed the servants to prepare the room with so many candles and oil lamps the space would be brighter than when sun flooded inside, to scent the sheets and pillows with her sweet rose fragrance, and see to the pup.

With Hortensia taking care of Rosa tonight, he and Sancha would be alone and undisturbed, except for what they did to each other. Grinning, he ran his hand beneath her dress to the top of her thighs.

She gasped.

"Quiet I said. Do you want the others to hear?"

"I might ask you the same." She cupped his buttocks and squeezed. "Do you truly expect me to be silent and still while you ravish me?"

He wanted her screaming in delight, panting in contentment. He wanted her delirious with love.

Once inside the chamber, he kicked the door closed and set her on her feet. She wavered slightly and righted herself, hair tumbling over her shoulders and face. On a huff, she pulled the tresses away.

He crossed his arms, affecting his most lordly expression. "Remove your clothing at once. I want to see what I got into this evening by wedding you."

She lifted her chin. "I wed you. Give me a show."

"In time."

"Now." She smiled. "Or I shall call a servant in here."

"To do what?" He stalked toward her. She didn't give an inch. He liked that. "You think any of them can keep me from you?"

"No, though my garments will. Remove my clothing, you say. How am I to do so on my own?" She gestured to the buttons and laces keeping her trapped in too much fabric.

He shook his head. "I should run your tailoress through."

"Free me from these things first, I beg of you." She flung out her arms. "They strangle me like a hangman's noose, crush me worse than a vise, flay my tender flesh as much as a—"

"I can see Tomás has ruined you with his blather. I need to remedy that."

"Please, no bloodshed. Running your brother through would be a crime."

"Indeed. I suppose I will simply have to keep you naked so you can never leave this room." He curled his forefinger toward himself, gesturing her closer.

With a wicked smile, she approached and promptly sank to her knees, her hands on his belly.

"What are you doing?"

She untied his hose. "Relieving you of your clothing so you can assist me with mine."

As though anything would ever keep him from stripping her. "Do so with haste. I do not intend to wait—"

He stopped. He had to. She had his hose and braies around his knees, shirt lifted, face pressed to his pelt.

"No, no, no, no." He eased her face away before her tongue made him forget what he truly wanted. "I demand your belly, not your mouth. As your husband, my word is law."

She licked the inside of his thigh. He shivered. She made a sound of approval. "A request would be far nicer."

"You have mine. Please take these garments off me so I may see to yours."

She made fast work of undressing him, tossing his clothes everywhere until he stood naked and fully aroused before her.

She reached for his shaft.

He pushed her hand away. "Now you." After he'd unbuttoned and unlaced her, he slid her clothing over her shoulders, past her breasts to her arms, trapping them. "Remain as you are. Not one move."

He padded around her as a master would with a new slave, taking in her partial nudity. In the candlelight, her hair shimmered more beautiful than a Spanish sunset. Her fair skin seemed too delicate for any man to touch. Her constricted nipples contradicted his notion, the pink halos tight with passion, tips hard with lust, breasts heavy and full, perfect for his hands.

The fabric trapped hers, not allowing Sancha to cover herself.

Enrique doubted she would, though she did seem a trifle daunted by his scrutiny. Good. He wanted her to feel his heated gaze before experiencing his touch as her husband.

He came up behind her, one arm around her waist, his hand skimming her breasts, lips on her throat.

She moaned, modesty forgotten, pleasure assured.

Her scent filled him, the light rose fragrance already surpassed by her musk, her excitement for her new husband.

He closed his eyes and restrained himself from pulling her to the floor, mounting and thrusting as his shaft demanded. The slightest brush of fabric against his crown was torturous, desire barreling through him, every part of his being demanding relief in her sweet, warm body.

In time.

She belonged to him now. No matter his oppressive desires, he wouldn't rush.

At a leisurely pace, he ran his hand down her torso and circled her navel as she'd so often done with him. He travelled lower, brushing his fingers over her belly.

Her muscles quivered. She made a gentle, yielding sound and pressed her buttocks into his thickened shaft. Shuddering, he forced himself to maintain control, at least for a few more seconds.

He released her to work on the rest of the buttons and laces. After freeing the last, he removed her garments and shoes, tossing the things over his shoulder, not caring where they landed.

She smiled.

He leaned down to her, their mouths almost touching. "Rest your arms on your head, present yourself to me."

Her cheeks flushed.

He liked her maidenly modesty, especially since there was a woman of deep passion beneath, one he had intimate knowledge of. "Do it now."

She lifted her eyebrows but did obey, arms on her head, breasts displayed, nipples raised to his mouth.

Not yet enough.

"Part your legs. I want to see what belongs to me."

Her blush deepened. Again, she submitted.

He padded around her. She turned, watching.

"Eyes to the front." He gestured, showing her what he wanted. "No moving at all."

"Can I breathe?"

He suppressed a smile. "Only if you do so gently."

She pulled in a huge breath and held the air.

He studied the dimples above her delectable buttocks, her sleek thighs and calves.

She exhaled finally.

He padded to the front, entranced by the lovely slope of her breasts, a mole near her left nipple. Her reddish thatch held him in thrall, plump folds peeking past the curly veil of hair, her flesh moist with desire.

He cupped her mound, slipped two fingers inside her sheath, and rested his thumb on her nub.

Moaning, she pushed into his hand, telling him what she wanted.

He gave her everything she required. Soon, her head lolled on her shoulders, her expression glassy, body and mind surrendering to release.

Denying her for the moment, he removed his hand. Her sex was drenched, ready for his shaft, not his fingers or mouth. Before she could protest at how he'd paused, he swept her into his arms, had her on the mattress, and knelt between her legs.

"At last." She pulled her knees back.

"I have a better idea." He grabbed her ankles and placed them on his shoulders, spreading her.

Sancha's face, throat, and chest turned as red as her hair, all of her suddenly one color.

He wasn't certain if he'd simply embarrassed or disgusted her. Possibly both. "Too much?"

She regarded his shaft, her mound, their positions. "No." Her eyes brightened. "Fill me, husband."

"With pleasure, wife."

They both grinned.

He drove his shaft into her yielding sheath, burying himself as far as a man could go, his mouth on hers, tongue inside, filling Sancha completely, claiming her, deepening their love.

* * * *

She suckled his tongue and hooked her feet behind his head, stunned at her wantonness. Even Isabella hadn't spoken of sharing anything like this with Fernando.

How Sancha adored this position and craved Enrique.

She cupped his face with one hand and ran her fingertips through his chest hair with the other, feeling his smile against her lips. His happiness was the greatest gift he could give her. She had to take care not to bring him pain.

How foolish she'd been in the dining hall, speaking of establishing a hospital, then nearly blurting that children died for lack of proper healing. He'd barely saved her from a confession with Dominico when she'd managed to bring attention to herself again and again, forcing Enrique to change the subject repeatedly, sparing her the priest's odd stare and questions that might lead to her work.

What was the matter with her? She'd always been reserved in the past and seemed to be making up for her prior modesty by speaking out of turn to his friend and brothers.

He stroked her nub, coordinating those movements with his exquisite thrusts.

Needing a full breath, she pulled her mouth free of his. The air didn't help. The room still lurched. She relaxed as much as she could and submitted to release, unable to deny herself any longer.

Unwieldy pleasure swept her away on a wave of brash lust. She was vaguely aware of squealing and crying out her release. Enrique's proud roar signaled his. Their fight for air afterward sounded as though they were both dying.

Finally, they filled the room with their shared laughter, her giggles tired. "Do you think we should take this more seriously?"

He howled with laughter. "I think we have the matter well in hand."

They did. No one could convince her that another husband and wife enjoyed each other more. Not even Isabella with her fantastic tales of delight with Fernando. He was a brave warrior and quite handsome, but he'd never be Enrique.

He held her during slumber, though rest didn't last long. There was so much to share. He stirred first, waking her with hungry kisses.

After he'd positioned her this time, she looked over her shoulder at him. "You *are* wicked."

"You are far too demure. Come now, arch your back to lift your buttocks."

She was on her hands and knees, legs parted, presenting her sex to him, her skin burning. Again, not from embarrassment but anticipation. "I thought you asked me not to move."

"I told you not to question. You have a habit of doing so."

"When?"

His shoulders bobbed with his struggle not to laugh. "The longer we speak, the longer you wait for me to fill you."

As far as she was concerned, converse was at an end. She blew him a kiss, did as he'd requested, then rested her forehead on the mattress and awaited his plunder and possession.

He mounted her easily, the bold position allowing his shaft to stroke her nub, each thrust reducing the world to the sounds of their passion, scents, and needs.

He rode her well, hands on her hips, bodies joined. They accepted release together, perfectly in tune, voices and breaths mingled.

Happy in the world they'd created for each other.

Chapter 11

If one could consider days golden when clouds blanketed the sun or when night cast the world into darkness, then Sancha's first weeks with Enrique satisfied the notion.

She found each moment precious.

They rode across the estate. He pointed out improvements he'd made to the vineyards, groves, wheat, and pasturage. His agricultural knowledge surprised her. She'd known he was a learned man, able to speak and read numerous languages as she did, but his understanding of how men could best use the soil and animals was a revelation. They talked for hours, him teaching, her absorbing facts she never knew existed.

Proudly, he showed her the great score of cattle, pigs, goats, and other animals on his land that she hadn't asked about before. She'd been too intent on study and protecting her heart, trying not to fall in love with him.

She'd never be so foolish again.

They rode through an area with hundreds of chickens. The creatures squawked and flapped their wings to get away from the horses. Enrique brought his gelding up short and stared at something to the left.

Several dead fowl lay amongst the others. He called a worker over.

"Patrón." The man inclined his head.

Enrique gestured to the fallen chickens, their bodies plump, feathers intact, blood absent. However, their wattles and heads were darker than normal. "What happened here?"

"The birds had trouble breathing a short time ago. I have no idea why. I gave them the same care as the others. Before I knew what to do about their trouble, they died."

Enrique studied the ground. "Remove the bodies and burn them. Move the rest of the fowl to another area. Clean this one thoroughly."

"Sí, patrón." The man hurried to the carcasses.

"Does this happen often?" Sancha asked.

"No. And it rarely lasts. Moving the creatures and cleaning the area has always stemmed the problem."

"Do you know what makes the birds ill?"

"The trouble seems to come from nowhere. A foolish thing to say, I know. The water and food we give the chickens is never tainted and has no ill effect on the other fowl that show no signs of distress. The source has to be something else."

She said no more until they rode past the workers who might overhear. "Have you ever considered animals might suffer similar illnesses to those afflicting people?"

"Are you saying the answer might be found in your books?"

"I have yet to read them all. When I experiment on my mice with potions I discovered in the volumes, the vermin respond as a human should. Not every time, of course, or with every mixture, though enough to tell me what may help us could help them."

"You mean to heal my animals now?"

"I thought you might enjoy learning what I know, the same as I savor everything you tell me about your land."

He squeezed her hand. "I would."

That day he joined Sancha in her study room and explored the volumes as she did for symptoms similar to what the chickens encountered. They discussed how she might duplicate the problem in her mice and what treatment might save them.

Whenever a method worked, he grew as excited as a child who'd mastered a new task. Laughing gaily, he'd swing her in his arms, then kiss her until neither of them could breathe. More often than not, his excitement and hers turned to passion. They forgot the books to indulge in carnal pleasures rather than knowledge.

An almost perfect time if not for her increasing impatience regarding the rumors. Since the wedding, there were no new claims against her, the previous ones dying down. Although she was grateful and relieved, she still craved visits to the villages to offer her skills if needed.

Already she'd seemed to have waited an endless amount of time.

Nearly two months into her marriage a missive from Isabella arrived, giving her hope she'd soon be free to move about undetected as she had earlier.

I am now speaking with more zeal than Tomás
ever had when I relate news of your and Enrique's
rides across his estate, you taking command of the

*house servants as a noble wife should, and how you
continue to capture Enrique's heart as you had the
first moment he saw you.*

*Everyone is quite weary of the way I go on about
your great romance, the men especially, who would
rather speak of war, Moors, the taking of Granada.*

*I hardly care what they think or want, relating
instead what you write in your missives, adding the
many smiles you and Enrique must surely share. No
different from my beloved Fernando and me.*

*I have promised those we know that you and I will
give birth within months of each other. You must make
certain this happens. I know our sons will be great
friends, both having dark hair like our husbands.*

*Happiness will never forsake you again, dear
Sancha. Only good will follow you now.*

*Your devoted sister,
Isabella*

Her letter cheered Sancha to the point that she kept the missive
with her at all times, using Isabella's words as a sort of charm. All she
had to do was act.

After troubling for days, she finally found the right time. She and
Enrique lay in bed, sated from their love. "When?"

He snuggled closer, arm across her waist, face to her neck. "Give me a
few moments. When my vigor returns, I shall have you again."

Smiling, she ruffled his hair. "Of course you will."

He yawned.

She sucked her lip, uncertain whether to ruin their wonderful moment
with talk of healing but told herself to go on. In order for their marriage to
succeed, they had to be open and honest, neither of them keeping worry
or problems from each other. "When will matters be safe enough for me
to heal again?"

He stopped running his thumb over her belly. Propped on his elbow,
he looked down at her, eyes and forelock sparkling in the moonlight
streaming across the bed. "Has someone requested your skill?"

"No. Though they will eventually. People harm themselves in all sorts
of ways or grow ill like your fowl with no known cause. Women have
trouble giving birth, endangering their lives and the infants'."

"None of this has happened yet. Be grateful everyone is well."

"And when they no longer are, what then? Do I still need to fear the rumors and remain confined here?"

"Confined? You make marriage to me sound like prison."

"Forgive me." She gathered him to her, running her fingers through his hair. "I have never been happier, but I cannot let others suffer when I have so much, especially the means to help them."

He sighed. "The rumors might have quieted, but we have no idea how long they may persist, smoldering like coals ready to burst back into flame, destroying everything in their path. You need to take care. Especially now. You could be carrying my son."

Her heart sank. Months ago, she would have resented his words, thinking he wanted to control her as husbands did with wives. She knew better now. His only concern was for her safety. "I would never do anything to harm our child or you. But I do need to know how long I must wait until I can return to healing as I once did."

He eased away to look at her. "If someone needs you, I can always bring them here for you to treat."

"The journey could kill them as it nearly did Fernando, and he was only a short distance from the convent when you brought him to me."

"Let me think on the matter. You should too. We can come to an agreement on the safest way to proceed."

"Do you want to do so now?"

He laughed softly. "I beg of you, let me rest." On a weary yawn, he sagged to the mattress. "We can consider the matter in the morning, to prepare ourselves when someone in the village will need your skills."

* * * *

Brave words Enrique had forced himself to speak. However, he'd given his oath not to stand in the way of her healing and had to abide by what he'd promised.

Repeatedly they discussed the issue and considered the perils involved, including her dressing as a boy during travel.

He rejected the idea. "Your garments would cause as much talk as your healing. Most people would consider you odd for disguising yourself as a male."

"Isabella did the same when Fernando escorted her from Granada to Papá's castle."

"He wanted to protect her against being raped. Neither of them made their presence known to others unless they absolutely had to for food or shelter. Isabella never strode into a village and healed anyone."

"I never stride. I walk demurely."

He smiled, pleased at her banter despite the troubling subject. "You know what I mean."

"What if I dress as a nun? Surely, we can get our hands on a habit. Who would question my intent if I resemble a sister?"

"The Church. A sacerdote. The inquisitors."

With each of his answers, more color drained from her face.

He couldn't stop. Too much was at stake. "To heal as you have been is one thing. To do so while pretending to serve God would be as bad in the eyes of the Church as a converso claiming fealty to Christianity while clinging to his former religion in private."

She sighed loudly. "What then? If I had the power to become invisible and walk around unnoticed I would, but I cannot."

Pity. Her going around unseen would make matters much easier for both of them. In fact, there was the answer. He frowned at an idea suddenly forming.

She leaned toward him. "Have I angered you?"

"No. You found the solution."

"I did? How? What?"

"Being a woman, you need to heal without being seen. Being a man, I have no such problem. I can visit the villages, especially those under my authority, without anyone questioning me. I have every right to be there to see what goes on."

She stared. "Are you saying you intend to heal?"

"No. Never." He made a face at having to deal with strangers' injuries and sickness as she had. In that, she was far braver than he was. "You can heal through me. When someone needs your skill, I could go to the villages with your materials and instructions on how to use them. After the raid, you taught the village women how to stitch a wound. I can read what you write, telling others what to do."

"How would I know what any of the people need in way of healing unless I saw them first?"

"By whatever physical complaints they have. You can ask whoever requests your help—one of the servants is my guess—if their ill relative or friend has the fever, is coughing, broke a limb, whatever the problem may be. The solution might not be perfect, but my idea is better than nothing, no?"

She looked past him, gaze absorbed.

"Sancha?"

Her expression remained pained. "Are circumstances truly so unsafe I have to do this through you?"

"Would I have offered to take time from my obligations to see to this if I thought the way was clear for you to heal?"

"Of course not." She melted into his arms. "How kind of you to help until I can do this on my own again."

"With luck, you should be able to do so shortly."

"How shortly?"

He wished she'd stop asking things he couldn't answer. "We need to take matters slowly. No one has even requested your help. Months may pass before anyone does."

* * * *

The matter came up little over a week later. Hortensia approached Sancha, since she knew of her healing.

Enrique cursed himself for allowing anyone other than his brothers to know of Sancha's gift, fearful she'd take off for the village before he could stop her.

To his surprise and relief, she discussed the matter calmly.

"The young woman Hortensia told me about is sister to one of the house servants." She paged through her largest volume as she spoke. "She resides in a village past the one the Moors raided, nearly a day's ride from here. For weeks, a cough has weakened her, producing small amounts of greenish phlegm with most of the matter remaining in her lungs. Unable to breathe well, she has no appetite and has wasted away, no longer the buxom woman she was."

Sancha paused on a page and ran her finger down the text, reading as she talked. "This book seems to mention such an illness. It may tell me what herbs and other materials to mix for a potion."

She read quietly, nodded, then jabbed her finger into the page. "Here it is. I shall write down every word for you to convey to the young woman and her family. If all goes well, she should slowly produce more phlegm when she coughs, in time expelling the vile substance."

He shuddered at the image she'd painted.

She caught his distaste before he could hide his feelings. "How brave you are to be doing this for the young woman."

"I do this for you, no one else. Not even for Hortensia, who had no right to go past me to get to you."

"She only asked my opinion on whether the young woman would survive. Not once did she request my help. I made the promise on my own. Rail at me, not her."

"Would you listen to me if I did?"

"I prefer a request."

He laughed, despite having to leave her for days on end. "How long will you need to prepare your materials? I want this done with quickly so I can return to you."

"I shall hurry." She didn't move.

"What now?"

"Will anyone question you suddenly going to that particular village?"

"Why would they? To ease your mind, I can check the other communities along the way, as I have in the past, to see if everything goes well."

"Even the one the Moors raided? Can you find out about Guillermo's cousin?"

"Who?"

"The man with the burned face."

He remembered and suppressed another shudder. "My first stop will be to see the poor man."

She threw her arms around his neck. "I ask too much of you. Most husbands would have murdered me by now."

He ran his hands down her narrow back and cupped her buttocks, loving their womanly shape. "Will you reward me greatly for my good deeds the moment I return?"

"I will be your devoted slave forever."

"You had better." He swatted her buttocks playfully. "See to what you must as I give my men their orders. They will assure your protection."

She pulled back and searched his face. "What of yours? Surely, you have no intention of travelling alone."

"Guards will ride with me as they always do, with others staying here for you."

Worry pinched her features. "Do you expect trouble?"

He didn't have to ask what kind. "I have kept an ear out for problems. Nothing is about, no worry about the Inquisition as long as you keep from fueling new rumors."

"I promise not to do anything to bring either of us grief. How could I? My days are spent here with you."

"Pleasantly, I hope."

"What else?" She leaned into him. "I have no need for parties, celebrations, or other pomp as you like to call those gatherings. The only person I do miss is Isabella."

"Upon my return we can make plans to have her come here or travel to see her."

"Two Lopéz de Lara sisters in the same castle? You are a good and brave man."

Laughing, he swung her around, kissed her deeply, and left to settle matters before his departure. The beginning of at least three days without her. A journey he would never have considered making for another woman.

Love certainly changed a man.

As passion did a woman. When the time came for him to leave, she kissed him farewell in their bedchamber, at the castle entrance, and again when he prepared to mount his gelding.

The guards looked off into the distance, pretending not to notice how she clung to him.

"You will take care?" she asked.

"Always. I have no desire to meet injury, illness, or death."

"No. Stop." She pressed her fingers against his lips. "Never say that word again in relation to you. I forbid it."

He pulled her farther away from his men, lest they hear her giving more orders to her husband. "The longer we take to say farewell, the longer my return to you will be."

She hugged him hard enough to impede his breathing, her face pressed to his shoulder. "I miss you already."

As he did her, though finally they had to part.

His last image of Sancha was her running down the path leading to the castle gate, hair and skirt flying as she tried to keep him in view.

* * * *

She missed him immediately and chided herself for having put him in such an awful position. If he'd refused to help, he would have broken his promise to her. By agreeing, he was possibly putting himself in danger from thieves, Moors, or the Inquisition if they learned what he'd done.

She wanted to shout or throw something to quell her anger at herself. She snatched a small volume but couldn't hurl it across the space. Even in her turmoil, the book was too precious. At last, she pounded her fist into her palm and tried to think of a solution so Enrique wouldn't have to act in her stead again.

Hours passed without an answer. She couldn't eat, study, or sleep, and spent an endless night in their bed. The sheets were too cool without him, the space too large. Every noise made her jump, not out of fear but her hope he'd returned to tell her all had gone well and they could move on with their lives.

Good sense told her he hadn't been gone long enough to have come back.

The following day, she ate eggs, bread, and cheese at Hortensia's urging. Although Sancha had ample nourishment, her mind suffered, her experiments and study going nowhere since she couldn't concentrate on anything for long. At last, she gave up and took Rosa outside, hoping play with the pup might relax her enough so she could think clearly again.

The galgo was initially timid at having so much to explore, though she soon bounded across the grass, sniffed flowers, and ran away from bees that buzzed near. Sancha threw numerous twigs for her to retrieve. Rosa ran to each, sniffed the wood then returned without a one.

Reclined on a blanket, Sancha fed the pup orange slices, boiled eggs, olives, and plenty of water, then ate her cheese, bread, and grapes, finishing with sweet wine.

The sun was heavier than before, while she was sluggish from food and lack of sleep. With her tension finally drained away, she cuddled next to Rosa and encircled the pup with her arm, content to have them nap.

* * * *

Something snapped. Sancha stirred, picturing Rosa chewing a twig, curious about its flavor.

A quick look told her the pup lay nearby, still asleep.

Another twig snapped. She wasn't alone.

On her feet hurriedly, she turned so fast she nearly lost her balance. One of Enrique's men, a short fellow with more fat on him than muscle, took a quick step back as if she'd alarmed him or he didn't want to startle her further.

"What is it?" She immediately thought of Enrique, fearing something untoward had happened. "Where is my husband?"

"With his men, señora. He left yesterday."

"You have word of him?" She advanced. "Something has happened?"

"No." He kept backing away. "A retinue waits at the gate requesting entrance."

Her pulse jumped. She knew of no one who would come here with servants, unless it was Isabella.

Sancha's hope surged until she considered the unlikelihood of her sister travelling. Fernando would advise against any unnecessary trip this early in her condition, the most likely time for a woman to lose an infant.

Rupert wouldn't have come either. He would have sent a missive to tell her if someone needed healing, which left no one except inquisitors. Did they travel with attendants?

She was afraid to know but had no other choice except to inquire. "Whose retinue?"

"Forgive me, I have no idea. The woman refused to say. She gave me this for you to read." He extended a missive.

Sancha turned from him, her hands shaking so badly she could barely lift the seal she didn't recognize. One from a woman. Wait.

She read the signature again. Luscinda.

Dizzy with apprehension, Sancha had to lock her knees to keep standing. Never had she needed Enrique as much as she did now, longing for his strong arms and assurances even though she was grateful he wasn't here. At least with him away, he wouldn't come to harm.

Bracing herself, she read the missive.

> *Dear Sancha, or should I say Señora de Zayas!*
>
> *What a surprise you gave us by wedding Enrique. None of our friends or acquaintances suspected what you were up to. Few could believe, given your somber ways. We thought news of your marriage was a trick to make everyone laugh.*
>
> *Isabella has assured us your and Enrique's union is one made in paradise.*
>
> *How wonderful for you.*
>
> *I offer you my heartiest good wishes on your sudden good fortune, and beg you to invite me inside your new home so we may visit.*
>
> *As you offered none of us a chance to help you celebrate, I do hope you and I can do so now.*
>
> *Señorita Doña Luscinda*

Sancha read the note twice more, clenching her jaw harder each time. What she was up to? Sudden good fortune? As though she'd threatened Enrique into marriage with him begging for his freedom.

The loathsome woman still wanted him despite his wedded state. What did Luscinda mean to do, murder Sancha in her own home?

She crushed the missive, ready to toss the vile thing into the pond and tell the guard to run the woman off the estate, but didn't. If she were to refuse Luscinda entrance, the wretch might claim Sancha had denied the visit because she wanted to continue her celebration with the Devil.

After smoothing the missive, she tucked the note in her sleeve. "Please escort the señorita to the castle entrance. I shall meet her there."

"Sí, señora."

Sancha brought Rosa inside and gave her to Hortensia. "Can you watch the pup for me?"

"Of course." The older woman regarded her closely. "Has something happened?"

"I have a guest."

"Oh. Would you like me to tell cook to prepare something special for—"

"No. The guest will not be staying. Wait. Perhaps she will." If she threw Luscinda out without food or drink, the next rumors might be that no meal was safe in the de Zayas castle, all tainted by spells and witchcraft. "Have her prepare our best."

"Sí, señora."

She smoothed her gown and hair, pulling a leaf from her tresses. Her shoulders sagged at how she must look, not that her taking time to bathe and put on fresh clothing would have changed Luscinda's mind. She already thought every woman was ugly compared to her.

Sancha tramped to the entrance, ordering herself to remain calm and dignified. Her throat tightened and her stomach rolled.

Luscinda's carriage pulled up, drawn by the finest horses, constructed of the best materials, with four footmen in immaculate livery. The tallest man jumped off his platform and opened the door.

Luscinda exited like a queen, a jeweled fan in one hand. Her dark rose gown shimmered in the sunlight, its tint matching the caul she wore. She raised her face to take in the castle's height, which exposed her long throat. The neckline of her gown was indecently low, the same as the one she'd worn to Isabella and Fernando's celebration. Her beauty undeniable.

She regarded the breathtaking grounds to the exclusion of everything else, staring especially at the lake and the sheer vastness of the land.

A flash of what appeared to be jealousy, or hatred, crossed her face before she turned to Sancha and blinked. "It is you. I thought..." She smiled sheepishly. "Forgive me. Dressed as you are, I thought you were one of the servants. How foolish of me to think so when you have never bothered with anything pretty. How good it is to see you. I was afraid you might turn me away."

She threw her arms around Sancha as one would a dear friend, rather than an acquaintance she'd just dismissed as plain and unworthy.

Sancha bared her teeth but patted Luscinda's back gently instead of kicking her for those insulting words. If Enrique had been here, he might have tossed the woman over the hill, smiling as she rolled to the lake.

"Are we to stay out here?" Luscinda shielded her face with her fan. "I fear the sun will damage my complexion. Being unwed, I must take care with my appearance. You, of course, have no need for concern as you now have Enrique. Is he inside? Does he know I come to visit?"

If he had, she would never have made it past the gate. Not wanting to discuss him in front of his servants, Sancha gestured to the castle. "We can speak inside."

The middle-aged servant opened the imposing door that was taller than two men standing on each other's shoulders, the carved wood depicting Moorish designs.

Luscinda regarded the grandeur longingly.

Sancha preferred her and Enrique's bedchamber, her study, and the pond, in that order.

Once they were inside and the servant had closed the door, she faced the woman. "Enrique is away on business."

Luscinda nodded absently and regarded the grand staircase, wide enough for twelve men to stand shoulder-to-shoulder without crowding each other. Silver candleholders stood on the engraved cabinet and tables. There were more holders secured to the stone walls.

Light poured through arched windows, sun flooding the area, turning the stone a dazzling white.

Luscinda looked over. "What business?"

Sancha froze, her mind racing to Enrique's visit to the villages, him helping her heal. A pulse ticked hard in her throat. She warned herself to calm down and think, not react. The woman was a menace, but couldn't read minds, and surely knew nothing of Enrique's actions. "I have no idea. I never involve myself in my husband's affairs."

Luscinda closed her fan and tapped the side gently against her cheek. "I marvel at a man who can leave his bride so quickly after wedding her. One would think passion could never allow such a thing. Oh well." She shrugged and smiled. "Enrique's home is more than I imagined. You must give me a tour."

She wanted her out of here yet feared any resistance to her request. Who knew what she would say or do. "Of course. Would you like something to eat and drink before we begin?"

"Food can wait. I long to see all you have."

Holding back a sigh, Sancha escorted her to the chapel first. Earlier, she'd lit every candle, praying for Enrique's safe return.

Luscinda stared at the flickering flames as Dominico had. "How fervently you pray. Or would Enrique be the one?"

"The dining area is this way." She showed her the grand room. Again, Luscinda's eyes brightened.

Once in the hall, Sancha passed Enrique's study.

Luscinda stopped and touched the metal handle. "What do you have in here?"

"Enrique's work on his holdings." She eased Luscinda's hand from the handle. "No one goes in there except my husband."

"Does he keep secrets from you? Do you keep them from him?"

"What are you saying?" She glared. "You come into my home to offend me? To accuse my husband and me of lying to each other?"

Luscinda rested her hand on her throat, her smile wilting. "Never to each other. I was merely playing with you. How serious you are." She tapped Sancha's hand with her fan. "You need to relax."

She stopped clenching her jaw, though only so she could speak. "Would you care to see the grounds?"

"No."

"The kitchen?"

Luscinda laughed. "I have never entered one in my entire life and have no intention of doing so now. Take me to the upper floors. I saw those lovely arched windows on the ride up the hill and long to see sun pouring into the rooms."

"Those are private chambers."

"I have no need to see Enrique's bedchamber or yours."

"We share the same one."

"Of course you do. How silly of me to believe otherwise. I was referring to the chambers you reserve for your guests."

Had she planned to stay the night? Appalled, Sancha wanted to refuse but wasn't certain she should. "Very well."

Despite Luscinda's insistence on touring the rooms, she took a brief look at each, leaving so quickly Sancha had to keep catching up with her. At last, she stopped at the door to Sancha and Enrique's bedchamber. "Is this where your husband sleeps?"

"Where we both do."

"Of course." She pointed her fan at the stairway across the hall, leading to the third level, the study room. "Where do the steps lead?"

Sancha grabbed Luscinda's arm to keep her from climbing the stairs. "We use the area for storage. Items from Enrique's boyhood, furnishings his family has had for generations but we no longer use."

"I adore old objects. Some of them can be quite beautiful. Show them to me. We may find a treasure."

She tightened her grip. "The items belong to Enrique, not me. I have no say in who sees them. Besides, the area is quite dusty. You would ruin your beautiful gown."

"If you hold my arm any harder, you will surely rip my sleeve."

Sancha released her. "We should go to the dining hall. I asked Enrique's cook to prepare something special in honor of your visit."

"No need." Luscinda swept past her. Upon reaching the grand stairway, she looked over. "I have others to see in this area. I shall take my leave of you now."

Within minutes, she'd left as mysteriously as she had arrived.

Chapter 12

The journey began with failure.

As Enrique had promised Sancha, he'd spoken to Guillermo's father. The peasant was a worn man with bent shoulders, showing a lifetime of hard labor, his hands still reddened from the fire that had taken his nephew's life.

"I saw to Vincente's face as much as I could," he'd told Enrique. "He was a good man, a hard worker who helped me greatly. He was in such pain because of the burns. During the raid, I shouted at him not to enter the hut again. The fire was too bad. He wanted to save what little we had and he…"

Enrique had squeezed the man's shoulder. Although Sancha had done what she could, she couldn't give Vincente the will to live in horrible pain with a disfigured face. Days after she'd left, the young man had ended his misery.

His uncle and Enrique had stood at Vincente's grave, new vegetation already growing over the dirt, life continuing. Being a practical man, Enrique accepted that one had to let loved ones go at times. No matter how skilled Sancha's healing was, some people deserved the relief death could bring, their terrible struggles over.

A sentiment he should have voiced to Vincente's uncle but couldn't. What words had ever eased the pain of those who'd lost a family member? The thought of ever losing Sancha wasn't something he could endure.

After making certain the man and the other peasants had what they needed, Enrique and his men had headed to the next community.

Upon arrival, he spoke with the village elders who greeted his group cordially, offering simple food and drink for the men, grain for their horses. Within a short time, Enrique and his guards had returned to the road.

They'd spent the night at a third village. In addition to the horses needing rest, a thick cloud cover hid the moon, casting everything into an inky blackness. They could have used torches to continue their journey, if they hadn't minded the light making their trip obvious to thieves. He didn't want a battle to keep him from the last village or Sancha longer than necessary. To return to his wife injured would be a cruel outcome for her good deeds.

Late the next afternoon, his group entered the village with the ill young woman. The men in charge directed Enrique to her hut. Despite the beautiful day, the hovel was stuffy and stank of illness. The young woman looked older than her years, body racked with brutal coughs followed by wheezing sounds as she struggled to breathe.

After introducing himself to the girl's mother, he explained that her other daughter, his servant, had mentioned the illness.

"I brought medicine for your girl." He handed over Sancha's mixture. With her note in hand, he read how often the daughter should drink the potion and what else she needed to do in order to treat her illness.

Her mother held up the large vial. "This will cure her immediately?"

Sancha hadn't told him when the remedy would start working. Wishing she had, he read her notes again and determined how long the potion would last. "The medicine is for five days. Within that time, your daughter should be able to expel the material in her lungs, making her breathing easier. You must also make certain she gets enough nourishment. San— ah, the physician said so here."

He showed the woman Sancha's note even though he figured she couldn't read.

She looked at the words then him, her expression questioning.

He called a guard in. The man left ample bread, cheese, figs, and oranges that Hortensia had packed for the woman and her daughter.

"Make certain your girl takes the medicine and eats," Enrique said.

She kissed his hand. "Gracias, patrón."

He hoped the outcome here would be better than Vincente's.

With the task finished, he visited with the other peasants who offered his group food and shelter for the evening.

Early the following morning, he checked on the girl. She was asleep finally, her color a bit better, cough not so pronounced.

The mother beamed. "She had a good night, the first in too long. I made her take the potion as you told me even though she said it tasted too foul." The woman clucked her tongue. "I even got some bread and cheese into her."

Enrique smiled. "Wonderful. Make certain she takes all the medicine. Every drop."

"You have my promise."

Finished with what he'd set out to do, he left for home. Sancha.

* * * *

No servant stood at the castle entrance. Sancha had sent him to his bed hours before. She waited alone for Enrique, the wind, moon, and stars her only companions. After pacing until her legs ached, she sat at the edge of the hill, peering at the road below.

Her eyes and mind kept playing tricks, showing her specks of light in the distance that she hoped were torches, Enrique and his men returning.

Twice, she pushed to her feet to see better. The cool breeze whipped her gown against her legs and tugged at her cloak and hair. Each time, the light proved no more than her foolish desire.

Back on the ground, she drew her knees to her chest, arms wrapped around her legs.

Sounds pressed in, the hard thump of her pulse, bushes rustling from an animal's exploration, a creature's shrill wail, tree limbs and leaves stirring in the wind.

She rocked in time with the noise.

Pinpoints of brightness flashed in the distance. Squinting, she concentrated on them. Rather than disappearing as the others had, these grew larger and more brilliant.

She jumped to her feet.

The lights neared, showing a vague outline of what she suspected were men and horses. The procession passed fields and vineyards. Instead of turning to the left, where another road led away from the castle, the group approached the gate.

She dashed down the path, heart pounding. After a brief distance, she had to stop and catch a bit of breath. With her palm pressed against her aching side, she tore toward the gate once more.

The horses approached so fast, Enrique reined in his gelding abruptly. He lifted his hand to his men and shouted, "Halt!"

Dismounted, he bolted toward her and embraced her as she did him. "What is it?" He hugged her fiercely. "What happened?"

Panting too hard to speak, she kissed his cheeks, chin, the tip of his nose, then fit her mouth over his, thrusting her tongue inside, cutting off his words.

He accepted her kiss for a moment then tore his mouth free. "Why are you breathing so hard and holding your side?"

"Hurts." She gasped for more air in order to speak. "From running."

"Why were you running?" He looked past her. "Was something chasing you?"

"No. Running to you." She cupped his face and kissed him harder this time, never wanting to let him go. Anything could have happened on his journey. He might not have returned to her.

Terrified at that ever happening, she thrust her tongue more deeply into his mouth.

Again, he broke free and stepped back, breathing as hard as she did. He turned to the man closest to him. "See to my horse. All of you, go." He flung his hand, gesturing them away. "My *esposa* and I will walk."

She wrapped her arms around his torso, not allowing him to move.

He touched her cheek. "Are you all right?"

She nodded then shook her head.

"Which is it?"

"I missed you."

"Oh. Is that all?"

She released him and stepped back. "All?"

"The way you were running and gasping, I thought—I have no idea what I thought, except something ghastly had happened."

"It had. You were away from me for days."

"At your request."

She whimpered, feeling guilty again. "Did you miss me even a little?"

"Greatly, and during every second."

She sagged into him once more.

He staggered from her weight and righted himself. She followed, staying close, running her hands over his chest, down his torso, and lower.

Enrique stopped her before she'd reached the hefty ridge between his legs. "We need to go to our bedchamber."

"The sheets are fresh and smell of my rose fragrance just as you like. I challenge you to race me to—"

He grabbed her wrist, keeping her from darting away. "What say we walk?"

With their arms around each other's waists, they strolled to the castle entrance, pausing frequently to kiss and embrace. Although dust clung to his clothes, he still smelled wonderful, musk scenting his skin. His hair was tousled, as she preferred, whiskers roughening his cheeks, everything about him better than she recalled.

She couldn't imagine how other women fell in love with men who left for war and didn't return for years or who never came back at all. How did those wives survive?

She was being childish, of course. The world was a cruel place where love seemed the least important matter, easily dismissed as everyone went about the business of simply staying alive. However, until she faced inescapable death, she wanted nothing more than to be with Enrique.

He opened the door for her.

Reluctantly, she let go of him to move inside and promptly took his hand once he'd joined her. "Fill me for hours on end—no, days—no, weeks. Please."

He fingered her cloak. "I should bathe first. The filth of the road clings to me."

"If mud covered you from head to foot, I would still want you without delay."

Rather than grinning at her admission, he regarded her closely. "What happened during my absence?"

Sancha didn't want to get into Luscinda's visit now, possibly ever. She still hadn't decided whether to tell him of the harpy's visit. "I played with Rosa until she tired of me."

He leaned close, his lips on her ear. "No study or experiments?"

"My mind refused to consider anything except you."

"And my task. We can speak of what happened in our room."

"I need your love first." Whatever he had to say wouldn't change anything for Guillermo's cousin or the young woman. Sancha had done what she could for them, praying repeatedly today, lighting more candles for their good health. Now, she needed her husband.

In their room, she removed her cloak and undressed him hurriedly, then bathed his face and hands with a damp cloth scented with her fragrance.

He kept sniffing. "You want me to smell like you?"

"You will anyway, in time. Rest your arms on your head." The words he'd once used on her. "Part your legs."

He lifted one eyebrow but did as she'd demanded. Her hunger for him tonight was too great for a request.

She ran the cloth over his chest and licked away moisture trapped in the short hairs.

He made a rumbling sound and edged closer, his shaft touching her skirt.

"Stay where you are." She pointed to the spot. "No moving, do you hear?"

"Are you quite certain you want that?" He flexed his member, making the lovely thing bob.

She forced herself to act stern. "Quiet. In this room, I rule."

He huffed but did keep his tongue.

She pressed her face to his chest and inhaled deeply of his now sweet scent with the delightful fragrance of man beneath.

His breaths quickened. "You tempt me far too much."

"Silence." She washed his arms and pits, then stepped behind him.

He turned his face to the side.

Again, she recalled his earlier words to her and gave him the same. "Eyes to the front."

He remained as he was.

Very well. She ran the cloth over his buttocks and down the insides of his thighs.

He pushed to his toes, wavered, then came back down, his heels smacking the floor. She dropped to her knees and licked away water trapped in the hair on his legs.

New sounds poured from him, male and uninhibited, fueled by lust and love.

Thrilled, she dipped the cloth into the bowl of scented water. With greater care than she'd shown the rest of him, she tended to his sac firm with passion, his shaft thick with need, and paid particular attention to the back of his crown, his pleasure spot.

He groaned louder than a man in mortal danger, snatched the cloth, and threw it across the room. "My bath is finished. I rule in here with you as my devoted slave, or have you forgotten?"

"Never. Your wish is my command."

He undid the fastenings on her clothes, stripping her nearly as fast as she had him.

On their bed, he burrowed his hard member into her sheath, thrusting until their curls touched, filling her completely. Needing to be closer, she pushed her hips into his and tightened her inner muscles around his shaft.

His head sagged to his shoulder. He sighed loudly, the noise sounding aroused yet content. "You do intend to kill me."

"And you me." She slid her fingers up his arms. He trembled at her touch, his reaction pleasing her more than she'd believed possible. "We shall go together, not even a moment apart."

"In fifty years or more. Promise me."

"You have my word."

They returned each other's assured smile, as though their bond gave them the right and power to predict an uncertain future. Getting down to the business of loving, they enjoyed each other until dawn arrived, after which they slept, then indulged even more.

* * * *

Enrique had Hortensia deliver the midmorning meal to his bedchamber. Neither he nor Sancha wanted to dress and leave each other yet.

She ate like a starved man, gobbling boiled eggs and olives faster than he ever had. After barely chewing the fare, she swallowed then polished off two oranges, three pieces of pork, crusty bread, and a large wedge of cheese.

She reached for more bread.

He caught her hand. "Did you eat anything while I was gone?"

She nodded, her cheeks puffed out with food.

He released her hand and placed his on her belly, silky and warm though far too flat. "Are you with child?"

She lifted her shoulders and finished her wine.

Disappointed, he brought his hand back from her. "No symptoms yet?"

"They will surely come." She took another orange.

"Why so hungry then?"

"The food is too delectable to resist? Your cook has skills beyond compare?"

He laughed briefly then regarded her. "Are you certain nothing happened these last days?"

She seemed different to him, edgier than he'd ever seen her except when Isabella had sent the first missive concerning the rumors. Surely more hadn't cropped up. He knew Sancha well enough now to expect her to say something on the matter, asking his advice, seeking his reassurance.

Another thing puzzled him. Not once had she inquired of the peasants, though previously she'd been concerned about their welfare to the detriment of her own. He hoped she didn't think him incapable of delivering her medicine, had presumed those sorry people were now dead, and didn't want to hear anything further about them.

Of course, her lack of curiosity might be for the best. He was loath to tell her of Vincente's tragic end. Thinking of the young man, Enrique grew restless, not knowing how to report the sad truth or figure out why she had yet to answer his question.

Worried she was trying to hide something from him, he pressed. "What happened during my absence? Tell me everything. No detail is too small. I love to hear you speak."

She chewed more slowly than she had earlier.

He waited, prepared to stay in their bed for the rest of the day if need be.

At last, she swallowed. "I did nothing to bring myself to an inquisitor's attention, if that concerns you. I kept our secret. I acted the part of the dutiful wife."

"Even though you are not?"

She smiled and dug into what fare remained.

Still concerned about her behavior, he took the last slice of beef before she could, wanting her mouth free of food so she had no reason to avoid their converse. "You have yet to ask about my journey."

She brushed crumbs from her lips. "I should never have asked you to go."

He'd been right. She did doubt his abilities. "I see. You had little faith in how I would perform the task, possibly even less now."

"No. Danger lies everywhere. Someone might have harmed you out there." She grew haunted. "Of course, you might have been harmed here too. It was best you went."

He shook his head, unable to follow her reasoning. "Who would have harmed me here?"

"Have you listened to nothing I said? The world is filled with danger."

"Here? In a castle on a hill behind fortified walls with guards at the gate and in other locations to see to our safety?"

She glanced past him to the window, the drapes pulled back. Even though sun poured inside, brightening everything, she seemed paler than she should have, drained of color.

Alarmed, he cradled her cheek. "Did a guard or servant say or do something to you during my absence?"

"No. What of Guillermo's cousin and the young woman?"

He didn't want to discuss them anymore than she wanted to tell him what had happened while he'd been gone. "I have bad news and good."

"Oh no." Her lovely mouth drooped in sorrow. "The girl died before you could get to her?"

"No. From what I could tell, she seemed better when I left. She was sleeping at least, her cough not as frequent. I told Hortensia what had happened when I asked her to bring our fare. Surely, the girl's sister has heard by now."

"I must tell Hortensia I can make more potion if the girl or anyone else in the village needs it. What bad news do you have for me?"

He picked an orange peel from the sheet and dropped it on the tray. "Vincente, Guillermo's cousin, perished—not because of anything you did." Her dismay killed him. "His uncle said Vincente was in great pain. He feared going through life horribly scarred and took matters into his own hands. You did everything you could. The Moors caused his death, not you."

"I added to his misery."

"You tried to help."

"What good is anything I know if I keep bringing people harm?"

"Vincente is the only one who died. I checked on the other peasants to see how they were. Everyone has mended as they should."

"For now. What of the future? What of you?"

He tossed the platters and plates to the other side of the bed and gathered her into his arms. "Did Isabella send you another missive? Did someone else, saying the rumors have started again? How could they? We wed. Soon our son will come. We have naught to worry about."

"Luscinda was here."

"What? At the gate?"

"In the castle. I feared turning her away, not knowing what my refusal would cause her to say or do. I still have the note she gave to the guard."

Sancha left the bed and swiped the missive off a cabinet. "Here."

He read the letter, rage building, his skin stinging with heat. "How dare she pen such a thing to you."

"She wanted to see your study and the rooms on this floor."

"Where I work and the bedchambers? Why?"

"I refused to let her inside your study, which made her more curious. As far as the rooms up here, I have no idea why she was so interested. She asked if we kept secrets from each other. I avoided as many of her questions as I could, telling her nothing. She even tried to take the stairs to my study room. I stopped her and insisted we go to the dining hall to eat. She left. All told, she was here less than an hour, despite writing of her desire to visit with me."

"I knew she was the one who started the rumors."

Sancha sat on the edge of the mattress. "What do you think she plans to say now?"

"What can she? You and I have wed. Nothing we have here would make anyone suspicious."

"Except the closed door to your study hiding what you have inside, and the room I kept her from with my books."

"The wretch has no right to see anything here, not even the grounds."

"She had no desire to tour them when I offered to show her."

"Did she ask to see the chapel, proof of our commitment to God?"

"No. I did take her there first. I had lit every candle earlier begging for your safe return. She asked which of us prayed so fervently, her words more accusation than question, as though you were pleading with God to save my soul because you knew I had given myself to the Devil. Everything she said pointed to the worst or mocked our union. What do you think will happen now? More rumors?"

"Not after I threaten her with everything I can think of."

"And make this worse? We have no proof she started the gossip. She twists whatever people say using their words against them. We have to find another way."

"If I could murder her, I would."

"You would not. I would beat you to it."

Laughing, he pulled her into his arms and tilted her backwards.

She squealed.

With his mouth molded to hers, he kissed her deeply, enthralled as always at her lips softness and heat, how wonderful she tasted. If Luscinda or anyone dared tried to harm Sancha or take her from him, he would kill them in a moment without regret.

Pity he had to think of another way to deal with Luscinda until she crossed the ultimate line. Her outrageous conduct had affected him and Sancha far too much. He was beginning to look over his shoulder, suspicious of things he'd never considered before. Poor Sancha believed she had to hide here, seeing no one except him in order to protect herself.

Of course, she never had craved parties and visitors as other nobles did. She preferred to live their life in solitude, save for her family, his, and Rosa. Unfortunately, that wouldn't do any longer.

Finished with the kiss, he pulled her to a sitting position. "We need to have a grand party to celebrate our union."

"What?"

"A party is the perfect solution, proving you and I have nothing to hide. Our guests can stay in the castle, roam around as they wish, look at everything, see us together, and know how happy we are."

"I have no need to prove our love."

"Not to me. However, if we cloister ourselves here, people will begin to wonder why, adding weight to Luscinda's words."

"I hate her. Wrong to say, I know, but I do." She lowered her voice further. "If we have a party and allow people to roam, what of my books?"

"This castle has more hiding places than Fernando's. Remember me telling you so, and your promise to pleasure me in each of them? I am still waiting."

"How can you jest at a time like this?"

"Would you prefer I scowl?"

She slapped his arm and groaned. "A party? The converse is always dull, the men arrogant, each trying to out position the other, the women looking for husbands, lovers, or a way to wound their rivals. I would rather face a murderous Moor."

"Trust me, you will shine at this celebration, wearing the finest gown in the kingdom, along with my mother's jewels."

"I have to take time for fittings?"

"Most women would be squealing with delight."

"Silks and jewels mean naught to me. I care only for you."

"And your healing. You know you never want to give up your study or experiments. A party is a small price to pay to have everyone leave you alone."

She rested her hand on his shaft. "Save you."

"Never will you be free of me." He brought her down to the mattress. "First love and then we plan the party."

Chapter 13

The gown Sancha would ultimately wear took longer to devise and execute than the most complicated potion or treatment.

What a waste of time and funds better used elsewhere. Sentiments she shared with Enrique, who kept assuring this one event would allow her enough peace to continue with her work.

She sighed at the fabric surrounding her, some silk, others velvet in a rainbow of colors. Just what she needed, more decisions. Should she settle on the lighter fabric, given some days were still nicely warm? Or should she opt for the heavier material, since the weather could change quickly, growing cool?

Holding a swatch of each weight, one in dark green and the other bright blue, she couldn't decide. "I have no idea what I should wear." She wiggled the fabrics at Enrique. "What do men like? What do you want to see me in?"

"Nothing. I prefer you naked."

With no help coming from his end, she was on her own. Pity that.

She'd never taken time to study fashions or to become skilled, as Isabella had, in spinning yarn or using a thread and needle. Except when she needed to mend wounds. Her only request to the women who'd made her garments was that the gowns be easy to wear and modest in appearance. Unlike other Spanish ladies, she hadn't tried to attract a husband or lover before or after her failed betrothal to Fernando. She'd wanted everyone to leave her alone so she could study and experiment.

Her books lay idle, the mice in no danger from her potions as she debated fabrics instead. Eventually, she settled on gold velvet, telling the tailoress to do with the material as she willed as long as she didn't cut the neck too low.

"What of the trim?" the woman asked. She showed Sancha a seemingly endless array of embroidered designs, some with beading or pearls, the cost surely outrageous.

How any woman could justify using wealth to clothe herself for one party when others went without food for days on end was a mystery to her.

Tired of the endeavor, she finally closed her eyes and rested her finger on one of the choices. "This one."

"Quite lovely," the tailoress said.

Sancha's finger had landed on a swatch of dark green embroidery threaded with gold, simple yet elegant.

The tailoress smiled broadly. "Once I add beads, the design will be perfect."

Sancha pressed her fingers to her temple. "If you must add beads, please keep them on the front." Enduring a party was torture enough. Having to sit through a long meal with beads biting into her back or legs would be too much.

She dreaded the event. Already Isabella had sent her regrets. Although she and her unborn child were thriving, Fernando had taken ill with a cough and slight fever that seemed to be going around with the change in the weather. *Nothing to worry about,* Isabella had written. *Fernando is already on the mend. Best to have him recover fully than chance a relapse.*

Sancha agreed, wishing she were at Fernando's castle, seeing to his welfare rather than preparing for an evening she couldn't avoid.

Responses to the missives Enrique had sent out arrived quickly. Everyone wrote how eager they were to help him and his new wife celebrate their union.

Or to learn if the newest rumors were true.

Hortensia told Sancha what a servant at another estate had said. The young man had overheard an exchange between his master and mistress, gossip on how Sancha must have bewitched Enrique to save herself from accusations of witchcraft. What else but a spell would have caused him to wed her so quickly and in secret when they barely knew each other? She had never wanted marriage before, and certainly wasn't with child.

The news had made her stomach roll. Her symptoms had increased with frequency, especially in the mornings. When she'd told Enrique she hadn't yet conceived, she hadn't experienced any signs of a coming child. Since he'd suggested having the party, she'd been increasingly queasy and attributed her condition to apprehension rather than impending motherhood.

Uncertain as to the cause of her nausea, she'd hid her symptoms from him. However, her worry about the newest rumors finally had her seeking him out.

She entered his study. He glanced up from his ledgers, his smile prompt and pleased until he had a good look at her face.

He stood. "What is it?"

She closed the door and joined him at his desk. "More rumors." She kept her voice low while she related what Hortensia had told her.

He swore.

"What are we going to do now? What if the party gives everyone more to wonder about, especially if you treat me nicely?"

"What are you talking about? How could I do otherwise? I adore you."

"Some would say because of the spell I cast."

"Not some. Luscinda." He brought his fist down hard on a ledger.

Sancha covered his hand before he pounded the thing to shreds, harming himself in the process. "Should we cancel the party?"

"No. We have nothing to hide and will prove so, leaving every door in the castle open, including the ones to this room and where you study. You and I will provide our guests with a lengthy tour to satisfy their curiosity. We shall charm them until they love us both."

"What of the hiding places? Will we also show them those rooms?"

"With them hidden, no one knows they exist."

True. "You and I best not spend too much time together during the gathering lest Luscinda accuse me of keeping you close so I can continue to bewitch you with my spells."

His complexion darkened. "I hope I can control myself around her."

"You must, though I do ask you to keep an eye on me. Especially if I have a knife in my hand whenever she comes near."

He smiled then sighed. "We shall watch out for each other. Forgive me for putting you through this. From the moment we met, my hope was to bring you naught but happiness."

"You have." She kissed his fingers. "The problem is mine."

"Ours. How are the preparations coming for your gown?"

"Nearly finished, thankfully. I had my last fitting today after dragging myself from the new hiding place for my books."

"Good thing."

"Because I forced myself to endure the tailoress pinning and readjusting the gown until I wanted to scream?"

"No. That your garment is nearly ready. We welcome our guests at the end of the week."

* * * *

Given Enrique's firm specifications, the castle sparkled with cleanliness: fresh candles filled each holder, lamps brimmed with oil, the servants wore their finest livery, and all doors were open, proving the de Zayas castle harbored no secrets.

He stood in the grand entrance hall with Sancha at his side, greeting their guests as they arrived. The hour was still early, which gave everyone a chance to refresh and relax before the celebration this evening.

As servants lugged trunks from carriages into the castle, he and Sancha accepted their guests' good wishes.

"You two look happy." Katia, an aged countess, took him and Sancha in with true warmth. "I remember being young and in love."

Sancha smiled. "A most wondrous feeling."

Katia patted Sancha's hand. "Never let anyone take it from you."

Enrique wondered if the old woman had noticed Luscinda's arrival as he had. Whereas the others had one trunk, she'd brought three. Enough to stay a month. He went ill thinking of it. With the authority of a commander giving orders to soldiers, she directed Enrique's servants on how to carry her things, where to leave them, and to take great care when setting the trunks down. She wanted no marks on the leather.

No doubt, the chests were part of her dowry, reserved for the unfortunate man who finally ended up with her.

Luscinda smoothed her gown. The bluish-green silk sported the low neck she preferred. She regarded the castle with an accountant's eye, seeing wealth, not a home as Sancha had.

Annoyed, Enrique turned to his wife, surprised she was already looking at him. "What?"

"The baroness asked as to your health."

He looked at the middle-aged woman. "Never been better."

She regarded Luscinda for a long moment before giving him a smile. "Something is surely going around. Several of my servants have fallen ill this last week with fevers and coughs, seemingly out of nowhere. As though targeted by an unseen force." The woman flicked her gaze at Sancha before speaking to him again. "Best you take care with your health. I understand true belief in God and prayer helps."

He bristled at the veiled accusation of witchcraft and Sancha having to defend herself repeatedly. Although the guests had been here only a short time, already she seemed tired of the ordeal.

He couldn't blame her and forced himself to smile at the baroness. "May God grant all of us good health."

"Indeed," Sancha said. "Especially in my condition."

Several nobles turned to her, Enrique included.

She offered a luminous smile, the first he'd seen since the others had arrived, her attention on him as though no one else existed.

Three women rushed over, the stoutest one pushing in front of the others. "Are you with child?"

"Sí. The first of many."

He grinned so hard his cheeks hurt, and he had to keep himself from hauling her into his arms and swinging her around like a lunatic, or a man hopelessly in love. "Do you need to sit? Do you want a glass of water or wine? Is it too warm in here? Should I have the servants open the windows?"

Women and men chuckled at his questions. A count clamped Enrique on his shoulder. "If you grow concerned at this point, within nine months you may have to take to your bed to recover."

Even those who'd seemed skeptical of Sancha's devotion to God laughed and applauded, voices raised in cheer for the coming new life.

Except Luscinda. She remained to the side, watching or plotting.

She couldn't possibly do anything more now. His and Sancha's marriage, along with their coming child, proved every rumor Luscinda had started was, at the least, a misconception, at most a vicious lie.

* * * *

Sancha hadn't meant to make a spectacle of her news that should have been for Enrique alone. The baroness's venomous comments and Luscinda's arrival had rattled her to the point she'd spoken without thinking.

Enrique didn't seem to mind, his joy obvious and lasting, even when a lone knight arrived, rather than Tomás, Pedro, and the men who'd been at Isabella and Fernando's wedding. Sancha and Enrique had agreed his brothers and the knights were the only ones they truly wanted here, delighted to have the men feast and enjoy the señoritas, who would appreciate their presence.

"A note from your brother." The man handed Enrique the missive.

The nobles stepped closer, an elderly duke in the lead. "Not more trouble with the Moors, I hope."

Finished reading, Enrique shook his head. "Tomás says a situation has come up that he and his men must attend to. Not a battle. We can rest easy."

Sancha touched his sleeve. "Have the Moors attacked another village?"

"No." He handed her the note. She read quickly.

Please give Sancha my sincerest apology for missing the gathering.

How greatly Pedro, my men, and I looked forward to the food and señoritas.

We must leave such enjoyment for a future time. Have no fear, there are no battles with the Moors keeping us away. Nor were any villages attacked.

As knights, we need to keep of sound mind and body, preparing ourselves for conflicts, rather than pleasure. We do so now.

Your brother,
Tomás

Although his assurances of no battles or raids eased her worry, she found the note somewhat strange, lacking Tomás's usual wit and charm. She couldn't imagine why he'd penned such a somber missive unless he feared inquisitors might intercept his words...because they were already on their way here.

She reeled, feeling sick, until she considered how foolish her thoughts were. Neither Tomás nor Pedro would write a letter to warn their brother of such an occurrence. They'd be here at Enrique's side, fighting those who dared harm him or her.

Still, the note troubled. She wanted to ask Enrique what he thought but didn't get the chance.

With the last of the guests here, he began the tour with her at his side. Earlier, they'd debated whether to bring everyone to the chapel first. If so, would more than a few lit candles seem odd? Would too few indicate a lack of devotion to good against evil?

He'd tired quickly of the debate. "We show them the dining hall first then the chapel. The route makes perfect sense as one area moves into the other. Light as many candles as you want. Worry what our Creator thinks rather than these foolish people."

She had no worries about God. The nobles, however...

One after the other glanced into the small room where flames bobbed on a fourth of the candles. A fair number. Not too much, nor too little. She hoped.

The elderly duke and Enrique laughed about something, everyone following them to another room then the study. She held back finally and checked faces to see if suspicions still held or had faded away.

Luscinda caught up with her. "How fortunate for you to be with child."

Sancha didn't trust the woman's good wishes, suspecting an accusation on its heels that she'd use the babe so no one would suspect her of witchcraft. Despite her annoyance, she smiled. "The fortunate one is the child growing within me. He will know the gift of life, the most powerful God of all, the greatest country on earth, and a wonderful papá."

"What of his mamá? What will he know from you?"

"Patience with fools."

Luscinda's sly smile faded, replaced by a look of pure hatred.

"There you are, dear Sancha." Dominico strode toward her, robe flapping around his skinny ankles.

She took his hands in hers and squeezed his fingers gently. "Enrique and I need to fatten you up. I hope you intend to eat your fill during these next days."

"More than my share, yours, and..." He glanced at Luscinda who remained nearby.

"Señorita Doña Luscinda," she said before Sancha could introduce them. "*Padre.*"

He smiled. "Dominico."

Luscinda lifted her eyebrows slightly. "How curious."

He leaned away. "My name? I rather like it."

"As well you should. What I meant is, I had no idea Sancha included sacerdotes as her friends. Nuns, yes, as one could always find her at the convent. Oh wait." Luscinda regarded her. "Word has it you have not been at the convent in months."

Word or rumor? "Were you looking for me there?"

"Me?" Smiling, Luscinda focused on Dominico. "Have you ever seen a woman with my looks in a nunnery?"

"If I had, I would have visited more often."

She laughed. "You missed the part of the tour with the chapel. Would you like me to show you the lovely stained glass windows and candles?"

"I saw them when I joined Enrique and Sancha in holy matrimony."

"Oh. So you were the one. You must tell me about the wonderful day. Dear Sancha is so shy she refuses to mention wedding Enrique."

Sancha dug her nails so deeply into her palms they hurt. "What would you like to know?"

"Dominico will tell me. Will you not?"

"Not much to tell. Enrique and Sancha could barely tear their eyes from each other to pay attention to me." He glanced past her to Sancha. "I have forgiven you for being so rude."

She smiled. "Gracias. Come with me." She gestured him toward her. "Enrique will surely want to see his best childhood friend."

"He had better."

Quickly, she led Dominico away from Luscinda.

* * * *

Most of the guests weren't interested in seeing every bedchamber or the room where Sancha had once studied, begging off for a rest or a nap in their rooms. Of those who remained for the entire tour, Luscinda was the most persistent, lingering at each spot as though she imagined herself reigning here.

Enrique would rather die or see her dead.

Once in Sancha's study room, Luscinda paced the now-empty area.

He gestured impatiently to her. "Come. There is naught to see up here."

"How odd." She spoke to Sancha. "You claimed this space had Enrique's childhood possessions and old furnishings. I see nothing here now."

He stepped between her and his wife. "The items were put to use for this celebration."

"I noted nothing different from the last time I was here. You must point them out to me."

"May I have a rest with my wife first?"

One of the men chuckled. The women averted their gazes at how Enrique had dismissed Luscinda.

He didn't care. He'd had all he could tolerate of her and entertaining guests he hardly cared about. "Sancha and I will see everyone later during the feast. Come." He took her hand.

She said nothing, nor did he on their stroll to their bedchamber. Once he'd closed the door, he pulled her into him and kissed her hungrily. She responded in kind, fisting her fingers in his robe to keep him to her, grinding her mound against his shaft, proving again how much she wanted him.

After tearing his mouth free, he held her within his embrace, his heart pounding. "Is it true?"

"Is what true?"

He rested his hand on her belly.

Her face brightened with the most exquisite smile. "Forgive me for telling you as I had. The baroness unsettled me and the words slipped out."

"Little wonder, the old crone would frighten a demon. Are you all right? Do you feel well?"

"Tired."

Of course. How stupid of him not to have realized such a thing. He swept her into his arms and carried her to their bed. "Sleep. We have hours before we have to continue this farce."

She scooted aside and patted the mattress for him to sit.

He joined her. "No love, only rest."

"We shall see. Except for the baroness, were the other nobles you spoke with convinced nothing is amiss here or with us?"

"Shortly after I started the tour, most of us were laughing as we always have." He frowned. "Where did you go? For several minutes I was unable to see you anywhere."

"You and the duke had moved ahead. Luscinda caught up and offered me good wishes on being with child."

"And?"

She related the exchange between her and the woman, then Dominico. "I suspect she wanted to be alone with him so she could question the poor man about me."

Enrique shrugged. "Even if she agreed to let him bed her, he knows nothing and can tell her nothing."

"Does it matter? She keeps twisting my words and actions to make everything I do seem suspect."

"Are you certain she admitted nothing about checking for you at the convent?" If he had even a shred of proof, he could confront and threaten her, putting an end to this.

Sancha sighed. "She was careful in what she said, far more than I have ever been."

"Because you have naught to hide. I want you to stop worrying about her. She has no way to harm either of us. Having this gathering has already proved a success in disproving the rumors. We hid nothing and soon you will have my son." He hugged her so hard he feared causing injury but couldn't stop. "Are you happy?"

"Not completely."

Surprised, he eased back. "Because of Luscinda?"

"No. You. Take these off." She pulled at his robe and doublet, each a deep red. "I want you inside me. I need your love to get through this evening."

"Only if you agree to rest after I have you."

She nodded.

He undressed quickly and helped her with her clothes. Together, they fell to the bed. He brushed her hair aside. "After we get through this night and the next days, we shall have our lives to ourselves again."

"None too soon." She kissed his neck.

A wave of warmth pulsed through him.

She nestled closer. "I wish Tomás and Pedro could have been here to make things easier on us, keeping the others busy, charming them. Especially Tomás. I found his note so somber and strange. Not like him at all. Poor man must have been terribly upset having to miss our gathering and the señoritas."

"I'm sure he was." Enrique smiled at her suckling his shoulder. "But he didn't write the note."

She pulled in her tongue and lifted her head. "Of course, he did. I saw his name."

"Pedro wrote it along with the missive. I know my brothers' scripts. Why he penned the letter for Tomás and signed his name, I have no idea."

She paled considerably. "Do you think they heard the rumors and tried to warn us something bad is about to happen?"

"With a note holding no information to help us?"

"Maybe they were afraid someone would seize the letter."

"If my brothers thought we were in danger, they would say so. This has nothing to do with the rumors, your healing, or the Inquisition."

"What then?"

He lifted his shoulders. "All must be well or they would have told me. Why keep bad tidings a secret?"

"You would from me if you wanted to save me worry."

He pulled her into him. "Men deal with each other far more openly than they do with women. Trust me, there is naught to worry about with Pedro's missive or our gathering. Everything will be over before you know it."

* * * *

Sancha held Enrique's sentiment in her heart as they dressed for what she feared would be an endless feast. Him in his usual clothes he found quite comfortable. Her in the new gown that didn't suit her in the least.

The sleeves and skirt were voluminous with enough yardage to make another garment, two if one created the items for a child. The trim Sancha had chosen, along with beadwork the tailoress promised, graced the square neckline, the edge of the sleeves, circled her hips, ran in a line to the hem with more beaded trim gracing it. Her gauzy kirtle, trimmed with lace, reached to her throat, at least presenting a more modest appearance than Luscinda had ever achieved.

Enrique took her in, his face naked with pride. "Smile. You have never looked more exquisite. The gown is perfect for your coloring and my mamá's jewels."

He opened the polished wood box he'd taken out earlier and removed an intricately designed emerald pendant with a gold chain attached. In the candlelight, the jewel flashed green, the same color as the trim on her gown.

The stone's beauty and the elaborateness of the piece overwhelmed and disturbed her.

In too short a time, she'd changed from the woman she'd once been. Now she dressed like a queen and wore a monarch's gem, her books and experiments forgotten, the peasants on their own. Thankfully, none had needed her these last days, but would. She had no business wasting time with a group of arrogant and pampered nobles when survival for others was at stake.

"Put it back." She stepped away. "I could never wear such a lovely piece."

"You can and will." He held it up. "Turn around, lift your hair, and accept my gift."

"I would rather be swimming in the pond with you, experimenting on my mice, or treating the ill."

"This is only one night, my love. The feast will end. Your mice will meet their doom once more."

Not fast enough for her. The gown was heavy, hot, and too ornate to move in easily. She was uncomfortable with the extravagance that would surely pull all eyes to her.

Once she was on the stairway, her worst fears came true.

Nobles glanced up, conversations stalled, eyes widened. Approval flooded the men's faces, envy the women's.

Luscinda stood within the glow of a dozen candles. The light skimmed her blue velvet gown, her caul bearing the same shade. The dark colors and her black hair made her skin seem exceedingly delicate and quite lovely. Young men surrounded her, each a minor noble without great estates. They'd been born second and third sons rather than the first. Their broad smiles and gentle touches on her sleeve failed to gain her attention. She eyed Sancha's gown and the jewel she wore.

No illness or wound had ever disturbed Sancha as much as Luscinda's calculating appraisal.

Enrique seemed blind to her presence. At the bottom of the stairs, he exchanged pleasantries with his guests.

The old duke smiled broadly at Sancha, his fat fingers wrapped around a goblet. "Your husband is a lucky man."

A count's wife edged close. "Your gown is exquisite. Do tell me the name of your tailoress."

Soon, the women had surrounded her, the men Enrique. Everyone talked at once about velvets, silks, jewels, gowns, war, Moors, property, the Crown, until Sancha's head spun as she tried to keep up. At past parties, she'd listened to others discuss trivialities, relieved the other nobles ignored her.

Now, these women sought converse on matters she'd never considered.

"I have yet to see the newest combs and fans," she said to an older woman, a marquis's wife.

The woman wagged her finger. "Your husband must take you there."

"Where?" Enrique joined them, proving to Sancha he'd listened all along, protecting her as he'd promised.

The women spoke at once, advising him to spend at least a day at the next fair so Sancha could have the latest fashions.

"Wearing what you have in the past will never do," a viscountess said.

The marquesa put up her hand. "I have an idea. We can go to the fair together. Ladies to purchase the most beautiful items they can find, men to haggle over weapons and animals as they drink themselves into a stupor."

Laughter rippled through the crowd.

Sancha smiled as well as she could, grateful for Enrique's arm when time came for the feast. She recalled how noisy the banquet had been at Fernando's castle. Tonight's was twice as loud given double the guests.

With Dominico seated on her right and Enrique on her left, she endured Luscinda's relentless scrutiny from across the table. Although the young woman kept up her end of converse with the men on either side of her, even toying with them shamelessly, her attention never left Sancha for long. Whenever Sancha spoke, Luscinda seemed particularly interested.

For the most part Sancha kept her tongue, concerned Luscinda might use whatever she said to put doubt back into the other's minds, destroying the hope and work Enrique had accomplished this night.

There was enough food to feed a sizeable village for a week. Two harpists and three men with lutes played a melody no one paid attention to and few probably heard given the din. Wine flowed freely.

The older men were the first to succumb to drink and their gluttony, sagging in their chairs with sleep or bending over the tables, arms pillowing their heads as they napped. A few ladies followed, lids closed, mouths slack.

Even Dominico grew sleepy. Although Sancha had seen him out-drink and out-eat Tomás, Pedro, and Enrique combined on the night of her wedding, he'd apparently reached his limit at this gathering.

"You should help him to his chamber," Luscinda suddenly said.

Sancha glanced at those who surrounded them, all busy with their own enjoyment, even Enrique, who had the duke laughing loudly at his tale. "Who do you mean?"

"Your priest."

"Enrique's boyhood friend?" She'd spoken louder than usual should anyone be listening. To claim Dominico was hers would be the first step to saying she'd corrupted his soul. The religious were favorite targets of demons. If she'd truly had the Devil's power, she would have made Luscinda burst into flames rather than having to endure her icy smile.

"Dear Sancha, call him whatever you want. He does seem ready to fall off his chair."

He swayed, jerked, and swayed once more, bumping Sancha again.

She helped him rest his head on the table.

Luscinda pursed her lips. "How uncomfortable he must be."

"No more than the others."

"Are you refusing to take him to his chamber because you fear being alone with a holy man?"

Her question shouldn't have shocked Sancha but did. If she didn't help Dominico to his room, Luscinda could claim she was afraid to be alone with him because he'd unmask her as a witch. If she did take him upstairs, speculation would arise concerning their time together and whether she'd tried to corrupt him carnally or he'd done so with her.

Sancha gestured for the servant behind Dominico's chair. "Help padre to his chamber. See he has everything he needs."

Unable to handle the priest alone, the young man called upon an older fellow next to him for help.

Luscinda stroked her goblet. "How clever of you."

Sancha stood. No one noticed, not the young nobles on either side of Luscinda who now spoke to others, nor Enrique who was telling his tale. She rounded the table to the other side and leaned down to the young woman.

With her cheek close to Luscinda's, Sancha whispered, "How sorry I feel for you. Wanting a man who will never share your desire, him having found you lacking even before he met me. Nothing has changed with Enrique in regards to you. Continue on your course and chance his reprisal at your own peril."

Sancha left the room.

Chapter 14

The duke's tale of an old romance had Enrique laughing so hard his throat grew parched. He reached blindly for his wine, misjudged the distance, and knocked over the beaker.

He shifted around to see if the drink had spattered Sancha. With his sudden movement, dizziness hit. After taking a moment to breathe deeply, clear his head, and curse himself for imbibing too much, he turned to Sancha once more.

Her chair and Dominico's were empty. Confused, he craned his neck to see if they were in another part of the dining hall visiting with others. There was no flash of her auburn hair, her gold gown, or Dominico's balding head.

Odd, unless…

His stomach twisted at the possibility of Sancha having fallen ill because of her condition.

His worry drove away the effects of his drinking, while good sense told him she wouldn't have left without telling him she was ill. She'd always come to him first, not Dominico, even if she believed his friend's prayers and blessings would help save the coming babe.

Enrique searched until a servant girl blocked his view, moving plates aside, mopping up the mess he'd made.

"Leave it." He scanned empty chairs, guests who still enjoyed themselves, those who had fallen asleep or had swooned, and finally came upon Luscinda across the table, staring at him.

His skin crawled. Never had he seen a woman's expression as intense and determined. The men on either side of her didn't seem to notice. Drunk, they talked loudly, each vying for her attention. To Luscinda, they seemed not to exist, as absent from her thoughts as Sancha was.

Enrique glared at her. "Where is she?"

She looked at him coldly. "Who?"

"My wife."

"Gone." She glanced at Dominico's empty chair, her expression knowing and accusatory as to what his wife and friend were doing alone together.

How dare she consider such a thing in regards to Sancha. He wanted to have it out with her but held back and cursed himself for paying more attention to enjoyment than safeguarding his wife. For those few moments of foolish pleasure, Luscinda had effortlessly forced him into a corner.

If he left to search for Sancha, as he should, Luscinda would likely point out his absence to the others, claiming he'd gone to find his wife and friend the moment he became aware of their absence. Luscinda wouldn't have to accuse Sancha of outright adultery or witchcraft. Spreading innuendo, then allowing others to come to their own conclusions would be enough. If he were to stay here, she could claim Sancha's absence had weakened the spell she'd cast on him, the one that had forced him to the altar. With Sancha's hold on him no longer firm, Luscinda might suggest he clearly preferred to be with her.

Whatever he did had no good outcome, a confrontation between them unwinnable for him. She could say anything to defend herself and would. Only a direct threat against Sancha would convince the other nobles of Luscinda's jealousy and avarice, causing them to dismiss anything else she said concerning his wife.

Luscinda had warned him not to spurn her and kept making good on her words.

More worried about Sancha than gossip, he left the room and sprinted down the hall toward his study. She might have taken refuge there. They'd shared many good moments in the room, her on his lap, keeping him from work.

At his approach, a viscount and a baron's young wife jumped apart, lips still wet from their impassioned kiss. Upon reaching his study, he opened the door and closed it quickly on the couple inside, both naked, their backs to him, the man prepared to mount the woman, who was on her hands and knees.

He climbed the stairs three at a time, reached the landing quickly, and raced down the hall to his and Sancha's bedchamber, his panting nearly as loud as his footfalls. Not caring how much noise he made, he threw open the door to the room. The handle struck the wall.

Sancha flinched, Rosa yipped, both on the mattress.

He kicked the door closed and dropped to one knee at Sancha's side. Her fingers were surprisingly warm, not icy as he'd expected. She didn't look upset either. Certainly nowhere near the rage tearing through him. "She said nothing to you?"

"Who?"

He frowned. "Who else? Luscinda."

"Oh her." She shrugged.

"Why did you leave the table without telling me where you were going? I thought something had happened to you and the infant."

Now, she frowned. "Without me telling you?"

"Are you feeling all right?"

"Fine. Tomorrow morning will surely be a different matter."

"What happened to bring you up here?"

"I missed Rosa."

He pressed his fingers to the inside of his eyes. "Must you always talk around things as though you have no idea what I mean when you most certainly do?"

"Forgive me. I want only to keep you from getting angrier."

"Too late." He lowered his hand. "What did Luscinda say to you this time?"

"The usual. She twisted my words to make them seem suspicious. In turn, I told her your feelings for her, or lack of them, would never change even if I were gone. I then warned her of your reprisal if she should continue her current course. I made no threats in public, whispering to her instead."

He nodded, proud she'd defended herself, though she'd done little to change Luscinda's mind. He'd seen her hatred at the table. For the first time, he realized the matter between them had gone beyond Luscinda wanting what his position and wealth could bring her. She meant to hurt him through Sancha, revenge her true goal.

Fury shot through him, burning his skin. He wanted to destroy her no matter the consequences.

"Are you all right?" Sancha gripped his arm.

He took a deep breath. The worry in her voice, her frantic touch, shook him back to good sense. "I am. Avoid the wretch as much as possible. Give her no chance to speak to you. Win over the other women, making them your allies."

"Must I go back down now?"

She looked so disheartened, tenderness welled in him. He ran his thumb over her bottom lip, stuck out like a little girl who pouted. "Tomorrow will be soon enough. Tonight, most everyone is too drunk or well on the way to notice your absence."

"The same as Dominico."

"I wondered where he went. Did he stagger away by himself?"

"Two servants dragged him from his chair at my request. I told them to put him in his bedchamber."

"How did I miss so much?"

She smiled gently. "You and the duke were enjoying yourselves, trying to outdo each other with tales of when you first became men, and the women who helped you reach those lofty goals."

His face stung. "How much did you hear?" He couldn't recall details of what he'd said.

"Enough for me to brag to Isabella regarding your indiscretions since she always goes on about Fernando's earlier adventures—no—stop."

He would not. He tickled Sancha until she sprawled on the bed, trembling with laughter, Rosa yipping at her side. He stroked the galgo's head to quiet her.

Sancha's giggles turned to contented sighs. "I love you, you know."

"For tickling you?"

"For not suggesting I go back to the gathering. I know you would never demand." She laced her fingers through his. "Will you stay here too?"

He shook his head. "I want to keep an eye on Luscinda. Turn over so I can undo your buttons."

Once she was naked, as he liked, he kissed her longingly, then hugged her in farewell.

When he reached their chamber door, she called out, "She will never win."

"Never." He'd see to Luscinda's ruin first, proving how ruthless he could be when it came to his beloved wife.

* * * *

He didn't return to the bedchamber until dawn and fell onto the mattress fully clothed.

Sancha hated to bother him, but she'd spent the night wondering and worrying what went on at the celebration. "Do you have anything to tell me?"

He finished his yawn. "Out of the corner of my eye, I saw the wretch staring at me. Not once did I glance her way, as though she was no longer at the table. At last, she gave up and went to her room."

"Are you certain she headed there?"

"I had a servant follow her and linger to make sure she remained, which he did and she did."

Good thing. She easily pictured Luscinda scouring the castle for something to use against them.

"Enough talk of her," he said. "Time for us to...to..." He fell asleep without finishing.

She followed him into slumber. Neither woke until nearly midday.

* * * *

He went off with the men to ride, fish, or hunt. Stuck with the women, she led the group to the area surrounding the pond. After servants had laid blankets over the grass and brought out chairs for the older women, they provided baskets of cheese, bread, grapes, olives, pork, boiled eggs, and wine.

Rosa couldn't seem to get enough eggs. She licked yolk off Sancha's fingertips, making her laugh.

Despite the month, the afternoon grew unexpectedly warm and lazy, the women still too tired or sated from food to speak much. Many sank to their blankets and slept beneath olive trees. Sancha smiled at Katia, the elderly countess who'd said she recalled being young and in love.

"Can I get you anything?" Sancha asked.

Katia's smile created a fan of wrinkles on the corners of her eyes. Otherwise, her skin was as fresh and fair as a young woman's. "I have already eaten far too much." She regarded the surroundings. "This area is lovely. Do you and Enrique come here often?"

"As much as we can. His work with the estates keeps him occupied."

"What keeps you occupied?" Luscinda asked from the next blanket. Seated beside her was the baroness who'd offered naught but frowns and insinuations since her arrival.

Pretending she hadn't heard the question, Sancha lifted the pup and presented her to the countess. "Have you met Rosa yet?"

"Bring her here." The galgo licked Katia's chin. She laughed gaily.

Luscinda and the baroness didn't join in, their attention on Sancha.

Whenever she said anything, one or the other would comment, trying to force her into a corner. She ignored them and followed Enrique's advice on making allies of the other women. Some she'd known for years, seeing them at countless gatherings, though they'd never spoken to her for long nor she to them.

Today, she forced herself to converse and finally asked mothers in the group for advice on enduring childbirth, tending to an infant, making certain her son or daughter would grow up healthy and strong.

Information she already knew, but pretended ignorance.

The change in the women's attitudes toward her was nearly magical. They surrounded her protectively and offered advice on what she shouldn't eat to avoid sickness in the mornings. One marquesa, who'd had seven children and was carrying her eighth, told her to ride every day, even when she was heavy with child, claiming the activity would make birthing far easier.

"And kill the horse from the weight," one young woman said.

Everyone laughed, save for Luscinda and the baroness.

Before long, Sancha forgot about them and genuinely enjoyed herself. She and a few women her age dipped their feet in the pond to cool off from the unseasonable heat, making certain they were always in the shade to avoid ruining their complexions.

"Men are so fortunate," a señorita with light brown hair said. "No matter how horrible they look, they can always find a wife."

"But not her tender regard," the young woman next to her said.

Somehow, the subject changed from love to wedding nights with tales more fantastic than what Sancha had heard the duke and Enrique discuss. She laughed heartily with the women.

A servant approached. "Señora?"

Still smiling, she turned to the young man.

He offered a small bow. "You have a visitor."

Surprised, she looked at him dumbly. "Me?"

"Sí. In the patrón's study." He offered another small bow and left without saying more, as though full disclosure wasn't his place in front of so many others, or perhaps such a thing wasn't allowed.

She suddenly thought of Isabella coming here, wanting to surprise her. Hoping for that, she pushed to her feet. "Please excuse me. I think my sister has made the gathering after all."

"Have her come out and join us," the one with the brown hair said. "Is she wed?"

Sancha nodded. "And with child."

"Wonderful. She can tell us even more tales about wedding nights."

"I warn you, hers are more outrageous than any of yours." With her words bringing on new laughter, Sancha left.

Barefoot, she ran into the castle and Enrique's study, stopping just inside the door. Pedro, not Isabella, stood inside.

"What are you doing here? Oh my, forgive me." Sancha felt horrible. "I meant to say, I was expecting Isabella, not you. Are you looking for Enrique? Is everything all right?" She inhaled sharply. "Has something happened to him? Had he been hunting? Is he hurt?"

"I have no idea where he is. I came to speak to both of you."

Her insides churned. The earlier worry she'd had about rumors and the inquisitors came back with a vengeance, making her dizzy and ill. "Why do you need to speak to us?"

Pedro strode past her and closed the door. "Tomás is ill."

"Ill?" She didn't understand. "In what way? How badly?"

He lifted his hand, grief and worry flooding his features.

"Tell me please."

"The surgeon doesn't expect him to survive."

"What? Enrique and I saw you and Tomás a short while ago. He was fine."

"He had a cough and a fever like so many are getting lately. The others recovered. For some reason he keeps getting worse. He asked me to write the letter for why we were unable to attend your gathering."

"You never wrote that he was ill."

"He told me not to. He feared ruining your and Enrique's gathering with worry. I argued if he came here, you could help him. He said no, refusing to endanger you because of your healing. The surgeon has bled him twice with him only growing worse. A third time will surely kill him. Something else must be done."

"I need to gather my things. Find Enrique. He and the men left hours ago. They should be on their way back by now."

She left Pedro to go to a storage area where she found an unused sack. Making certain no one watched or followed her, she ran to the hidden room where Enrique had moved her books, mice, herbs, and other materials.

Just inside the door she stopped, tears blurring her vision.

Tomás couldn't die. He had too much to live for, charming countless señoritas, taunting his brothers good-naturedly. Of all Enrique's siblings, she was closest to him. He'd always smiled and teased her.

She packed her materials quickly, adding her largest volume should her initial remedies fail to help. Given what Pedro had told her, the illness sounded the same as what Isabella said Fernando experienced. The symptoms also matched what the baroness claimed in regards to her servants.

With everything ready, she left the sack in the room, returned unnoticed to the study, and paced for what seemed an eternity. Finally, footfalls rang in the hall. Enrique and Pedro hurried inside the room, breathing hard, their faces flushed.

She closed the door. "I have everything ready in the room. As soon as I fetch the sack, we can leave for the fortaleza."

Enrique shook his head. "Not you."

"What do you mean? I can use everything I know to heal him."

"At a stronghold filled with knights and a surgeon who sees to their care? Pedro never should have asked you to do this."

"I offered. None of this is his fault."

"What does it matter? If any of the men sees you healing, they will tell the authorities."

"You want me to let Tomás die?"

"No. Give me your medicine. Write down what I must do and I can—"

"Listen to me. I need to tend to him as I did Fernando, not through you. Hoping you achieve what I can may cause your brother's death."

"How can you treat him at a fortaleza?" He turned to Pedro. "Tell her how foolish her idea is."

"Enrique is right. I was wrong to have come here. Tomás would never want you to risk your safety, no matter his need."

"No one will know what I do. No different than at the convent. The sacerdote was there and never knew I treated Fernando. He thought I was holding prayer vigils. The two of you can say the same to the knights and the surgeon."

Enrique glared. "You hope that will keep them out of Tomás's room?"

"Telling them how contagious the illness is will keep them well away with none of them seeing what goes on inside. We can say the fever and cough brought down one of the nobles we know after he dealt with his manservant who had the same symptoms. Now he, the servant, and everyone in his castle are ill."

Enrique shook his head.

She cried, "Each moment you force me to reason with you is another lost as Tomás grows weaker. You promised before we wed you would never stop me from healing. You would help me. Do so now."

His face turned red.

"Please. If not for your brother, for me."

"What of our child you carry?"

"You are with child?" Pedro asked.

"I am, but my condition changes nothing." She went to Enrique. "You asked about our babe. When he becomes a knight and needs a healer I would hope one would chance everything to keep him whole and alive."

He swore beneath his breath then spoke to Pedro. "Gather what she packed so she has everything she needs." He told his brother where to find the secret room, then held out his hand to her. "We need to tell our guests of our departure. If we leave without word, they will wonder."

With Luscinda's encouragement, they would talk.

The men were in the dining hall, enjoying their repast after a day of sport. Enrique told them of Tomás's grave illness.

The nobles offered sympathy and their hope the young man would survive.

Sancha led the way to the pond where the ladies rested, talked, and laughed until they noticed her and Enrique's approach.

With a glance, he took them in. "Forgive my wife and I for leaving you so suddenly. My brother, Tomás, has taken quite ill."

Several of the women inhaled sharply in surprise and dismay, hands to their throats. A flurry of wishes for renewed health followed.

"Sancha and I will be leaving for the stronghold immediately," he said.

"Why her?" Luscinda stood. "What can she do there?"

He took a step toward her, hands tightened into fists, face dark with fury.

Sancha grabbed his arm, stopping him. "I can pray for Tomás's good health, as I would hope each of you will do in the chapel."

The ladies glanced from her to Enrique, then Luscinda.

Katia came forward. "Of course, we will. I can take care of Rosa in your absence. Go. See to Tomás. Make certain he survives his illness."

Chapter 15

Given Sancha's condition, Enrique asked her to ride in the carriage. For him to insist would have proved futile. Repeatedly, his wife did whatever she willed.

She shook her head. "A horse would be faster."

"And more dangerous. You keep forgetting about the child you carry."

"Riding a horse is good for both of us." She recounted what the marquesa had advised. "She and her children are in perfect health."

"Until a horse throws one of them."

"We have no time to debate this with Tomás lying near death."

He loved his brother and wanted him to survive, though not at her expense. To lose Sancha would be more than he could bear, but he couldn't sway her.

With each league they travelled, his mood darkened, convincing him they rode toward certain doom. Although Tomás's men were brave warriors who would stand beside him to their deaths, their first loyalty was to God and the Crown. A hint of anything involving heresy and they would seek out the authorities even if the suspected witch were Tomás's sister-in-law.

The knights would spare no one arrest, an interrogation, torture, or death at the stake when their souls were at risk.

His shoulders ached with tension. He couldn't seem to catch enough breath. Each time he glanced at Sancha, her attention was on the road, as was Pedro's, both lost in their own thoughts.

The fortaleza was several hours' ride from the castle. To Enrique, the horses seemed to move at a pace greater than what seemed possible, fate's invisible hand guiding them toward destruction.

By the time the stronghold came into view, the sun had already dipped behind the trees, its rays casting long shadows, the air cooling.

Enrique ordered his guards back to the castle. He, Pedro, and Sancha reined in their mounts, dust swirling around them. Two knights rode hard in their direction, their expressions grim, swords drawn.

Pedro shouted, "Ignacio, Juan, I bring my brother and his wife to see Tomás."

"How is my brother?" Enrique asked.

Ignacio shook his head. "Not good."

Sancha put up her hand for their attention. "You must stay away from his room. The illness he has will spread." She related her tale of the noble, his manservant, and the others they infected.

Juan's features slackened. "Most of us have been in his room wishing him well, doing what we can. Will we now fall ill as he had?"

"Only if you continue to stay close to him. Be grateful none of you has taken sick. You must clear all rooms surrounding his."

Ignacio spoke to Enrique. "Who will see to his care? Bring him food, water, and whatever else he needs?"

"Pedro and I will. His care is our duty and privilege." He patted the alforjas with her materials inside. "We bring much of what he loves to eat and drink to help make him strong again."

"Sancha will pray for God's mercy," Pedro said. "He answered her pleas when Fernando lay injured at the convent."

Juan and Ignacio nodded. They'd been with the group when Sancha's uncle had waylaid Fernando, nearly murdering him before Fernando had struck the final blow and killed the puto.

"If you please," she said. "I need a prayer bench in the room next to Tomás's."

Juan gestured to the stronghold. "You can have full use of our chapel."

"I need to remain as close as I can to Enrique and Pedro to see if they show signs of the illness. Any worry I have for them will interfere with my pleas to God."

"The prayer bench is yours," Ignacio said. "Along with whatever else you ask. Be prepared, though, for how ill Tomás is. He is not the same man."

He and Juan wheeled their horses around, leading the group to the fortaleza. A chill settled in Enrique for his brother's state and what Sancha was about to do.

Once at the entrance to the stone building, Juan alerted the men to stay away from Tomás's room. "Spread the word. Tell the knights in the chambers next to Tomás's they must leave the area at once."

The men fanned out, many running into the structure.

Torches lit the interior. Everyone's footfalls rang loudly on the stone floor.

"Wait," someone shouted behind them.

An older man hurried toward the group, his unshaven face ashen even in the dim light.

"Xavier, our surgeon," Ignacio said.

"Is it true the illness spreads?" the man asked.

Enrique nodded.

Xavier backed away and made the sign of the cross over himself. "I did all I could for Tomás. Nothing else can help him." He left as fast as his age allowed.

Enrique and the others stopped long enough for Ignacio to locate a prayer bench. He and Pedro hauled the item up a narrow flight to the next level. In the hall with Tomás's chamber, knights hurried past them, possessions in hand, clearing the area as warned.

A rattling cough mingled with the men's footfalls.

"This is the closest chamber to Tomás's." Ignacio inclined his head to the room before he and Pedro put the bench inside.

Ignacio came out first, trying to catch his breath. Enrique rested his hand on the man's shoulder. "Leave food and drink at the bottom of the steps for my wife, Pedro, and me. We can fetch the items, so you have no need to go further. Tomás would never want you risking your health for him."

"I know. I will keep him in my prayers." He backed away slowly.

Enrique suspected the man was ashamed to show his fear of the illness. "Go. Before you fall sick."

Ignacio smiled gratefully and hurried away.

Pedro gestured to a room on the left. Light from torches spilled from within the space to the hall.

Tomás's coughs were relentless, followed by a thin wheezing sound.

"Come." Sancha led the way into his room.

* * * *

Although Ignacio had warned them of Tomás's state, no words could have prepared Sancha for his condition.

He'd lost so much weight his cheeks and eyes were sunken, face reddened from the force of his coughs, hair plastered to his head. The beautiful blond locks she remembered were far darker and greasy, his upper lip and cheeks bristly with his beard.

His lids were partly open, but she didn't think he recognized them. He was far too ill. She made the sign of the cross over herself and begged God to give her the skill to make him well.

After her quick prayer, she gestured to Enrique. "Please bring my materials to his bed."

He lowered the alforjas to the floor and unpacked the items quickly. After Pedro had closed the door, he joined his brother to help.

She rested her palm on Tomás's forehead, biting her lip at the heat. The fever was burning him alive, his skin dry, lips swollen and cracked. "I need clean water. The coldest you can find. As much as you can bring immediately."

She opened the shutter over the narrow window, letting the cool night air inside.

Pedro hurried past Enrique to her. "Tomás is shivering already. More chill can do him no good."

"I need to bring his fever down. If not, he will die. Bring me the water now."

"Listen to her." Enrique pulled Pedro from the room, their footfalls fading quickly.

She yanked the blankets off Tomás and undressed him until he wore naught but his braies. His wasted body, once so solid and strong, brought tears to her eyes. "You will be well." She touched his cheek. "I promise you."

He jerked away with another violent, rattling cough.

She dipped a square of clean linen in the basin of water and bathed his face, throat, chest. Wind blew inside, ruffling her skirt. The torch flames danced.

He shivered violently.

She dampened the cloth again and laid it across his forehead. On her knees, she paged through her book for the best potions to treat his illness. Her search seemed endless, but at last she found the needed passage and lined up containers containing yarrow, ginger, and peppermint. She prayed for Enrique and Pedro to hurry.

By the time they returned with four pails of water, she'd already measured the herbs and cleaned Tomás's cup with wine.

"I need to brew a potion for his fever." She handed Enrique the cup. "Fill this with clean water. Can you set up the torch so the water boils?"

"Of course. Whatever you need."

"Do so quickly." She lifted small squares of linen tied with string, the herbs inside, and handed them to Pedro. "These go into the cup after the water bubbles."

As the men worked on the potion, she lifted the ladle from the first pail and brought the water to Tomás.

"Drink." She settled her hand on the back of his head to keep him up.

More water poured over his lips than inside his mouth. He moaned, wheezed, coughed.

Soon, his upper chest and her skirt were soaked. She filled the ladle repeatedly until he'd managed to get some of the liquid inside. Next, she ladled water on his throat and chest to bring down the fever and used a sodden cloth to dampen his face. He coughed and wheezed, struggling for breath.

She put her palms on his cheek and forehead. He seemed slightly cooler, though not enough.

"What of the potion?" she asked.

Pedro bounced on his heels. "The water has yet to boil."

He, Sancha, and Enrique kept vigil over the cup and Tomás. No one spoke. Tomás's agonized coughs filled the chamber.

At last, the potion was finished and cool enough to use. She gestured to both men. "Please hold him up for me."

Enrique and Pedro supported their brother. His head flopped forward, shoulders jerking with his cough.

She slipped her hand beneath his chin and lifted his face. "Drink. You must finish every drop."

The effort took a painfully long time before he finished. Immediately, she handed the cup to Enrique. "Please brew more water. I must now see to the potion for his cough."

* * * *

Sancha focused so much on tending to Tomás hour after hour, day after day, she would have forgotten to eat or sleep if not for Enrique. At his command, Pedro brought a mattress into the room for her to lie on. Enrique fetched the cheese, bread, wine, and beef Ignacio always left for them, urging her to eat her fill.

Swallowing any food was an effort, given her worry over Tomás and her condition. With every dawn, her queasiness returned. Pedro provided a bucket for her to use. Afterward, Enrique wiped her face with damp linen. They took care of her when Tomás was the one in need.

He still looked terrible, his coughs pronounced. While Enrique and Pedro slept, she read her book to see if she'd missed a better remedy.

The words finally swam in front of her, her mind too tired to make sense of the text. What seemed only seconds later, someone shook her shoulder, waking her.

She ran her hand over her eyes and glanced up at Enrique. "What is it?"

"Tomás is shivering more than he has been."

Sweat rolled off him as water would after taking a bath. She hurried to his side and pressed her palm to his forehead. Much cooler. "His fever broke."

He wheezed, coughed then gagged.

"A square of linen." She wiggled her fingers.

Enrique handed her several pieces of cloth.

She held one close to Tomás's mouth. He coughed, made a face, and spat into the linen. His phlegm was a deep green streaked with blood.

Enrique paled but didn't look away. "Will he live?"

She took his hand, wanting to comfort. "The first of his sickness is leaving."

"The blood…"

"His throat is raw from trying to expel the phlegm. Once he clears his lungs, he will heal."

A new cough racked Tomás.

Enrique looked as helpless as she'd ever seen him. "When will that be? Him healing?"

"In time. We must wait."

* * * *

Enrique communicated Tomás's progress to the men with notes he left on the steps. Ignacio left his own missives. His last concerned him not having to send again for the sacerdote to anoint Tomás for death.

> *Padre arrived two days ago. When he heard the*
> *illness could spread, he declined to go to Tomás's*
> *room, saying the matter was best left in God's hands,*
> *and to send for him after we had buried Tomás.*

Enrique didn't want to consider what would have happened had the priest seen Sancha here along with her materials.

Although Tomás grew better for a few hours at a time, his health always seemed to worsen toward the end of each day. Sancha poured potions down his throat. Enrique and Pedro threatened to thrash him within an inch of his life if he didn't eat.

He finally curled his upper lip at them. "Sancha will stop you." He gave her a weak smile. "Will you not?"

"Eat, or I will thrash you." She pushed another spoonful of broth between his lips.

Dutifully, he swallowed the watery stock. "You used to be so nice. What happened?"

He'd almost died on them. Enrique had never been more grateful to see anyone survive.

Within a few days, Tomás was able to leave simple broth behind to partake of bread and cheese. He soon asked for meat. The heartier fare put some weight back on him.

One afternoon, he threw back his covers. "I need to leave this bed. I want to walk."

Enrique and Pedro caught him before he fell to the floor, his legs too thin and weak, wobbling worse than a newborn colt.

With their help, he walked a bit more each day, at last growing strong enough to cross the room on his own. The short journey left him panting and leaning against the wall for support.

Worried, Enrique pulled Sancha aside. "Will he ever be hearty again?"

"Once he fills out, he will be the same as always. You need to stop worrying."

"If I could, I would. Have I thanked you for your courage and skill? Without you, he would have died."

"I like Tomás far too much to let such a thing happen."

Laughing softly, he pulled her into his embrace. "You are a wonder. Promise never to do anything as foolish as this again."

She eased away, her lovely face drained of enthusiasm, heavy with disappointment.

He sighed. "When you do proceed, I insist on being at your side."

"Always."

* * * *

At last, the time came to leave for the castle, Tomás accompanying them to convalesce in a comfortable bedchamber with servants available to indulge his every need. Enrique had already sent word ahead for Hortensia to prepare for their arrival.

Outside the stronghold, Tomás stopped and wrinkled his nose. "You expect me to ride in a carriage like a mere woman?"

Sancha crossed her arms beneath her breasts. "A mere what?"

He gave her a sheepish smile. "In no way did I mean you, dear Sancha, wondrous Sancha, beauteous Sancha, glorious—"

"Here he goes," Enrique said, happy to have his too-charming brother back. "If you keep going on as you always do, we will never arrive. Get in."

"How can I with these blankets wrapped around me? I am not a helpless babe."

Enrique slung his arm around his brother's neck and pulled him close, not wanting anyone to overhear. "Would you prefer to stay and have the surgeon bleed you again?"

"I have no wish to die. However, I refuse to get in that thing until I say farewell to my men."

"Do so quickly."

He took an inordinate amount of time to wish his fellow knights well, taking every opportunity he could to state how his brothers' care and Sancha's pleas to God had saved him.

"Yes," he said, answering one warrior's question, "Enrique did shove food down my throat despite my protests. Did I tell you how Pedro tried to outdo him by forcing me to drink whatever he could get his hands on? None of my oaths stopped either of them."

The men laughed.

"If not for Sancha, they would have surely killed me." Tomás gave her a sweet smile. "Much to my delight, she called Enrique and Pedro away from my bedside to see if they were also growing sick. She made certain they ate their fill and had enough rest before returning to torment me." He sighed. "Many times at night I heard her fervent prayers, begging for my good health, asking God to spare me, the same as she prayed for Fernando. My brother Enrique is a lucky man and hardly deserves her."

How true.

The knights clamped Enrique on the shoulder or patted his back, respect in their expressions for Sancha.

She smiled shyly, playing the demure wife.

What a woman he had in her.

At last, they were on their way home, guards around the perimeter, Sancha riding in the carriage with Tomás, Pedro driving the conveyance, Enrique on his mount, lighthearted for the first time in weeks.

He glanced at his brother. "How long can you stay with us?"

"After a few days of your excellent food and wine, I must go back to the stronghold." He gestured Enrique closer so they could talk without the guards overhearing. "Sancha was magnificent. If we had left Tomás to the surgeon, the fool would have bled him dry."

"He and the sacerdote seemed more concerned with saving their own hides than their patient's."

"Not everyone is as brave as your wife. Speaking of which, what of her sisters besides Isabella? Are any of them as courageous, beautiful, and knowledgeable as Sancha is?"

"None of them are around. Carmen and Concepcion are at Court under the Queen's tutelage. From what Sancha has said, they prefer jewels, silks, velvets, and combs to any kind of knowledge. However, they are supposed to be quite beautiful and not for you or Tomás to woo or even think about."

"Why not?"

"Two brothers wedding two sisters is enough for any family. Find a wife somewhere else."

"Who said I was looking for a wife?"

Enrique shot a look at Pedro. "Stay away from Sancha's sisters. Tell Tomás the same."

"How good it is to have him back."

Yes. After the recent turmoil, Enrique couldn't wait to get home, relax, eat a good meal, and sleep in his own bed with Sancha at his side.

* * * *

They reached the castle at midday. A servant and Pedro helped Tomás to his room.

With the alforjas over one shoulder, Enrique slipped his arm around Sancha's waist. "Too tired to eat?"

"I would love several helpings of whatever the cook has prepared. Have you ever seen a lovelier day? Still quite warm for this time of year. Can we have our meal by the pond?"

"Of course."

"Patrón. Señora." Hortensia hurried to them. "You have a visitor. I asked her to wait over there." She gestured to the small room off the entrance.

He exchanged a glance with Sancha, then leaned down to Hortensia to avoid other servants hearing the converse. "Is the visitor Señorita Luscinda?"

"No. Countess Katia."

Sancha brightened instantly. "What a delightful woman. She was so kind to take care of Rosa when we left to see Tomás. She must be here to find out about him. Come."

She tugged Enrique's hand.

At the sound of their footfalls, Katia turned from the window, her red velvet gown as regal as her bearing.

"How wonderful to see you." Sancha ran across the room and threw her arms around the woman.

Katia's face glowed with affection. Enrique couldn't have been more pleased. She would make a great ally for his wife.

After he greeted the old woman, Sancha bounced on her heels like a young girl. "We have good news. Tomás is here, making his recovery."

"How wonderful. I am so glad."

"Come." Sancha slipped her arm through Katia's. "We can enjoy a repast at the pond."

"I fear not." Katia patted Sancha's arm then stepped away to close the door.

Enrique grew apprehensive again. "You have something to tell us?"

"I do." She looked at them both with kindness and sorrow. "I attended a gathering last night. Luscinda was there. She knew Tomás had survived. How, I have no idea. Perhaps the servants talked as they always do." She spoke to Sancha. "She told a group of women your pact with the Devil was the only thing that could have possibly spared Tomás from death. As soon as she can, Luscinda plans to take her suspicions to the tribunal."

Chapter 16

Everything stopped. Sancha's breath, the wind brushing past the castle, Katia's words. The countess's mouth moved but Sancha didn't hear anything further. She squeezed Enrique's hand, though she couldn't recall having reached for him.

He led her to a leather chair, his arm around her waist, supporting her. She could barely walk, her legs heavy, the rest of her bristling with loathing for Luscinda.

She hated the woman not only for what she'd do to her, but Enrique and his brothers. The tribunal would find them guilty too, because Tomás had survived and Enrique, along with Pedro, had taken her to the fortaleza to do the Devil's work.

"You have to flee." She dropped to the chair. "Is there time enough?"

He sank to one knee at her side. "What are you talking about?"

"You must go. Tomás and Pedro have to leave with you. When the tribunal learns you and your brothers were with me at the fortaleza, all will be lost."

"No one will learn anything because you have done nothing except pray for my brother's recovery. Nor will I ever flee. Not from the tribunal and certainly not the wretch's lies." He spoke to Katia. "Do you know where Luscinda is now?"

Sancha grabbed his sleeve. "What do you intend to do?"

"Finish this as I should have from the beginning."

She cried, "If you harm her, there will be no end to this for you. Please, you and your brothers need to find somewhere safe to live. Leave me to deal with this alone—oh no." She tried to get up, but her legs wouldn't hold her.

"What happened?" Enrique took her hand. "Is it the babe?"

"No. The inquisitors will pull Isabella into this too. I have to send a missive at once to warn her and Fernando to—"

"You need to relax before you harm yourself and our child." He lifted his face to Katia. "Would you ask Hortensia to bring Sancha some water and to have Pedro come in here?"

"Of course." She hurried from the room, closing the door behind her.

"I will never leave you." He gathered her to him. "Nor will I allow anyone to harm you, Isabella, or any of my family. This stops now."

Holding back tears, she slipped her arms around his neck, cherishing his warmth and strength, savoring his scent. How many more moments would she have to simply embrace him before circumstances separated them forever? She pulled him as close as she could and it still wasn't enough. "Forgive me for bringing you such pain."

"You have given me naught but joy and will continue to so for the rest of our lives."

A sob tore from her. "We have no life left. Luscinda will never stop. You heard what Katia said. The wretch will go to the tribunal. Whatever I do or say, she will continue to accuse."

"Accusations go in both directions."

Pedro rushed inside followed by Katia. She closed the door.

"What do we do?" he asked Enrique.

"Send missives to Fernando, Alfonso, and Gabriello. Have them come here immediately."

"To do what?" Sancha fingered tears from her eyes. "Fight against the authorities when they come to arrest me?"

He smoothed back her hair. "No one is going to arrest you."

"Not with us here." Pedro tapped Enrique's shoulder. "Tomás wants to join us in whatever we plan. He insists. There is no way we can sway him."

Enrique muttered an oath but nodded.

"No." Sancha frowned at him and Pedro. "I will not have Tomás risk his health for me. I forbid it, and for any of you to put yourselves in danger on my behalf."

"The only one in danger will be Luscinda." Enrique pecked her tear-stained cheek. "Thanks to the countess, I now have proof the rumors began and continued with the wretch. As I said, accusations go both ways."

"You believe accusing Luscinda of being the one who started this will cause her to stop or recant?"

"No. But accusing her of witchcraft will."

"What?"

"Time to give Luscinda a taste of what cruel rumors can do."

* * * *

Pedro's twin, Alfonso, arrived late the same evening along with Gabriello. Enrique told his brothers he expected Fernando to join them early on the morrow without Isabella. Sancha insisted her sister stay home to avoid being part of this or in danger from Luscinda.

Gathered in Enrique's study, the brothers devised their confrontation with the woman. How they would trap Luscinda with her own words, as she loved to do with others.

According to Katia, Luscinda would be in Córdoba during the next week, she and her mother the guests of a wealthy merchant. Luscinda's original intent had been to attend the fair once the festivities began, several days from now. Her purpose at this point? Everyone knew the Inquisition had tribunals in Córdoba and Sevilla.

Enrique and his brothers didn't seem alarmed by that fact or her earlier threats.

"We should be able to find her at the merchant's home, plotting as always," Gabriello said. His hair was dark like Enrique's, his features almost identical to Tomás's.

Though weak, Tomás was alert, his expression as determined as his brothers. No one would keep him from this meet.

Nor would they do so with Sancha. She finally interrupted the men's converse. "When do we leave?"

Enrique turned from Pedro who'd been speaking. "We?"

"I intend to come with you."

He frowned. "No. My brothers and I will handle this."

"You want me to hide here while you confront her?"

"I want you to stay here and be safe."

"No." With the passing hours, outrage had replaced her worry. "If you fight, I fight. When you fight, I fight."

"In your condition?"

She threw up her hands. "I am with child, Enrique, not dying."

Gabriello and Alfonso smiled.

Tomás leaned toward Enrique. "Sancha should join us. Prove to Luscinda we stand together on this. She harms one of us, she harms all."

The other brothers nodded.

Enrique sagged in his chair and sighed loudly. "You let us do the talking."

"Forgive me, but no, I intend to have my say."

He regarded her. "What exactly?"

She smiled. "Something I just thought of." A truth so impossible to challenge, she was surprised not to have considered the notion earlier.

Enrique and his brothers looked intrigued. Tomás grinned conspiratorially. "Come, tell us, dear Sancha, sweet Sancha, lovely San—"

"Yes, please tell us," Gabriello said. "Before Tomás goes on all night."

Tomás grumbled at his brother's teasing. Sancha kept her peace.

* * * *

Fernando arrived early the next morning and hugged her first. He looked virile and strong, as though his battle with her uncle had never occurred. Pleased to see him, she returned his hearty embrace.

"I hear you are with child," he said.

"The same as Isabella. How is she?" Sancha eased away and planted her hands on her hips. "Are you treating her well?"

He pulled a letter out of his pouch. "I have a feeling she told you in this."

Delighted to have word from her sister, she scanned the note quickly.

> *My dearest Sancha,*
> *How I wish I could be there for this meet, but I agree with you and my husband that by staying here I will keep you from worrying about me.*
> *I have no more fear for you.*
> *Your Enrique, my Fernando, and their brave brothers will protect you well.*
> *I cannot wait to learn what happens.*
> *Make the puta pay for the pain she has caused you.*

Sancha laughed at Isabella's foul language. No matter how many times Fernando had warned her not to use terms such as puto or puta, Isabella kept doing so.

"What did she write?" Fernando asked.

Sancha held the missive to her breast. "A note to me, not you."

"Best you never know what the letter contains," Tomás said.

Enrique took Sancha's hand. "Are you still certain you want to go?"

She nodded. Nothing would keep her away.

* * * *

The merchant's home was at the end of a narrow street in the lovely city, vines with waxy green leaves climbing the building's white walls, ironwork grills over the windows.

The female servant who opened the front door stared at so many men and one lone woman.

Enrique took charge immediately. "Señor Guzman is here?"

"No. He had business to attend to."

"Señorita Luscinda Cortés is inside?"

"In the courtyard, awaiting her mamá's return. Who should I say is calling on her?"

"We will tell her ourselves." He moved past the woman.

"No." She waved her hands frantically. "You must wait for me to announce you."

Ignoring her pleas, Sancha and the rest filed in.

The home was cool, clean, shadowed against the day's lingering warmth, and quite luxurious. Its many Moorish touches, including arched entryways, colorful mosaic tiles, silk pillows and drapes called to mind a Sultan's harem Sancha had heard so much gossip about.

In the courtyard, water poured from a fountain. Orange and lemon trees created sweet scents and abundant shade in the enclosed area. Enough to save a señorita's flawless complexion from the sun.

Luscinda relaxed on a grand Moorish chair beneath a large tree, a yellow silk pillow behind her back, a green one beneath her feet. She, or more probably a servant, had braided her hair. The thick black coil dangled over her shoulder, the end touching the waist of her crimson gown.

"You must wait," the servant called once more.

Luscinda glanced up from the letter she held. Shock crossed her face at Sancha, Enrique, and his brothers' approach as one, a united force.

She stood so quickly, her feet caught on the pillow, nearly sending her to the ground.

"Forgive me, señorita." The servant wrung her hands. "They gave me no chance to announce them."

Luscinda glared at Enrique. "What are you doing here?"

"What else?" Sancha folded her hands in front. "Accusing you of witchcraft."

"As is our duty to God and Spain," Enrique said.

The servant made the sign of the cross over herself.

Luscinda lost what little color she had. She backed away. Enrique advanced. "There." He pointed at her throat. "I see the Devil's mark."

"I do too." Fernando strode close. "And another on her hand."

Luscinda dropped her letter.

With his boot on the missive, Tomás turned to the others. "I heard her at the gathering a few days ago. She promised the baroness eternal youth if only she'd give her soul to the—"

"You lie," Luscinda said.

The servant fled.

Luscinda shouted, "Come back here. Throw them out."

Gabriello rubbed his jaw. "She even sounds like the Devil. We need to do something about that." He crowded Luscinda as Enrique and his other brothers had.

"Get away from me," she shouted.

Alfonso spoke to his brothers. "I think she sounds worse than Satan."

"How dare you." Despite her outrage, her fear was greater. She backed away from the men, ran into a lemon tree, and flinched. She hurried around the trunk. Enrique and his brothers followed.

She cried, "I will see all of you arrested by the tribunal."

"You will keep your tongue," Sancha said. "Or I will have it along with your youth and beauty. Have you forgotten I consort with the Devil? You said so yourself and have told others the same many times. If what you said is true, I should have the power to strike you dead or disfigure you horribly."

Luscinda shook her fist. "Touch me in the least and you will regret doing so."

"You threaten a woman who has the Devil's power behind her? How brave you are." Sancha smiled and approached Luscinda, prepared to say what had suddenly occurred to her yesterday. A truth she should have always seen but hadn't. "You claimed I was the one who could destroy lives. Why then have I held off with yours? You certainly deserve the same anguish you caused my husband, our families, and me. Could it be you remain unharmed because I have no dark power? Could it be, you are the one under Satan's control, given what you have done, the lies you repeatedly told about me?"

"Witch." Enrique pointed at her.

Alfonso circled Luscinda. "I see another mark from the Devil on her neck."

She spun away and came face-to-face with Tomás, so wan and thin from his illness.

"You made me sick," he said to her then spoke to the others. "She put a spell on me, hoping I would die to ruin Sancha and Enrique's happiness."

Gabriello stepped forward. "The crops on Papá's estate withered this year as they never have. You did that." He pointed at her and shouted, "Witch!"

She tried to run into the house. Alfonso blocked her. Sancha, Enrique, and his other brothers surrounded her again.

"Leave me alone," she cried.

"Never." Enrique's expression was dark with disgust. "The time has come for you to learn accusations move in both directions. You claim my wife engages in witchcraft. Now my family, Sancha's, and I are going to say the same about you. Our ties to the Crown are closer than your family's will ever be. Before your lies harm us, we intend to destroy you."

She shrank from him. "I never went to the tribunal. I spoke to no one except those at the gathering."

"You mean you lied to no one but them," Sancha said.

Luscinda glared at her but finally nodded.

Enrique crowded her. "During the next hours you will write missives to every noble we know, telling them of your jealousy and greed. How you intended to destroy Sancha because you wanted—"

"No. I could never show my face again."

"After you write your letters," he said, "you and your mother will move to the north, your people there, never to return to Andalucía again."

"No!"

"Pedro." He looked over. "You know where to find the tribunal?"

"I do."

"Leave now. Tell them we have a witch who needs questioning."

Pedro left the courtyard.

"Wait!" Luscinda cried for him to stop until he had. "I would never have let the lies go on. I would have stopped them before the inquisitors came."

"You will stop them now," Sancha said.

Enrique gestured to Alfonso and Gabriello. "Take the señorita inside. Tell her what she needs to write in her letters."

Once they'd led Luscinda away, with Pedro, Fernando, and Tomás following, Sancha held Enrique as tightly as she could.

He stroked her hair. "Are you all right?"

She couldn't stop trembling. "Is it over finally?"

He embraced her, his size and strength a balm. "Our future is only beginning."

Epilogue

Months later…

The spring day proved warmer than usual, its heat tempered by a mild breeze.

Sancha lifted her face and inhaled deeply of fragrant grass, sweet flowers, rich earth. She smiled at the ducks on the pond, surely the same mamá and papá as last year, looking forward to their new brood.

Instinctively, she rested her hand on her swollen belly, the child inside.

"You need to eat and so does our son." Enrique offered her three orange slices.

She gobbled the food without pause or apology. Since conceiving, she couldn't eat enough fruit, craving its sweet juice endlessly, almost to the exclusion of everything else. Katia had said her desire for oranges proved she carried a son.

The old woman sat on a chair beneath an olive tree, smiling at Rosa and Diego, Isabella's galgo. The dogs turned in circles, sniffing each other. Rosa tired of the activity first and darted away with Diego in fast pursuit. A game they'd played since meeting. In a few months, Rosa would be old enough to breed. Sancha and Isabella had promised her to Diego.

"We should have a betrothal ceremony for them," Isabella had said, laughing at the idea.

How wonderful to have her close.

During these last weeks before she gave birth, she and Fernando had come here to await their child's arrival. They lounged on a blanket beneath the next tree, sharing soft laughter and intimate smiles, Fernando's hand on her belly, their infant's kicks delighting both.

When Isabella's time came, Sancha and Katia would be on hand to usher the new life into the world. The countess was a dear friend now and a blessing to Sancha and Isabella, the mamá they'd missed since their own had died.

Finished with peeling a new orange, Enrique stretched out on the blanket, legs crossed at his ankles.

"Sleepy?" Sancha asked.

He propped his head in his hand and glanced to the left. "Not with the noise."

A group of señoritas surrounded Pedro, Gabriello, Alfonso, and Tomás. The young women's gowns were as vivid as any flower, the silks in red, yellow, green, and blue. The girls' loud giggles interrupted their chatter, after which they continued to speak without taking a moment to breathe.

The brothers laughed and flirted with the young noblewomen, except for Tomás. He offered a bland smile, continually glancing off in the distance, his thoughts elsewhere.

His health wasn't an issue. He'd regained his lost weight, becoming the same man he'd been before his illness, tall and strong, blond hair quite beautiful, his handsome features drawing more than a few of the señoritas to him.

Again, he listened politely but seemed distracted.

Sancha leaned down to Enrique. "What ails Tomás?"

She'd hoped these young women would please all his brothers, giving them an incentive to settle down. Enrique, even more than she, thought it was high time his brothers found wives.

He handed her another orange slice. "Trouble at his castle, I think."

After his brush with death, he'd returned to the fortaleza for a short time to turn his command over to Pedro. The sovereigns had granted Tomás land and a castle for serving the Crown courageously, the same as they'd done with Fernando. Both brothers were now rich men like Enrique.

"What kind of trouble? Surely not raids by the Moors."

"No. A new servant."

She frowned. "If Tomás finds the man unacceptable, he should simply dismiss him."

"The servant is female. I believe her name is Beatriz. And I can assure you, Tomás does not want her to leave. He seems quite besotted with her."

"How awful."

Enrique lifted his eyebrows. "Why? Because the woman lacks our noble heritage?"

"Of course not. Tomás rules at his castle. For him to be infatuated is a small matter as he has naught to lose. What of the girl? When things go badly, as they surely will, where will she go? You should have a talk with him about not taking unfair advantage."

"Already have. Given the look on his face, not a word I said got through."

She'd have to talk to him later. "Do you think it will ever be any different?"

Enrique lifted his face to her, hair dancing in the breeze, his forelock a startling white against his dark hair. "Will what be any different?"

"A woman's place in this world. Females being at such a disadvantage to you men who have every privilege."

"Have I been so awful to you?" He cupped the back of her neck and eased her down to him, his lips on her ear. "Have I not accompanied you on every journey to the villages? Have I not brought the ill here for you to treat? Did I not catch a score of mice last week for you to torment during your experiments? Will I not continue to do these things and more for the rest of our days?"

He had and would. "You are a man among men."

Chuckling, he eased back to the blanket, his beautiful features filled with love.

Her heart opened even more to him. How lucky she was to have Enrique, and him to have her.

"What of my question?" she asked. "You have yet to answer."

"Forgive me. Your praise chased every other thought out of my head."

She waited.

He looked sheepish. "What question?"

"If the world will ever be different for women, allowing them to be all they can?"

A time when universities would welcome them, praising their thirst for knowledge rather than calling them witches. When they stood beside men, rather than behind, helping to build great cities, improving life for everyone, not only nobles, and had a say in their own future.

Sancha's had once been promised to Fernando without her consent. As awful as Luscinda had behaved, she'd simply followed a woman's only allowed goal: to find a husband. What might she have been like if given as many possibilities as men had?

"The world had better," Enrique said.

She shook her head. "Had better what?"

"Change. You never will."

Praise, not indignation, rang in his words, filling her with hope.

For their daughters, at least, the world would be a different, better place. Those girls would continue to bring more change, one man at a time through understanding, friendship, love. The same as their mamá and papá had done with each other.

She ran her fingers over his bottom lip. "I tire of this spot. What say we go to our chamber?"

With a pleased smile, he led her to their room and closed the door on the outside world.

Meet the Author

Tina Donahue is an Amazon and international bestselling romance author in historical, contemporary, paranormal, fantasy and sci-fi. She's received numerous industry writing awards and is featured in the Novel and Short Story Writer's Market. She lives in California.

Keep reading for a sample of book three in Tina Donahue's
Dangerous Desires series

PASSIONATE PURSUIT

Forced into a betrothal by her ruthless papá, Beatriz wants only to escape
marriage to a cruel Marquis. Fleeing an impossible situation, she assumes
another identity and seeks work as a servant despite her father's wealth.
Tomás doesn't know what to make of the new woman at his castle.
Beautiful and well spoken, Beatriz doesn't seem suited to a life of
drudgery. Captivated, he pursues her.
Determined to resist a man she can never have, Beatriz soon falls under
Tomás's spell as he does with her. Passion turns to love.
All while the Marquis sets a trap to make her his forever.

A Lyrical Originals novel available August. 2016

Learn more about Tina at
http://www.kensingtonbooks.com/author.aspx/24772

Chapter 1

Andalucía, Spain—1489
The castle of Tomás de Zayas

The siege had begun. Not from bloodthirsty Moors. Oh no. Tomás de Zayas would have welcomed such a prospect. He'd fought Spain's enemies with ruthless determination during his service to the Crown. Those battles were frequently grisly, but the conflicts had always ended.

What he'd face in the coming hours could turn into a miserable lifetime sentence if he wasn't careful.

Tomás planned to be.

He didn't budge from the parapet.

The first wave of carriages approached his estate, the transports less than half a league apart, though far enough for the drivers and their charges not to spot each other from the heavily vegetated ground. Inside each conveyance was a señorita and her mamá with naught but marriage on their minds and him the unwilling suitor.

His gut churned.

A mild breeze ruffled his hair, robe, and doublet. The sky was clear, sun heavy, air sweetly scented with new vegetation and spring flowers. Balmy weather that was too splendid for their visit. A day a man should spend outside riding, laughing, loving…with the right woman.

An image filled his mind of the one he craved. Her hair so dark the tresses were nearly black. Eyes light brown, softened with desire. Pale skin with a hint of color in her cheeks, her response to his intense and eager gaze. Plush mouth, pink as an Andalucían dawn, her lips parted to welcome his.

He released a yearning sigh none of the arriving females would ever hear from him.

He'd held them off for months, declining invitations to countless gatherings. The mamás had persisted with endless requests to visit his estate, claiming they and their daughters wanted to see how he was doing after his brush with death.

He was hearty as ever and wanted to enjoy life again, though not with them. The woman he craved was already here.

A rush of heat poured through him, unbidden and insistent.

"There you are," Nuncio said.

He turned to his manservant, an ancient fellow who'd been with his family well before Tomás's birth. Despite Nuncio's sixty years, the man held himself as erect as a Spanish knight. While his bearing and white hair gave him a courtly appearance, his casual manner was more intrusive uncle than groveling servant.

Nuncio regarded the goblet Tomás held. He arched one of his bushy white eyebrows.

Gleefully, Tomás finished his wine, wanting more to fortify himself against the coming hours.

Clattering horse hooves and wheels quieted.

The first carriage had arrived. Mother and daughter left their conveyance, chattering endlessly, too far below for him to catch any words. Their voices, however, rang with excitement. Their silly giggles grated.

He pictured the one woman he did desire but shouldn't, at least according to his brother Enrique and sister-in-law Sancha. Both had lectured Tomás on his wayward passion that couldn't amount to anything, ever, except trouble and heartache.

Precisely what he'd get from the women intruding upon him today, even though they were noble born, their backgrounds similar to his. A supposed incentive for him to find a bride. With his service to the Crown over, everyone seemed to expect him to wed without complaint or delay. After all, the señoritas vying for his attention were young, most lovely, all educated, and trained to please a husband in every possible manner, to bear his sons willingly and with great frequency as duty demanded. Everything a man should want, except stirring his carnal appetite with lust so deep the feeling stole his breath and thickened his blood.

How could any man live without such delight? Enrique certainly hadn't. He adored Sancha as she did him. Fernando, his other brother, was the same. He and Isabella were inseparable.

Why should he settle for less?

How could he avoid doing so, considering the woman he wanted wasn't of his station.

Sighing, he leaned against a stone column and regarded the valley beyond, endless fields of wheat, orchards, and vineyards that made up his land. How he wished he were out there riding, running, or even walking, rather than having circumstances trap him here.

"Are you planning to throw yourself off?" Nuncio sighed tiredly. "Should I be alarmed?"

Only when Tomás tossed him off the side. "You should do your duty and see to my desires." He held out his goblet. "I need more wine."

Nuncio remained planted to the spot, wrinkled hands folded in front, striking a lord of the manor pose. "Your guests might believe otherwise."

Tomás pushed away from the column and glanced at the area below. The carriage and footmen were off to the side, the women nowhere in sight. Presumably, mother and daughter were within the castle, waiting for what they believed would be a private visit with him.

Pity that.

He turned his pleased smile on Nuncio. "As they have no regard for my feelings, I hardly care what they think. If you remember, I politely declined their requests to come here, until you hounded me about my indifference to their marriage plans with me as their grudging victim. Now, I have a chance to tell the mamás I have no intention of wedding any of their daughters."

"By gathering all of them here at the same time."

"Clever, no?"

"Some might say reckless, considering their families are your political allies, though they may not be after today."

Tomás waved away Nuncio's comment. "Better to get this over with at one time rather than dragging the matter out through countless visits. Besides, my public declaration will keep gossip to a minimum. None of the women will be able to say I rejected any señorita because of her shrill laugh, slow wit, poor shape, or dull converse. They were all equally lacking."

Nuncio looked heavenward. He might have even started to pray.

Tomás held back a sigh. "In my desire for them. Never fear, I shall be unfailingly polite and let each of the ladies know how wonderful she is. More beautiful than stars sparkling in the night sky, more promising than the hint of spring after a brutal winter, more—"

"Forgive me for interrupting, but one would hope they would still be listening at that point." He squared his narrow shoulders. "Cook prepared a feast for your guests. If any of them have an appetite after your pretty speech, I propose we hide the knives. For your safety, of course."

Tomás smiled. "I can take care of myself." He sobered. "I refuse to settle for less than what Enrique and Fernando have."

"You mean the families they started."

Not entirely. However, Isabella had given birth to her and Fernando's first child, a daughter. They named her Juana after Isabella's late mother. Sancha hadn't yet delivered. Given what Enrique had repeatedly said, he didn't care whether she bore him a son or a daughter. He simply wanted her and the child's health and happiness.

Nuncio cleared his throat delicately. "If I may be so bold…"

"You will be anyway. Get on with it."

"Very well. If you seek children, I advise you wed first as your brothers had."

"They fought for the women they wanted. Neither let convention get in his way."

"Your brothers wed women from their own backgrounds."

"They fell in love with them first and overcame numerous obstacles to be at their sides, even though none were originally meant to be together. Have you forgotten Fernando's betrothal to Sancha was long before she married Enrique instead? What about Isabella pretending to be Sancha and wedding Fernando before he knew the difference between the two sisters? Despite such chaos, all are blissfully happy now."

"Miracles do happen at times, though in your case you best not hope for one."

Tomás shoved his hair back from where the wind had blown it. "As the youngest son, who I end up with, or if I end up with anyone, is of no consequence. Enrique inherits everything from Papá. Building upon the family dynasty is his duty. I can do as I please."

Nuncio looked off into the distance, his expression suddenly a mask, though the lines in his face seemed to have deepened. Clearly, the man should have been riding, running, or walking through the fields rather than being here bothering him.

He turned back to Tomás. "Is this about Beatriz?"

His heart slammed into his chest. Lightheaded, he rested his hand on the stone for support and pretended to drink from his empty goblet. A ruse to buy time, since he was unable and unwilling to answer Nuncio. Above, a bird cried out, its wings outstretched to catch a gust. Below, wheels rattled against stone, announcing more guests. This time, several carriages drew near.

He wanted to run. His legs were too leaden to move. "Where is she?"

Nuncio shook his head.

Tomás frowned. Frustration oiled his limbs, allowing him to move as he couldn't seconds earlier. Fists clenched, he approached the older man, prepared to thrash him to get an answer.

Nuncio stood his ground and kept his tongue, clearly not cowed.

Tomás glared. "Answer me. Where is she?"

"Seeing to her tasks as the other servants are doing."

And would most likely finish her work before Nuncio offered anything more than he had. "Inform my guests I shall be delayed slightly."

Before the manservant could respond, Tomás slapped his goblet into Nuncio's hand and hurried down the steps, his shoes ringing on the stone. On the next level, he rushed through the castle once owned by a Moor, the same as Fernando's castle had been. Their service to the Crown had won them the re-conquered estates. Although Tomás's home was far smaller than Fernando's and certainly Enrique's, he still had to search numerous halls and countless rooms for Beatriz.

He wanted to see her. No. He needed to. A compulsion he couldn't seem to resist despite her being a servant. A matter obviously important to Nuncio, Enrique, and Sancha, with them advising him not to take advantage of his position and Beatriz since a dalliance between them could lead nowhere.

He was well aware of the perils and hadn't done anything except watch her whenever he could.

She was remarkably different from his other servants, her air, manner, and speech refined. Intelligence shone in her eyes. She even seemed able to read. Weeks ago, he'd come upon her tidying his study. She'd regarded the book spines at length, the way one would when reading titles. Remarkable and odd. If she were educated, he couldn't imagine why she'd willingly spend her days here in endless drudgery.

When he'd asked his housekeeper about her, Señora Cisneros said Beatriz came from one of the many villages Tomás owned and that she needed work to support her ailing mother. He hadn't bothered to check out the story, sensing Beatriz might have an ill parent, which drove her to seek work here. As to the other part of her background…deep inside, he sensed she hadn't come from any village.

Not that he cared whether he was right or not.

Seeing her again, settling his overwhelming desire was his only goal. Today, he could compare Beatriz to the other women and determine if his desire for her was only a passing whim. Once he'd had another look at her, he might be able to dismiss his feelings as mere fantasy and have peace at last.

Where had she gone?

He strode toward the first hall and the bedchambers, this area open and airy. Sun spilled through arched windows that stretched from the floor to the ceiling. Several rays shone on intricate mosaics in blue, yellow, green, and red, decorations beloved by the Moors. In the brilliant light, the stone columns and floors were white as milk.

Upon reaching the chambers, he checked room after room, each filled with rich wall hangings and Spanish furniture, the dark wood and leather carved with ornate designs. Every chamber was spotless and duly aired to smell quite fresh. Also empty. With only two more rooms to go, he sensed Beatriz might be in another part of the castle, tending to those rooms.

No matter. He'd run her down in time.

After a quick check of the remaining chambers, he turned.

Beatriz stood several feet away, a basket of linens in her hands, her gaze on him.

His mouth went dry.

Despite her red gown, white tunic, and linen cap, the same livery his other female servants wore, she might as well have been a queen.

She was certainly beautiful enough. Her skin was paler than most, the color of a fine pearl, features delicate, eyes lushly lashed and softened with what appeared to be need.

His chest tightened, breathing became difficult, the air suddenly too thick.

Her lips parted in what seemed to be an invitation.

Everything grew quiet. Colors and the surrounding area faded into the background, leaving nothing except her to feast on. Dewy skin, sensuous mouth, full breasts, lush hips.

His shaft thickened and grew hard, craving her heated sheath damp with moisture, proof of her excitement.

She was no more than a few feet away. His for the taking. He merely had to cross the small space separating them.

The distance seemed wider than the ocean with too many warnings bombarding him. Sancha's advice that he not ruin Beatriz, leaving her few options for marriage to a respectable man. Enrique warning about the child Tomás would eventually sire with her. Nuncio's repeated admonitions about her peasant background, which wouldn't allow them a future together no matter how much Tomás may have wanted one.

He shouldn't have sought her out. His plan to dismiss any feelings he'd had failed miserably. He wanted her far more than he had earlier even though a liaison between them was impossible.

He should have run from the hall and not looked back. He couldn't move. His longing for these few moments with her were far too compelling, even though they'd never amount to anything.

He tipped his head. "*Buenas tardes.*"

Color rose to her cheeks, and her eyes cleared, no longer dreamy or aroused. She stepped back.

Pity. The distance between them was already too great, she didn't need to add to it. Although he understood her prudence, he hated that they had to resist their desire.

"Buenas tardes, patrón." She propped the basket on her hip and retreated two steps this time.

In another moment, she might bolt, leaving him.

He prayed not yet. "Are the linens too heavy?" He gestured to them. "Do you need help?"

She shook her head, making her tendrils dance around her cheeks.

The bobbing tresses captivated him. He imagined winding the dark, silky strands around his fingers, using the locks to ease her closer. "Are you quite certain?"

He wanted to help, needed to be near.

She gripped the basket so hard her knuckles turned white. "I can see to my work. I can work all day and night if need be."

Such dedication. "Have you ever needed to do so in order to finish?"

His housekeeper better not be working her too hard.

"No." Beatriz frowned slightly, then made her face a mask again, the kind servants show a master, leaving the poor fool with no way to know what they thought. "I finish my tasks quickly. Without problems."

"How wonderful." He stepped in her way before she could get around him. "How is your mother doing? Does she need a potion or poultice?"

She stared.

He grew quite somber. "Señora Cisneros mentioned your mamá's troubles in passing. How sad I am for you and her. However, I know a physician who may be able to help. Tell me the symptoms and I can bring you what she needs."

No matter what ailed the woman, Sancha could prepare a remedy. She was a healer. When Tomás had fallen ill at the fortaleza, she'd saved his life. A dangerous matter for her because of the Inquisition, which led to accusations of her being a witch. Thankfully, he, Enrique, and their brothers had handled the matter, leaving her free to practice healing in secret.

Beatriz hefted the basket again and settled the thing more firmly on her hip.

"Those linens are too heavy for you." He grabbed the basket.

She held on to it.

Surely, she didn't think she'd win against him. He was a head taller than her, nearly twice her weight, and far stronger.

He tugged.

She let go.

He locked his knees to keep from staggering back at the weight. Far too cumbersome for such a delicate flower as her. He'd have to talk with Señora Cisneros about Beatriz's future duties.

Rather than offering a sweet smile for his help, she bit her lip.

Tenderness welled within him, along with unruly desire. "No reason to be afraid. Your position is safe. I merely want to help. Tell me what ails your mamá."

"Nothing at the moment. She recovered fully from her latest illness. I must get back to work." She reached for the basket.

Tomás didn't hand the linens over. "Is my housekeeper demanding too much, even with you willing to work day and night?"

"Señora Cisneros is a lovely woman."

She had a mustache, hairs on her chin, the girth of two women combined, and a high-pitched voice that set his teeth on edge. However, she did keep the castle running smoothly without being too overbearing. "I find her efficient in a slightly masculine way. Is that what you meant?"

The corners of Beatriz's mouth lifted slightly with his teasing, though she didn't allow herself to smile.

Making her laugh meant everything to Tomás without him understanding why. "Do you promise not to tell her I said such a thing?"

More color stained her cheeks. "She and I rarely speak. Work keeps us busy."

"So you do promise. Wonderful." He grinned and lifted the basket. "Where did you plan to take this? I can bring the linens to whatever room you—"

Loud throat clearing flowed down the hall.

Either Señora Cisneros or Nuncio had just entered from behind. Hard to tell which, since they both made the same noises when displeased with the help. He looked over.

Nuncio.

Beatriz pulled the basket from Tomás with surprisingly strength, though she did totter from the weight.

"Careful." He reached for her before she fell into the wall.

She twisted away seconds before he could touch her sleeve or any other part of her.

Nuncio cleared his throat once more.

Tomás frowned at the man. "Did you inform the guests of my delay?"

"Several times. They still await your presence. Every one of them in the same room."

Surely without knives if Nuncio had anything to say. Tomás turned to her. "If your mamá should fall ill again, please tell me. I can help."

Her attention remained on Nuncio.

Wanting to speak softly to her, Tomás leaned closer and caught her scent...the fragrance of freshly washed clothes and clean skin. His head swam, unbridled desire coursing through him again. For a moment, he found speech difficult. "If Nuncio rails at you for keeping me here, let me know. I shall thrash him soundly."

Laughter bubbled from her, which she quelled without pause.

Her joy, no matter how brief, was a balm for everything wrong with today. How marvelous if they, at least, became friends, speaking freely, laughing, enjoying themselves. An odd notion for any man when faced with such a delectable woman. However, he didn't see many other options at this point.

Holding back a sigh, he left her side and strode to Nuncio. "Shall we go?" Halfway down the hall, Tomás spoke first. "Make certain the ladies' carriages, drivers, and footmen are ready to depart. I trust no one will be staying long once I give them my speech."

"As you wish. Whatever you wish. Whenever you wish."

Tomás rolled his eyes. If wishes were his for the asking, he'd still be speaking to Beatriz, inviting her to ride the grounds with him, having a late supper with her on the hillside overlooking his estate, finally carrying her into his chamber for some much-needed passion with both of them discovering wondrous things about the other.

He surely wouldn't be facing a group of women who might want to harm him once they knew he had no intention of wedding anyone.